MURDER

MANUSCRIPT

The first Baines & Bohr Mystery

Lynn Maver

Thank you to Ann, Ian, Katleen, Mark and Rebecca.

For my Elise

CONTENTS

Prologue 1

Tuesday 9 April 3

Wednesday 10 April 57

Thursday 11 April 81

Friday 12 April 98

Saturday 13 April 149

Sunday 14 April 162

Monday 15 April 178

Epilogue 199

Monday 10 July 202

Thursday, 13 July 203

PROLOGUE

Emma Baines rushed up the six steps two by two, eager to get in out of the rain. The front door swung open as she approached and Marie appeared.

"Morning Emma."

"Morning Marie. Very wet today."

"Terrible. And you know who'll have to check all the drains again."

Emma fled further in to the building and up the stairs before Marie could start listing all the horrible jobs she was required to do. She'd heard this particular diatribe often enough and wasn't in the mood today. She could just hear Theresa come through the door and make the fatal mistake of stopping as she said her good morning – ah well, she was still new, she'd learn.

Tim had beaten her in this morning and was already at his desk.

"Hi Em. I really thought spring was finally starting and now we've got all this horrible rain again."

"I know Tim. It is sort of normal weather for April though."

Emma switched on her computer, hung up her coat and began to sort through the surprisingly large amount of emails that had appeared overnight.

"Olivia asked if you could deal with this letter first; she says it's urgent." Tim handed Emma an envelope, then wandered down to the kitchen to make them both a cup of tea. Emma quickly scanned the letter; nothing too out of the ordinary, but requested by a professor of some university in America, which must be why Olivia had seen it as a priority. And she'd have been charmed by the old fashioned real letter touch. While sipping her cup of green tea Emma searched the catalogue database and noted the location of the documents she'd need to consult. With the cup half-drunk she set of to the basement, expecting to be back long before the rest had gone cold.

One minute – or three flights of stairs and a walk along the corridor – later, Emma switched on the lights, keyed in the code and entered the large strongroom. As the fluorescent tubes slowly flickered into life, she began to move to her right - she needed a box from the far end of the room. She looked along the line of black steering wheels to see where the mobile racking had been left open and spotted the gap right at the other end. Of course. She let out a gentle expletive, moved to the middle of the room and turned the wheel; about nine heavy rows of shelving laden with boxes and ancient volumes began to creak into action and rolled to the side. Then they stopped; Emma was surprised and looked over – no there was still quite a gap there. She heaved the wheel round again, the gap decreased considerably, but she could feel that there was an obstruction. A very different expletive escaped her lips. Who had been such an idiot as to leave something in between the stacks? Last time this had happened, a small stepladder had been destroyed and all staff had been given a lengthy lecture about their responsibilities. The obstruction didn't feel solid enough for something as rigid as a kick step though. Surely no one had left a box of documents on the floor? Jennifer would have a seizure! And there would be another lecture. Emma had been rolling the bays back as she passed them, angrily turning at each wheel until she reached the open space. She looked into the gap as the metal shelves shuddered to a halt and everything became a blur, except for the blood. So much blood. She steadied herself by grasping the cool metal edge of the shelving and tried to tear her eyes away from the red mess on the floor. She noticed with detached surprise that she hadn't screamed or fainted, then managed to persuade her feet to start moving. Slowly at first, then faster, out of that room, past Conservation, up the stairs, into the light of day. Her voice caught up with her several seconds later as the long-expected scream materialised.

TUESDAY 9 APRIL

One

The dark green Golf pulled up behind the blue and white police car, narrowly avoiding a collision. Sergeant Fletcher unclenched his fingers and tried not to breathe out too loud.

"Nick, can you go and find out what's going on?"

As he watched his sergeant approach the uniformed officer standing by the door, Lucas Bohr counted to ten to calm down. He ought to be used to driving by now, but even after two years he just didn't trust the car to do as it was told. For years he'd managed to avoid getting his driving licence, but when he'd been promoted to inspector it had been strongly suggested he needed to be independently mobile. How he had managed to pass his test, no one knew.

"I wish I could say the body is in the library, but apparently it's called a repository," Nick grinned through the window.

"Whose body?"

"Unknown male."

Lucas got out of the car and noticed the large banner over the front door of the Victorian red brick building, proclaiming it to be 'Literally London'. What would it have been built as, he wondered? It didn't look right as a family home: it was too wide even for its imposing height, and no ordinary house would have quite so many windows. Or such a striking oak front door; even left wide open as it currently was, it delivered a clear message that it was there to keep the unwanted out. Or the inhabitants in. A school, perhaps? As he ascended the four steps leading up to the entrance, he noticed the second door, a modern glass one, which slid open as he approached. The spacious entrance hall with the broad, majestic staircase enhanced the school feeling. Modernity had crept in here as well, with a whole wall of glass this time, through which Lucas could see a bright room with wooden tables and colourful bookshelves. That was to his left though; Nick had disappeared through a small door to his right, which discreetly declared to be 'staff only'. Lucas followed and descended the much smaller staircase into the basement.

3

Nick had already reached the constable who stood guard in the middle of the corridor. Lucas preferred to take his time and ambled along towards the first door on his left; this opened up into a room that had a vague laboratory feel to it, but also included an ancient iron press and sheets of paper lying everywhere. He went on, past the constable, to the only other door on the left hand side. This area had a clearer purpose: full of overflowing racking and cardboard boxes it was obviously used as a storage space. Lucas retraced his steps to the middle of the corridor and entered the only door on the right hand side, through which he could hear Nick in conversation with the pathologist. He smiled as he recognised Flo Vermander's voice; as bright as she was petite, she was always a pleasure to share a case with.

The rectangular room was unlike any he'd ever seen before: rows and rows of metal shelving on rails, the tops almost touching the fluorescent tubes on the ceiling. Rather boring looking brown boxes filled the shelves, although there were a few grey parcels visible as well. There were about thirty of these bays altogether, each with a large steering wheel at the end for moving them along. The only gap was several bays to his left, where Nick and Flo had just stepped out.
"Hello Flo."
"Ah, there you are Lucas." Flo was wearing her extra small forensics suit, her long blond hair hidden in its hood. "It's pretty gruesome in there."
"Any idea who we're dealing with?"
"You're in luck. I was just telling Nick I found your victim's wallet and phone in his jacket pocket."
Nick opened up the black leather wallet and took out the driving licence.
"Hugo Bonner." He raised his eyebrows as he read the address and handed the ID to Lucas. "Posh address."
"Fits with the posh suit." Flo remarked. "Of course, we can't be certain it's him. The head has been squashed between two of those rolling stacks."
Lucas looked up from examining the driving licence.
"How is that possible? Surely his shoulders would hit the racking first?"
"When you look in there, you'll see he was lying on his side. And you'll see the big rubber stoppers along the bottom of these bays to stop them banging in to each other. His head was right in between a pair of those."
Nick looked at his boss.
"An unlikely coincidence, don't you think?"
Lucas hesitated before replying.
"True...but what for? To hide his identity? Then why leave his wallet in his pocket?" He turned back to Flo. "Or to hide the cause of death?"

"Could be," Flo agreed. "it's not going to be easy to get any forensic evidence from his head. Of course," she added with a mischievous smile, "he could have only been unconscious when he was put there."

Lucas grimaced.

"Trust you to come up with the most pleasant scenario. How about a time of death?"

"A calculated guess would be sometime between one pm and six pm yesterday. I'll try to narrow it down after the autopsy."

Nick stepped aside so Lucas could walk in to the gap in the racking. The first thing he noticed were the shiny black leather shoes. Even at the impossible angle they were sticking out, you could see how expensive they were. The dark blue suit had survived reasonably unscathed and was hand made. Despite the many murdered bodies Lucas had seen in his career, he had to swallow hard when he allowed his eyes to settle on the head. Those rubber stoppers must have nearly touched each other, resulting in the face being totally squashed and a ridiculous amount of blood and brains having oozed out. No wonder the usually unflappable Nick had been looking a bit pale. Back in the corridor Lucas asked the constable who'd found the body.

"A Miss Emma Baines, Sir, one of the girls who works here. She was taken to the staff room by some of her colleagues."

"We'd better have a chat with Miss Baines and the rest of the staff."

Emma wished everyone would just leave her alone now. The confusion in the entrance hall as she tried to describe what she had seen, the walk back up the stairs surrounded by concerned – and extremely curious – colleagues, being pushed into one of the chairs in the staff room, someone handing her a cup of milky tea; her recollections of all that were hazy, especially compared to the dreadful image that had seared itself onto her brain. She needed some peace and quiet, a decent cup of tea and a chance to think.

"You look awfully pale, Em."

Tim had crouched down next to her and was looking worried. Granted, Tim usually looked worried, but she tended to be the one to try and cheer him up, not the cause of the concern. He gently took the cup of milky tea out of her hand and replaced it with her favourite yellow mug full of gorgeous green tea. Emma gave her friend a grateful smile, but still didn't trust herself to say anything – she knew how hysterical her voice had been earlier and she definitely never wanted to sound like that again. Her eyes wandered across the room, with its mismatched hotchpotch of furniture. Olivia was sitting on her usual straight-backed chair, staring at the open door and the constable who stood there. The brave constable, who hadn't given in when Olivia had argued with him, insisting she be allowed to go to her office and get on with work, rather than having to wait in the staff room along with everyone else.

Not many people managed to stand up to Olivia's onslaughts and the policeman was still looking a bit flustered, but he had prevailed. Richard appeared into view, pacing up and down the room as he had been doing since they'd got there. Poor Richard. He was trying hard to look in control, but was probably wishing he hadn't postponed his retirement last year and was now at home playing with his grandson. He'd almost walked over to her several times, but each time Frederick had cut him off. He undoubtedly wanted to ask the same question he'd posed as soon as he'd realised what had happened – who is it? With all staff accounted for, Emma's answer that she didn't know, hadn't seen his face, hadn't been able to make out a face amidst the mash of blood and brains, hadn't stopped Richard from asking her if she was sure. Several times. Frederick had just caught up with him again. It was quite a comical image, the tall imposing Frederick, impeccably dressed in his tweeds standing next to their much shorter director in his grey off-the-peg suit. Emma realised she'd started to giggle and was in danger of becoming hysterical again. She dug her nails firmly into the palm of her hand, closed her eyes and took a few deep breaths. Opening her eyes again, she looked towards the other end of the room, where Tim had re-joined the others on the big orange sofa. Theresa was taking a swig from her coke bottle and looking at her phone. Presumably making sure her friends were kept up to date with all developments. Does it mean I'm old, Emma wondered, that I'm not constantly glued to my phone and don't feel the need to share every second of my life with the world at large? Probably not; even when she'd been nineteen she hadn't been anywhere near as vibrant and outgoing as Theresa. Tim and Jennifer were having an intense conversation now, accentuated by surreptitious glances in her direction. Jennifer looked pale; her shoulder length henna'd hair framed her face and accentuated its lack of colour. Just what she'd looked like after her husband's suicide two years ago – of course, this situation must be bringing back awful memories. Marie walked up to the sofa and joined their discussion. She was standing with her back towards Emma, her long grey ponytail swishing from side to side as she moved her head. Images of actual ponies leapt into Emma's head and she could feel another burst of hysterical giggles coming on. Just then Marie turned round and started heading towards her. Emma braced herself for the inevitable monologue and was completely taken aback when Marie only suggested she come and join them on the settee. She just wanted to be left alone, but it was easier to give in, so she rose from the chair and found herself taking hold of Marie's outstretched hand as her legs felt like jelly. She let Marie lead her to the sofa, where Theresa had jumped up from the seat and was now perched on the end, while Tim and Jennifer moved apart so she could sit in the middle. The uneasy silent glances were more than Emma could cope with; she took a deep breath, exhaled slowly and hoped her voice would sound a bit more normal.

"Well, this wasn't how I imagined today would go." Not exactly normal, but a lot better than hysterical screaming.

Jennifer gave her a watery smile and put her arm round her.

"So you have no idea who it is then?"

"You're as bad as Richard," Theresa exclaimed ,"leave poor Emma alone."

"It's all right," Emma said, managing to sound a lot more like herself. "I have been wondering that myself. I'm sure it was a man, but beyond that..." Emma could hear her voice change as the vision of the squashed head re-appeared. She swallowed hard and was about to continue when she noticed two men standing in the doorway. The older one was quite tall and had a surprising head of thick blond curly hair; he was wearing a suit, but without managing to look smart. The younger one – younger than she was, surely – wasn't particularly tall, but looked athletic. His muscles practically burst out of his clothes; Theresa's skirt seemed to have become a bit shorter, so she must have noticed as well. The serious policemen had arrived.

The first thing Lucas noticed was the horrendously orange sofa; someone with little taste must have decided the room needed some colour. He assumed the tall young woman with the short black bob was the one who'd found the body, as her face was as pale as the hands that were clasped round the yellow mug. The slightly older woman with the long vaguely red hair was looking a bit ashen, but had her arm round the younger one so must be doing the comforting. The young girl at the end was already flirting with Nick, so unlikely to have seen the mess in the basement. And the woman standing behind the sofa was definitely too old to be described as a 'girl', as was the rotund and stern looking woman glaring at him from a lonely chair. By now their arrival had been spotted by everyone in the room and the oldest man, who seemed to want to make up for his receding hairline with his grey beard, started striding towards him.

"I'm Dr Richard Owen and I'm in charge here," Richard said, trying to sound forceful. "Who are you?"

"This is Sergeant Fletcher," Lucas replied, gesturing towards Nick, "and I'm Inspector Bohr. I'm in charge of the murder investigation." He always managed to surprise people by sounding a lot more authoritative than he looked and Richard took a tiny step back.

"Perhaps you could introduce the other people in the room?"

Richard gestured to the tall, slim man he'd been deep in discussion with.

"This is Frederick Samuels, our librarian."

Frederick nodded a greeting from where he was standing.

"On the sofa are Jennifer Marr, our conservator and Emma Baines and Tim Edwards, our researchers. The young lady perched on the end is Theresa Woodward, the searchroom assistant."

Three pairs of eyes stared at Lucas; the fourth pair was kept firmly on Nick.

"There is also Dr Olivia Dunstable, our archivist," Richard continued as he vaguely gestured towards the woman sitting apart, "and..."

"I'm Marie Thorpe, caretaker, cleaner and general dogsbody." Lucas shook the hand proffered by the stocky fifty-something woman with the greying ponytail.

"I look after the building, you see, and..."

"Thank you Mrs Thorpe. We'll need to talk to all of you, of course – is there a room available we could use?"

"You're welcome to use my office, inspector," Frederick offered. "It's right next to this room."

"Thank you, Mr Samuels. I'd like to ask you all to remain here until we've spoken to you; after that it would be best if you went home. You should be able to return to work tomorrow morning." He turned towards Richard. "Could we start with you, Dr Owen?"

Two

The large office exuded a sense of order and calm: a place for everything and everything in its place. The far wall was lined with glass-fronted book cases, full of dust free hard covers and paperbacks, while several artistic photographs of London landmarks decorated the other wall. Lucas wandered over to the window and the antique mahogany desk, with its sleek computer and comfortable office chair. He didn't dare touch the framed photograph of two young men in their late teens; Frederick Samuels would know if he didn't replace it in the exact right spot. Nick had invited Dr Owen to sit down at the small conference table in the middle of the room and had joined him there, notebook at the ready.

"Tell me, Dr Owen," Lucas asked still standing at Samuel's desk, "what exactly is Literally London?"

"We are the library and archive for London born authors, inspector. We collect both their publications and their personal papers, letters, diaries, manuscripts... anything connected to them." Richard was sounding much more relaxed now. "We're open to the public on weekdays and Saturday mornings and undertake research for those who can't come here in person."

Lucas had walked over to the glass fronted cases and was looking intently at their contents.

"I see. Collecting all those books and documents must be costly – how are you funded?"

"We're a charitable trust. The basic collection was put together in the early twentieth century by Sir George Bonner; his grandson decided to make the archive available to all by having it run by a trust and housed in a separate building, rather than hidden away in the family home."

Lucas sauntered across to the table and looked closely at Richard.

"Is the Bonner family still involved?"

Richard nodded.

"Yes, Hugo Bonner is the Head of the Trustees. It was his father who turned the collection into a trust."

Lucas pulled a chair over and sat down.

"Could you describe Hugo Bonner for me?"

Richard shifted uncomfortably in his seat.

"Why on earth would you want me to..." He stopped and all colour drained from his face. "You don't think...?"

"Please, Dr Owen, describe Mr Bonner. Is he tall, short, fat, thin,..."

Richard swallowed hard.

"A little less tall than you are and perhaps just slightly overweight. But you're wrong, you know, it can't be him, he hasn't been here in weeks."

"How does he dress?"

"Hand-made suits, everything very expensive. It's still a wealthy family."

"So if I were to tell you that the dead man wore a Saville Row dark blue suit, fits the general description you gave and had in his leather wallet the driving licence and credit cards of Mr Hugo Bonner..."

Richard lowered his head and stared at the floor for a moment. Then he looked back at Lucas, with tears in his eyes.

"Hugo was not just my boss, he was my friend." His voice broke and he paused for a moment. "I would like to see him."

Lucas leant in closer and said in his friendliest voice:

"I'm afraid that won't be possible. Even if it were, I wouldn't recommend it."

"Was Mr Bonner married?" Nick asked.

Richard jerked his head to the side.

"Oh, poor Helen. And Matthew." He stared out of the window for a while. "Matthew is about to sit his A-levels. Hugo is...was so proud of him."

Lucas glanced at Nick, who went out of the room and returned with a glass of water. Richard gratefully drank a few sips.

"I must call Helen."

"A kind gesture, Dr Owen, but it would be better if we could inform Mrs Bonner ourselves." Seeing the doubt in Richard's eyes, Lucas continued. "We'll be very considerate."

Richard shrugged his shoulders.

"I suppose you know what you're doing."

"You said Mr Bonner hadn't visited the archive recently?"

"That's right. He only visited occasionally; the last time was about six weeks ago, to discuss our next fundraising event."

"Do you have any idea what he might have been doing here yesterday afternoon?" Richard shook his head.

"If he had an appointment with one of my colleagues, I didn't know about it."

"Did anything unusual happen yesterday?"

"No, inspector, it was a fairly typical Monday."

Richard stood in his usual Monday morning place, waiting for the room to fill. When Marie confirmed all staff were in the building and Olivia had deigned to arrive, he began.

"Marie has asked me to remind you to remember to sign out in the evening – it's annoying and time-wasting for her when she wants to lock the building if she can't be sure that everyone's gone. And of course, we did all agree to be out by twenty past five at the latest."

He glanced at Olivia, but she merely continued to stare straight ahead.

"Now then," he continued "is there anything else anyone would like to mention?"
Silence reigned, so Richard declared the meeting closed and walked to his office, followed by Frederick and Olivia.

"Is it normal for your meetings to be over so quickly?" Nick asked.
Richard nodded.
"To be honest, the weekly meeting is more of a courtesy to the staff, so they feel involved. Mr Samuels, Dr Dunstable and I always have a lengthier conversation in my office afterwards."
"Was there anything in particular you discussed yesterday?"
"Just both their hobby horses."

Richard sighed as Olivia turned straight away to her favourite subject.
"You've got your head in the sand with our financial situation Richard. We must make some cuts."
"The trustees are happy, they don't need us to make a profit."
"They don't want us to lose money either. I've said it before, conservation is far too expensive, we can't keep subsidising it."
"Jennifer's work matters, even you must see that Olivia. The way she turns documents that are so badly damaged, so far gone that no one has ever been able to study them back into useable ones that can be studied."
"But at what cost? What she does takes forever and what's the point of having all these newly available documents when I don't have anyone to catalogue them properly and therefore make them available to all these eager researches. It would be much more cost effective to have another archivist."
Ah finally, thought Richard, so that's what's she's after.
"I'll talk to the trustees and see whether they'd be willing to employ someone extra." "With what money?!" Olivia said incredulously. "Besides, only Hugo matters. If you could convince him of the inefficiency of conservation..."
"Hugo takes great pride in Jennifer's work, as we all should." Richard was beginning to lose his patience. "There's no way he would get rid of her. Instead of complaining, why don't you come up with something positive I can take to the board — see whether you can apply for funding somewhere to get an extra archivist. Or give Theresa some training."
"Oh, of course, anyone can do cataloguing, especially a brainless party girl!" Olivia hissed.
"Come now, Olivia, not everyone without a degree is brainless," Frederick interrupted.
Olivia stared at him in disbelief and was about to reply when he went on:
"Can we move on to a different subject now? I would like to talk about the amount of rubbish the Trustees keep insisting we take in."
Oh great, thought Richard, this again too.

"I had a word with Hugo last week; he's going to talk to the others about involving us more in the accessioning side of things, so there's nothing to worry about." He looked at both in turn. "If there's nothing else, I think it's high time we got on with some work."

"Is there a problem with the archive's income?" Lucas sounded surprised. "With wealthy patrons, surely..."
"A perceived lack of money," Richard snapped. "Olivia thinks our budget should be spent in a different way. It is merely a matter of how to spend the resources we have, not lack of resources."
"What did you do next?"
"I spent the morning in my office, going through various bits of paperwork."
"What are the lunchtime arrangements like?" Nick asked.
"Lunch is an hour, to be taken at some point between noon and two pm. Theresa - Miss Woodward - is on duty in our public research room and has her lunch from twelve to one, while Olivia covers for her. Olivia then has her lunch between one and two; all other staff are able to have their break when they like."
"When did you have yours yesterday?"

Richard had spent the morning going over the accounts, annoyed with himself for letting Olivia worry him. Of course having their own conservator was expensive, but so was buying manuscripts at auction or simply heating this cavernous building during the winter. They weren't spending much more than last year and as long as the trustees were happy there was no need to panic. Maybe it would be worth asking Hugo to come over and discuss the finances; they could head off any concerns the other trustees might have by organising another big fundraiser. There were always American universities keen to work with Literally London and they seemed to have plenty of money to spend. Funny how it was so easy to get them interested in an archive housing collections from London born authors while most Londoners had no idea the place even existed. A quick knock on the door brought Richard back to the present as Marie dashed in with the post.
"Nothing much today" she cheerfully announced.
"Thanks Marie." Richard looked up as Marie was still standing there "Is there anything else?"
"Fire drill Richard. It's a year ago today since we had one, I told you last week. We should hold one today or we'll be in trouble with the fire brigade."
"I'm sure they'll allow us a few days' grace."
"I could arrange one this afternoon easily enough." Marie insisted.
"No" Richard replied, raising his voice. "I've already got a headache from looking at these accounts, I'm not making it worse with that dreadful alarm."
Seeing the look of disquiet on Marie's face, Richard added: "Friday. You choose what time."

"You're the boss. I checked the drains this morning – they're all fine now – and I've mopped the stores. I'll get on with dusting the book shelves this afternoon."
Praise was clearly expected and Richard dutifully obliged.
"Excellent, I know the building's in safe hands with you around."
Marie beamed as she left the room, but Richard's attention was now on a new email that had just arrived. Oh dear, she'd copied Fred into it as well. Richard looked at the clock: already after twelve thirty, he'd better get some lunch. Frederick would have to wait till this afternoon. Richard put on his Burberry raincoat and headed down the stairs, nodding to Jennifer who was on her way up.

"When did you return?"
"I'm not sure...no wait. Theresa was running down the stairs as I was heading back up, so it must have been one o'clock. Fredrick was waiting for me outside my office, I'm sure he'll know *exactly* what time that was."
Lucas noted the emphasis on the 'exactly'; tension between Mr Samuels and the director, perhaps?
"We went into my office and had a brief discussion; I spent the rest of the afternoon at my desk."
"On your own?"
Richard thought for a moment.
"Yes, on my own. I don't remember any interruptions."
"Does everyone leave at the same time?"
"Around the same time, yes. We close to the public at four and leave the building shortly after five."
"Who locks up?"
"Marie Thorpe, our caretaker."
"And what time did you leave yesterday?"
"Around ten past five."
Lucas got up from his chair and held out his hand.
"Thank you Dr Owen, you've been most helpful."
Richard shook the proffered hand, but remained seated.
"You said we would be able to come in to work tomorrow?"
"The store where the body was found may still be out of bounds, but, yes, you should be able to use the rest of the building as normal."
Richard slowly rose.
"You also said we should go home after having spoken to you."
"Yes, it's best if..."
"I would prefer to stay until you've spoken to all my staff," Richard interrupted. "I'm sure you understand."
Lucas hesitated.

"As long as you don't re-join them in the staff room." He looked straight into Richard's eyes. "I'm sure *you* understand."

Richard nodded.

"I'll be in my office."

Lucas waited until the door had closed before reaching for his phone.

"Any word on Hugo Bonner?...I see... No don't talk to Mrs Bonner yet, I'd rather do that myself. Keep everything discreet at the moment."

He put the phone back in his pocket and turned to Nick.

"No sign of Bonner anywhere. It seems likely that it's him."

"Surely his wife would have missed him by now and reported his absence?"

"That's one of the questions we will ask her when we see her this afternoon."

Nick walked over to the door.

"Miss Baines?"

Lucas nodded. Time to speak to the young lady who'd found the body.

Three

Emma followed the sergeant into Frederick's office, where Inspector Bohr greeted her with a friendly smile and ushered her onto the chair. She tried to keep her gaze steady as she looked at him, but her trembling hands betrayed how upset she still felt.

"Please tell me about this morning."

A kind voice to go with the smile. Emma took a deep breath and recounted her morning's discovery; she managed to keep her voice even until she reached the mess of brain and blood and could feel the hysteria starting to rise up again.

"Thank you, Miss Baines," Lucas interrupted, "no need for further details.

Nick had brought a jug of water and several glasses back with him and offered her one, which she gratefully accepted as it gave her fidgety hands something to hold on to.

"I just have one more question about this morning," Lucas continued after Emma had taken a few sips. "Do you have any idea who it might be?"

Emma gripped the glass even tighter and looked intently at the colourless liquid.

"I didn't at first...and I don't really still...it's just that suit..."

"Yes, Miss Baines? What about the suit?"

She lifted her head and looked at both of them in turn.

"I can't be sure...but I only know one person who wears suits like that. But then he wasn't here yesterday, so how could it be him?"

"Who, Miss Baines?" Nick was also using his friendliest voice.

"Hugo Bonner, the chair of the trustees."

"Do you know Mr Bonner well?"

Emma's grip relaxed as she looked at Lucas.

"You're not surprised. Is it him?"

Lucas nodded.

"We haven't had formal identification yet, but it does look like it is Mr Bonner."

"That doesn't make sense, he wasn't here..."

Emma stared into nothingness, lost in thought.

"Miss Baines? I asked whether you knew Mr Bonner well?"

"Sorry, yes you did. No, I didn't." She stopped, took another sip and started again. "I didn't know him at all. I've seen him around the building a few times and we held a big fundraiser a while ago which he hosted, but apart from that..."

"How long have you worked here?"

"Just over four years."

"And what do you do?"

"We get a lot of enquiries from all over the world – people who can't come to us in person but want to know things about the collection." She saw the puzzled expression on Lucas' face. "Do we have correspondence by this particular author? Did such and such ever write to such and such in America? In which draft of the manuscript does this sentence first appear? Those kinds of questions."

"And you answer them?"

"Some of them. Olivia shares out the enquiries, so I get the questions she believes I will be able to answer."

"I see." Lucas leant back in his chair. "What was yesterday like?"

Emma let go of the glass.

"A normal Monday. We had our weekly meeting and then got on with work."

Emma clicked on the folder of current enquiries and opened the file containing the research she'd started on Friday. Scanning through what she'd written so far she worked out which documents she needed to get from the store to finish her reply and got up to head to the basement.

"Tim?"

Tim looked up from behind his computer screen.

"Does Jennifer seem a bit, well, happier to you?"

Tim considered this for a moment.

"She does seem to have recovered somewhat. It has been more than two years, you'd hope she'd have managed to move on by now."

Emma looked doubtful.

"I'm not sure I would have. But I have noticed her smiling a bit more lately, so let's hope the worst is over."

As Emma walked out of the room and headed down the stairs she remembered that awful day when Richard had called them all together to tell them about Simon's death. Jennifer had been so worried about her husband, trying to make sure he took his medication, but in the end the darkness had won and he had taken an overdose. Emma could picture it so clearly, Jennifer arriving home after work calling Simon's name, Jennifer opening the door to the bedroom and seeing him lying lifeless on the bed; she could hear the sob that escaped before the scream, feel the shaking of Jennifer's body as she touched the ice cold hand... Emma took a deep breath and stopped herself – as usual her imagination was getting wildly out of hand. Jennifer had never spoken about what had happened or how she'd found him. When she'd returned to work several months later she'd looked pale and extremely fragile; they'd all been warned to treat her as usual and not to bring up the subject unless she did so herself, which she never had. They'd agreed among themselves to keep an eye on her, not to let her languish on her own in the basement all the time and even now they would pop in to conservation any time they needed to go to the basement store.

There was no reply to Emma's knock, so she tried again, a bit louder this time.

"Come in," Jennifer called.

As soon as she opened the door Emma realised why her first attempt hadn't been heard: the fume cupboard was switched on. This enormous Perspex contraption dwarfed Jennifer, who was sitting in front of it, her gloved hands inside the ventilated area. The noise of the extraction unit was, as always, awful. But at least it meant there was only a hint of the aroma in the room of whatever solvent Jennifer was currently using.

"Hi Jennifer, how's it going?"

Jennifer looked up from her work and pointed to a folder of documents lying on the large table in the centre of the room.

"Some kind person has repaired all of these with the most disgusting self-adhesive tape they could find" she sighed "and now of course the tape is falling off, even though the adhesive is still horribly sticky in places."

"What are you using to get it off with?"

"Any solvent that will work! Toluene is getting the adhesive residue off, but it's not getting rid of the stains. I can try a few others, but we may just have to live with those."

The smell was stronger near the fume cupboard and reminded Emma of especially nasty nail polish remover.

"Don't have that contraption on for too long, you'll go deaf."

"What?" said Jennifer, flashing a big smile.

"I'll save you a muffin at tea break," Emma responded, "you definitely deserve one."

Emma was relieved to be back in the corridor and made her way to the blissfully quiet store. She hoped Jennifer wouldn't need to be in that noise all day. Of course it was better than inhaling the fumes and risk getting all sorts of health problems, but only just. She keyed the code in the keypad - as if no one would be able to guess 1,2,3,4,star - and the lights flickered into action as she entered the room. It never failed to impress her, this large echoing room, filled with rows upon rows of metal shelves laden with the most boringly drab looking brown boxes. But the treasures that lay in those boxes! Even after four years of working there she'd only seen a fraction of what the archive contained. The shelf she needed was two rows down from where the racking was currently open and she rolled the two intervening mobile stacks to one side. She took the box of its shelf, placed it on the little table next to the door and found the folder of letters she needed. The box back on its shelf she scampered up the stairs again, all the way to the top floor and back into her office, where Tim was staring at his phone.

"Everything ok, Tim?"

"Olivia just called." He looked worried. "She wants to see me in her office. Now."

"What have you done?"

"Don't know."

"Better not keep her waiting. Maybe it's something good."

Tim gave her a nervous half-smile, got up and walked out of the room. Poor Tim; it never took much to upset Olivia. Ah well, she couldn't do anything to help him just now, so she sat down and started looking through the documents she'd just brought up.

"Do you know why Dr Dunstable wanted to see Mr Edwards?" Lucas interrupted. Emma shook her head.

"When he came back he'd obviously been told off. It was just about tea break time, so went to the staff room and had a drink." She smiled at the memory. "Frederick had baked blueberry muffins, which cheered Tim up no end."

"When did you go for lunch?"

"Most of us meet up in the staff room around half past twelve."

"Most of you being?"

"Tim, Marie, Jennifer and I. Theresa is always there already as she has her lunch from twelve to one."

"Did you see anyone else around that time?"

"No...not see." She grabbed hold of the glass again. "I'm sure it was nothing."

"What was nothing Miss Baines?"

"Angry voices coming from Richard's office as I was leaving the staff room. Two male voices – I assumed Richard and Frederick."

"Do they argue often?"

"No, absolutely not." She looked directly into Lucas' eyes. "As I said, I'm sure it was nothing."

Lucas was taken aback for a moment by those clear green eyes.

"What did you do in the afternoon?"

Damn. Emma couldn't believe the database was playing up again. It wouldn't even let her close it now. She looked up as Tim dashed into the room, quickly sat down and started tapping away on his keyboard. Emma glanced into the hallway – yes, there was Olivia, heading for her office.

"Did you hear the arguing coming from Richard's office?" Tim asked. "I wonder what that was all about."

"I saw Frederick go out with his coat on earlier, but he's back now. Maybe he needed to cool off." Emma replied. "Odd though, Richard doesn't often get that upset." She looked at her computer screen, sighed, switched the computer off at the plug and switched it on again. A few minutes later she was back in the catalogue database, attempting to add the information she'd found. Suddenly the screen froze; "Oh will you behave!" she shouted.

"Is Tim misbehaving?" Frederick stood at their doorway, coffee in hand, looking puzzled. Emma burst out laughing when she saw the annoyance on Tim's face.

"No, it's only the database, it's acting up again. You wouldn't take a look at it would you?" Frederick walked round the desk and looked at the screen.

"Have you tried…"

"…switching it off and on again." Emma interrupted. "Yes, I did that about ten minutes ago."

"May I?" Frederick asked, gesturing with his cup in the vague direction of the screen.

Emma got up. "Please do. I have some documents to put back in the store, so I'll leave you to work your magic."

As Emma walked to the stairs she looked at Richard's office; should she go in and ask what the arguing had been about? Maybe better to leave it, she decided, and walked down to the basement store. Having replaced the document, she knocked on Jennifer's door and was greeted a few moments later with a "come in". 'Worst nail polish remover ever' Emma thought as she walked through the door.

"Hey Jennifer, found even more gooey tape?"

Jennifer looked up from the document she was examining.

"It's a never ending battle" she said calmly. "What can I do for you Em?"

"I just popped into the store to put a folder away and thought I'd say hello. But I'd better get back upstairs – Frederick is trying to fix the database."

"Ok, I'll see you later then," Jennifer replied and turned her attention back to the letter.

In the office Frederick had vanished and Tim was looking decidedly unhappy.

"What's wrong?" Emma asked as she sat down.

"I popped down to see if Richard was ok, but he didn't want to talk."

I guessed that right then, Emma thought.

"Don't worry about it Tim, I'm sure things will be back to normal tomorrow. Hey, I think Frederick actually managed to fix this!" Emma was so delighted to finally be able to make the addition she'd found, she completely lost track of time.

"What time was it when you went into the store?" Nick asked.

"Around half past two."

"Did you see anyone else down there?"

"No one except Jennifer."

"Did you go back to the basement later?"

"No. I was in my office till about four o'clock, when we had a quick afternoon break."

Lucas chipped in.

"We?"

"Tim, Jennifer, Marie, Theresa and I. Then I was on the computer till five, when I went home."

"Did you see anyone else leave the building?"

Emma paused for a moment.

"The daily exodus is always pretty similar; it gets difficult to distinguish one from another." She closed her eyes, trying to picture the previous night. "I walked downstairs with Tim...we met Jennifer in the foyer...Tim rushed off, while I chatted to Jennifer...then Theresa joined us...Marie walked past and said goodnight...the three of us left the building." She opened her eyes again. "That was it."

"Thank you, Miss Baines." Lucas rose from his chair and held out his hand. As they shook hands he realised she was nearly as tall as he was. And that her smile made her eyes sing. "We'll probably need to talk to you again, but that's it for now."

"I have to admit, I'll be glad to get home."

Nick waited till Emma had left the room.

"So who's next?"

He looked up from his notebook, wondering why he hadn't received an answer.

"Sir?"

Lucas was staring at the closed door, deep in thought.

"Lucas?"

That did it.

"Sorry Nick. Marie Thorpe next, I think. Let's find out how secure this building actually is."

He walked over to the window and looked at the leaden sky, trying to get his mind back on the case. It was a long time since a woman had made such a powerful first impression on him. Not since Chloe, in fact. And she'd left nearly ten years ago.

Four

The door flung open; Lucas spun round to be greeted by the sight of Olivia Dunstable striding into the room. She waddled straight up to him, her hand outstretched.

"Inspector Bohr, a pleasure to meet you."

It was difficult to marry the honeyed voice with the memory of the woman who'd been glaring at everyone earlier. Lucas shook her hand – she had a weak grip – and invited her to sit down at the table.

"Thank you, that's very kind of you. I fear I have reached an age where I do prefer to sit rather than stand."

She heaved herself onto the chair, ignoring Nick who had already taken up his position at the other end of the table.

"Dr Dunstable," Lucas began, "would it surprise you to hear that the victim is likely to be Mr Hugo Bonner?"

A flicker of immense satisfaction was hastily replaced by a more suitable, serious expression.

"Hugo? Why would you think it might be Hugo?"

"The general description fits and we found Mr Bonner's wallet in the dead man's pocket."

"Oh dear, how awful."

She didn't quite pull it off – there was still a triumphant tinge mixed in with the sorrow. Lucas decided to play along and put on his grave face.

"Did you know him well?"

"Reasonably well. After all he was our head of trustees."

Lucas moved in slightly and lowered his voice.

"I'm sure you must have spoken to him often about the archive."

She beamed back at him.

"I made many suggestions, yes. He completely trusted my opinion on our collections. And of course, whenever Richard isn't here I'm in charge and I would meet with him."

"Did you meet Mr Bonner yesterday?" Nick asked.

She seemed surprised at his contribution and kept her gaze firmly on Lucas as she answered.

"No, I did not. He must have come to see Richard and not spoken to anyone else."

She'd almost managed to keep the hurt out of her voice.

"Tell me about yesterday, Dr Dunstable. I believe it started with a meeting?"

"The weekly waste of time Richard insists on, yes. Then we had our management meeting and then I was finally able to get back to my office."

"I believe you had a meeting with Mr Edwards?"

She looked rather contemptuous at the suggestion.

"I spoke to Tim, yes. Then I went to the search room so Theresa could have her break, after which I made myself a cup of coffee in the kitchen." She started to shift impatiently in her chair. "Do you need to know all this detail, inspector?"

"I'm afraid so, Dr Dunstable."

"Very well. I stayed in my office until one minute to twelve, when I went to the search room to allow Theresa to have her lunch..."

"Did you see anyone else?" Lucas interrupted.

"No. Theresa was late back as usual, so it was about five past one when I left the search room. I then went downstairs to the strongroom to retrieve a document..."

"Was anyone else down there?" Nick tried again.

Olivia rolled her eyes.

"Do you think I would leave out the bit where I ran into Hugo or someone behaving suspiciously?" She shifted her attention back to Lucas and gave him a pitying smile. "As I was saying, I retrieved a document from the strongroom. It was in rather dire condition, so I took it into Conservation and had a conversation with Jennifer."

"When did you arrive there?"

Nick could be very persistent.

"About twenty past one. I stayed a few minutes, then went back upstairs." She glared at Nick as she continued. "Tim came out of the library on the first floor just before I reached there and continued up the stairs in front of me. Marie was dusting book shelves as I walked by. I made myself a cup of coffee in the staff room and spent the rest of the afternoon at my desk."

"You didn't have lunch?" Lucas checked.

"I always eat my sandwiches at my desk. Some of us have too much work to do to have lengthy lunches."

Lucas forced out a smile.

"And when did you leave at night?"

For the first time, Olivia looked uncomfortable and didn't meet his eyes.

"My usual time, a quarter past five."

"Just one more question." Nick interceded. "Dr Owens introduced you as the 'archivist' – what does your job entail?"

Olivia gave him a cold stare.

"I am in charge of our archive, sergeant. That means the original documents, rather than printed books. I catalogue them and answer enquiries about them; I also look out for suitable material we might wish to purchase at auctions."

Nick felt like a schoolboy who had just been told off by the head teacher.

Lucas got up.

"Thank you Dr Dunstable, that will be all for now."

Olivia gave Nick a curt nod, Lucas a beaming smile and left.

"Sorry Sir, she walked straight past me when I went into that room. There was no stopping her."

"She does seem rather fierce. Doesn't say anything more than she absolutely has to, either."

"I'll get Mrs Thorpe."

Within five minutes of Marie Thorpe sitting down, Lucas felt he knew her entire life's story, from leaving school at sixteen, through marriage, various jobs including driving a taxi, three children and now being caretaker here at Literally London. Finally realising the hoped for pause would never come, he interrupted Marie as she was regaling them with her daughter's wedding plans.

"That's all useful to know Mrs Thorpe, but I would like to ask you a few questions now." Seeing she was about to speak again as he dared to pause, he continued. "We believe the victim may be a Mr Hugo Bonner. Did you know him at all?"

Marie's mouth opened wide in amazement – she actually seemed speechless. For a moment anyway.

"Mr Bonner? Our Mr. Bonner? Such a gentleman he is, always says hello when he sees me, always interested in the building and all the maintenance..."

"Did you see him yesterday?"

Marie shook her head.

"No I didn't, which just shows it can't be him. He always says hello to everyone, even if he only seriously talks to Richard and..."

"Thank you Mrs Thorpe. I believe you open up the building in the morning?"

"Yes I do, every morning, come rain or shine, I'm here at eight on the dot. And that's not easy with traffic being what it is and the bus never being there on time..."

Lucas could hear Nick groan.

"Was there anything unusual about yesterday morning?"

Marie looked at him wide-eyed.

"You mean the murderer might have already been in the building? And there I was, walking round everywhere on my own, never knowing there was someone watching me..."

"No, no, Mrs Thorpe, I don't think anyone would have already been there," Lucas hastily clarified. "Please just tell us what you do when you open up."

Marie settled back in the chair.

"Ah well, that's easy. I switch off the alarm, leave the outer door open and the sliding door locked. All the staff have the code to open the inner door, so they can come in, but the public can't. Then I walk round the building, checking all the fire exits are clear: top floor first, where the offices and the staff room are, then the first floor..."

"Is that where all the books are?" Nick asked.

"The library yes, on both sides of the stairs. The books people want to look at most are on the shelves in the search room, but the others are on the first floor, all on open shelving, which are a nightmare to dust I can tell you..."

"And then do you check the ground floor?" Lucas tried not to sound too impatient with yet another interruption.

"That's got the fire exit at the back of the building and of course the front door counts as one as well. Down in the basement is only one way out, right at the end of the corridor. We use that one when we get big deliveries. Of course we only keep it propped open when there are people around, I'd never allow a fire door to be left open, that would be against all regulations and I'm always careful..."

"I believe the day started with a meeting?" Lucas stopped trying to sound apologetic for interrupting – Marie was clearly used to holding conversations this way.

"Just the usual Monday get together. Then I checked the outside of the building and made sure all the drains were clear. By the time I got back in it was tea time..."

As Marie and Emma entered the large staff room, Frederick was already in the little kitchen area, pouring boiling water on some instant coffee. Marie joined him to discuss the weekend's football; Emma watched Olivia stride past the open door, on her way to the Searchroom to relieve Theresa so she could have her break.

"I baked blueberry muffins yesterday" Frederick smiled at Emma as he walked past her to go back to his office. "Don't let Marie gobble them all up."

Emma returned the smile and went into the little kitchen. Marie had made herself a cup of tea and was indeed eating a muffin; Emma got her cup and green tea bag and put two muffins on a plate. She heard Tim and Jennifer come in, so added another one and took the plate and cup out with her. They'd all just settled into the various chairs when Theresa ran in, grabbed a muffin, took her coke bottle from the fridge, jumped onto the bright orange sofa and heaved a great big sigh of relief.

"Five people in! Five at once! From the moment we opened!"

"Oh, poor little Theresa, you must be exhausted" Marie laughed.

Theresa didn't look too pleased, so before she could say anything, Emma asked her about her weekend.

"What a party on Saturday! Best one ever!" Theresa exclaimed.

"Was it insanely loud and ridiculously overcrowded with ludicrously expensive drinks?" Emma asked.

"Of course it was", Theresa replied, beaming. "You should come with me sometime", she added sweetly, "or don't you go to clubs anymore?"

Emma shuddered.

"I've never enjoyed places like that, where you have to shout to let yourself be heard and you can feel the bass beating in your chest."

Theresa looked at her in utter disbelief.

"Then what on earth do you do to have fun?"

Jennifer burst out laughing.

"Theresa, there are lots of other ways to have fun. Meeting up with friends for a chat, going to the theatre, reading a book..."

"Going for walks, visiting museums," added Emma, "I bet you'd love the V&A – all those old clothes and weird fashions, they'd be right up your street."

Theresa looked doubtful.

"If you want something more active," Marie chipped in, "try going for a run or a swim or an aerobics class; all great ways to relax."

"No, I have to agree with Theresa," Tim said to everyone's surprise. "Nothing beats a pounding beat and a heaving dance floor."

He blushed a little, realising everyone was staring at him in disbelief.

"I used to go clubbing a lot," he explained, "but I haven't been in years. I guess it's just not something you do once you're in your thirties."

"That's just silly!" Theresa exclaimed. "Why don't you come with me to the Black Circle next Sunday – it's going to be epic."

Tim looked wistful.

"I just might," he sighed.

"Sorry to interrupt this fascinating discussion" Jennifer interjected "but it's quarter to eleven."

Theresa yelped, chucked the half-full bottle back in the fridge and dashed downstairs. Tim and Emma both got up and headed for the door.

"She'll be here in forty seconds," Tim warned.

"I'll wash up," Marie offered.

"And I'll head back to my self-adhesive tape."

Thirty-five seconds later, Olivia walked into the staff room. Marie was busy washing the mugs and watched her enter the kitchen, switch on the kettle, put some instant coffee in her mug and walk straight out again. Always the same routine – even waiting for a kettle to boil was too much of a waste of time.

"What did you do the rest of the morning?"

"A parcel arrived for Frederick, so I took that up to him. A van dropped off a large delivery for Jennifer, which I took through to her. Frederick was there in conservation, he helped me shift it all. Then I got my duster from my little cubby hole..."

"Where's that?" Nick wanted to know.

"On the ground floor, underneath the stairs. I call it a cubby hole, but it's a nice space, with a desk and a chair and room for all my bits and bobs."

"What time was this?"

"About eleven. I dusted shelves in the library until the post arrived," she looked at Nick and added, "just before twelve, that was. There were a few letters for Richard, which I took to him. Then I had lunch." Her eyes widened as memories from yesterday flooded back. "Of course, we had all that commotion in Richard's office. Just after one, Richard and Frederick having a real go at each other. Couldn't hear what was being said, though." Disappointment radiated from her face.

"You didn't ask?"

"I tried to at tea time, but Frederick didn't really respond. So I just went back to my dusting."

Marie looked round the large library with satisfaction; she'd managed to dust a quarter of the bookshelves in only two half days, a new record. She tidied away the stepladder and duster and popped in to Richard's office to tell him about the good progress. By then it was twenty to five, time to start locking up. Marie liked routines. Every day she opened the building in exactly the same way and every day she closed it in exactly the same way. First down to the basement to check that the back door was locked. She didn't have to worry about anything else down there, Jennifer could be relied on to turn off the lights on her way out. On ground floor level she shut down the computer in her little cubby hole, before checking all the windows and the back door. Theresa didn't usually forget anything in the search room, so she could leave that for a quick check right at the end. She switched off the lights in the two first floor libraries, then up to the staff room to check the windows and make sure no food had been left lying around. She could hear Emma and Tim getting their coats on – yes, five o'clock on the dot. As soon as they'd left the office she checked everything was turned off in there. Coming back into the hallway she could hear Emma in the foyer, chatting with Theresa and Jennifer – that just left the managers. They never tended to rush, so she went down, said goodnight to the girls and went into the search room to make sure the fire door was closed. Back in the foyer she checked the signing-out sheet next to the door: Frederick had left as well and she could hear Richard coming down the stairs.

"Good night Marie, see you tomorrow."

"Good night boss."

Marie knew better than to hang around and be seen to be waiting, so she popped back into her little office and read some more of a particularly gruesome thriller, until she heard the final footsteps heading for the door.

"Good night Olivia" she said quietly to herself. Marie put her coat on and switched off the stairwell lights. Even now, when it was still light way beyond half past five, she didn't much like being on her own in the building in the evening. With all the blinds down the Victorian gloom permeated into the twenty-first century and it became all too easy to imagine the ghosts of whipped schoolchildren haunting the corridors. Not to mention all the history seeping out of those innocent looking brown boxes in the stores. She glanced at the signing-

out sheet – wow, they'd actually listened this morning and had all signed out – set the
alarm, and locked the door behind her.

Lucas looked puzzled.
"I thought Dr Owen and Dr Dunstable had left at nearly the same time?"
Marie burst out laughing.
"You've got to be kidding! Olivia leaving on time – whatever next. They're all
supposed to be out by twenty past, but I'm lucky if she's gone by half past, like she
was yesterday. Honestly, she'd stay half the night if Richard'd let her. She's even
asked him if she can lock up, but no, he said, that's Marie's job and she always does
it properly. In a right mood she was after that, I can tell you. Of course..."
"Who locks up when you're not here?"
"Richard does."
"Thank you Mrs Thorpe," Lucas added "you've been extremely helpful."
Marie rose from her seat, but didn't leave.
"If I go home, who locks up tonight then? No disrespect, but you don't know all the
ins and outs of the building and I wouldn't want..."
"We'll call you before we leave and let you lock up." Lucas offered.
Marie nodded, said "That's all right then" and left the room.
Lucas sighed.
"I need coffee."
"I thought you'd stopped drinking..."
"I need coffee," he repeated, emphasising each word. "See if they can spare us some
mugs and instant from that kitchen, Nick. And we'd better talk to Frederick Samuels
next."

Five

"Let me hold the door for you, sergeant."

"Thank you."

Nick entered carrying two mugs, placed the black coffee on the table in front of Lucas and took the milky one over to his seat. Lucas took a quick sip, remembered he didn't like instant and turned his attention to Frederick Samuels.

"So, Mr Samuels, I believe you are the librarian?"

"That's right." Frederick had brought along his own mug, which he now put down on the table. "I am in charge of our collection of printed books and make decisions about which volumes to add, different editions we need to have, etcetera." There was still a faint hint of a Jamaican accent in the way he talked, although a public school education had tried its best to extinguish it.

"Does that mean you are second in command?"

A great bellowing laugh filled the room.

"Don't let Olivia hear you say that, inspector. We are both *second in command*, although she may have other ideas."

"But you know Hugo Bonner?"

The laughter vanished as confusion spread over Frederick's features.

"Of course I know Hugo –why on earth do you ask?"

"We have reason to believe the body found in the basement is that of..."

"Hugo? How astonishing. I had no idea he had even been here yesterday."

"He didn't come to meet you, then?"

"No, not at all. He comes to see Richard, but usually drops by to say hello."

Lucas attempted another sip of his coffee, while Nick chipped in.

"Could you tell us about yesterday, sir? After the staff meeting..."

"We had our weekly management meeting. I wasn't happy with the way the trustees keep accepting utter rubbish for our collections. Richard rather brushed it off." Frederick put his mug down on the exact same place it had stood before. "I spent the rest of the morning at my desk, until Marie brought up a parcel."

Frederick had just gulped down the last remnants of his coffee, when Marie came in with the post.

"Great muffins again Fred" Marie said "but my favourites are still those chocolaty ones."

"Hint taken, I'll get the cocoa powder out this weekend." Frederick smiled as Marie continued her post run. It had been difficult to indulge his favourite hobby since the divorce, but his

colleagues had become appreciative of the weekly bake and he enjoyed sharing his wares. That it annoyed Olivia to see smiling faces in the staff room was a nice bonus. He turned his attention to the post; not many letters of course, most correspondence happened digitally now, but there was an interesting looking padded envelope. As he opened it, a note slid out: As promised, Kev. A memory crawled its way into his mind of a fundraiser a few weeks ago and an overbearing man promising him to send a 'nice book' to the archive. Well, they had thousands already and most were bound to be a whole lot 'nicer' than this one, but still, you never knew. He disentangled the book from the envelope and swore as the boards immediately fell off – really, people had no idea how to look after books! He turned to the front page, read the details twice and almost slid off his chair. A first edition Whitmore! First edition! He took back his previous thought; after all if more people knew how to look after old books, they'd realise how precious and valuable some of them could be and they'd never offer them for free to his library. No way, they'd go straight to an antiques dealer – or worse, put it on eBay! A pity about the boards, but Jennifer should be able to fix those. He picked up both– originals, surely? – and the rest of the book and set off for the basement.

There was no response to his gentle knock on the conservation door, but he opened it anyway, saying "Jennifer?" as he went in. Jennifer was sitting at her computer with her back to the door, unable to hear him thanks to the dreadful whirring of that horrendous fume-contraption. "Jennifer?" he said again, a bit louder this time. Jennifer turned round and looked surprised: "Frederick, I didn't hear you at all there. Let me switch this off, it's only mopping up the leftovers on the blotters now."
The sudden cessation of noise was deafening in itself and needed a moment to adjust to. Still speaking a little too loudly Frederick asked 'What horrors have you been dealing with this morning then?' Jennifer showed him the now no longer sticky documents and the remnants of tape lying in the fume cupboard. Then it was Frederick's turn to show the dismembered book he'd just received.
"Anything you can do for this, Jennifer?"
She took a good look at the binding, boards and textblock and showed Frederick how it would be feasible to attach everything back together again.
"Just mention it to Richard and I'll add it to my planning for next month."
Frederick was about to be profusely grateful when a loud tap on the door was followed by Marie bursting in.
"Oh I'm sorry, am I interrupting?"
"Of course not Marie" Jennifer replied "what can I do for you?"
"A van has just dropped off all that disaster equipment you ordered – there's boxes and boxes of it, all in the corridor."

"That's great, just in time for the big exercise I'm planning for next month. Would you mind bringing it all in here Marie" she added sweetly "so I can go through it all and check everything's there? I'll make some room for them."

"I'll give you hand Marie," Frederick offered; it still took the two of them about ten minutes before they had all the boxes neatly stacked up to the left of the door, between the big table and the majestic iron press.

"Thank you both very much."

"I suppose you'll want a hand getting it all into the store as well?" Marie asked, not sounding particularly enthusiastic.

"Don't worry about that Marie. It'll take me a while to sort all this out – I'll put it next door bit by bit."

Frederick waved a goodbye to both and headed back to his office, where he put the book on the new accessions shelf so he could show it Richard later. Unfortunately his excellent mood vanished as soon as he read his next email.

"What email was that?" Lucas interrupted.

Frederick moved his mug about 3 millimetres to the left.

"One of the trustees announcing they had accepted another 'wonderful' collection of books for us." The coffee cup was repositioned about four millimetres to the right. "I have to admit, I got rather angry, especially as Richard had just assured me this wouldn't happen again."

"What did you do?"

"I went to see Richard." The mug slid another two millimetres to the right. "He wasn't in his office, so I waited outside his door until he came back, just after one. We had a slight...altercation, after which I went outside to get some fresh air."

"Did you see anyone on your way out?"

Frederick shook his head.

"I'm afraid I wasn't in a mood to see anything. I do know I didn't see anyone when I came back in; I stayed in my office a little while and then decided to have a wonder round. I didn't get any further than the office though, as Emma was having problems with the database."

"And once you'd helped Miss Baines?"

"I spent the rest of the afternoon in my office; left the building at my usual time of ten past five."

The mug was now back exactly where it had been to begin with.

"Thank you, Mr Samuels, that's all for now."

"Who next?"

Nick was still sitting at the table, finishing off his coffee, while Lucas wandered over to the bookcase.

"Remind me who are left?"

Nick checked his notes.

"Jennifer Marr, Tim Edwards and Theresa Woodward."

Lucas hesitated; did the order matter?

"Surprise me."

He turned his attention back to the books while Nick was out of the room. A whole wall of beautifully bound first editions, neatly arranged according to the Dewey system. He expected no less from Frederick Samuels.

"Please sit down Miss Woodward."

Nick had re-appeared, followed by the bundle of youth that was Theresa Woodward. She pulled out a different chair, nearer to where Nick had sat down, and gave him a dreamy smile. A good thing Nick was so thoroughly down to earth, Lucas thought. Better let him take the lead on this one. He sat down on his usual chair and gave Nick a brief nod.

"How long have you worked here, Miss Woodward?" Nick began.

"It's Theresa," she smiled, "no need to be so formal."

Nick gave her a broad smile back.

"Very well, Theresa. How long?"

"A year and a half. I worked in a baker's for a couple of years after I left school and then got the job here."

"Do you like it here?"

"It's all right." She paused for a moment. "Actually, it's been pretty good. I've learned a lot and now that I'm alone in the search room, dealing with the customers, I've got quite a bit of responsibility."

"A good place to work then?"

"It would be, if only..." She leant in closer to Nick and whispered. "Olivia's a horrible old bag; the rest of them are all right."

"Have you ever met a Mr Hugo Bonner?"

Theresa nonchalantly placed her right hand on the table, so it almost touched Nick's arm.

"That's the big boss, isn't it, the one who's in charge of the trust? I met him at a fundraiser we all had to go to; he was pretty charming, but the do itself was horrendously boring. I left as soon as Richard said we could go."

"We think the body Miss Baines found is that of Mr Bonner."

Her eyes opened wide in surprise; she pulled her hand back and sat up straight.

"Really? Someone killed our boss?"

"You seem surprised."

"Well, it just seems like a stupid thing to do. All those old fogies at the fundraiser loved him, I'm sure they gave him lots of money." She slumped back in her seat. "Maybe I should start looking for another job."

"Can you tell me about yesterday, Theresa?"

She nodded without much enthusiasm.

"It was pretty much like every other day. I'm in the search room all the time, so I don't know much about what goes on in the rest of the building. I even missed the fight between Richard and Frederick."

"But you heard about it?"

"Oh yes, at afternoon tea break. I was there already when Marie came in."

Frederick was making himself another cup of coffee in the staffroom; as soon as she walked in Marie asked:

"What was all that commotion about with the guv'nor earlier? It sounded like you two were at each other's throat."

The others tried to look disinterested, but no one wanted to break the silence and possibly miss whatever Frederick had to say.

"Things did get a bit heated, yes," Frederick admitted, "but it was nothing. I suppose it was just an argument that had been brewing for a while."

Frederick wandered back to his office, delicately holding his hot mug so as not to spill anything or burn his fingers. Marie turned to the others:

"Why would you get that worked up over 'nothing'?"

"It must have just been the last straw," Emma suggested, "It's never good to bottle things up."

"I always tell people exactly what I think" Theresa said "That makes life much easier."

"Really?" Tim sounded incredulous. "You must have had lots of interesting chats with Olivia then."

"I'm forthright, not an idiot!" Theresa exclaimed. "And before you say anything else, there's a big difference between saying what you think and being mean and nasty with it."

"If you say so." Marie replied.

Jennifer got up before Theresa could take the bait, took her mug to the kitchen and asked "Any volunteers to wash up?"

"My turn I guess." Theresa went into the kitchen while the others all trundled back to their desks.

"I was only joking Tessie, you know that don't you?" Marie said as she handed her her mug. Theresa gave her a quick 'no hard feelings' smile and handed her the tea towel.

"We finished the dishes, then I went back to the search room to tidy up." Theresa's hand had slipped back onto the table; Nick pulled his arm back slightly.
"When did you leave?"
"Just after five, like I always do. I hopped on the bus, met some friends in a pub and got home about eight."
"Thank you Miss Woodward."
The sound of Lucas' voice made her jump.
"We may need to talk to you again, but you can go home now."
Theresa just managed to brush Nick's arm as she got up from her chair.
"I bet you like parties, sergeant."
Nick laughed.
"The last party I went to I was surrounded by three year olds and balloons. Mind you, my son had a great time and it *was* his birthday, so..."
Theresa looked decidedly disappointed.

Six

A very pale Jennifer Marr sat down and reached for a glass of water. She gave Lucas a faint smile.

"Bad memories. They've been flooding back this afternoon."

He pulled his chair closer to the table and softened his voice.

"Memories of what?"

"My husband's death, just over two years ago." Tears welled up in her eyes; she grabbed her purse, pulled out a tissue and dabbed her eyes.

"I'll try to make this brief Mrs Marr. Did you know Hugo Bonner?"

Jennifer stared at him in utter disbelief.

"Hugo? It's Hugo?" she whispered.

"You knew him well?"

Jennifer looked down at the grainy surface of the table.

"Reasonably well." Her gaze shifted to the window. "He took a keen interest in my work."

Lucas waited a while, but she didn't add anything else.

"What *is* your work?"

Jennifer continued to look in the direction of the window, her eyes unfocussed, unseeing.

Lucas tried again, a little louder this time.

"Mrs Marr?"

Gradually Jennifer turned her head in his direction.

"What exactly is your work, Mrs Marr?"

Her eyes took another moment to re-focus, but found his face as her hands found the cool glass of water.

"I'm the conservator. I repair damaged books, documents, photographs, maps. Anything in the archive. So they can be looked at again."

"And Mr Bonner found this interesting?"

She nodded her head.

"He found it fascinating, how you can turn a disintegrating, torn, extremely fragile piece of paper back into something that is safe to be held and studied." She took a sip of water. "He loved books. Had a big collection of his own." Another sip. "I did some work for him privately, re-binding volumes that were falling apart." She gave Lucas an apologetic smile. "I'm not being very coherent, I'm sorry. It's just all a bit much."

Lucas leant in slightly closer.

"You're doing fine. Did Mr Bonner come to see you yesterday?"

"No." She sounded puzzled and her eyes flitted through the room, unable to focus on anything. "I don't understand why he was here...no one mentioned he was coming...no one mentioned seeing him...I don't understand..."

"Mrs Marr?"

Lucas waited until she'd focussed on him again.

"Tell me about yesterday."

Jennifer retrieved her soup from the fridge, heated it up in the microwave and joined Theresa who was munching away on her cheese sandwiches and crisps, listening to her Ipod.

"Still busy down there?" Jennifer asked.

Theresa pulled out her earphones.

"Not too bad now, only three left. And one's Mr Harrison – he's never any trouble."

"I shouldn't say anything," Marie whispered loudly, as she, Emma and Tim joined the table, "but it's a year since we had our last fire drill."

Jennifer nodded along with the others, but still couldn't understand why she always insisted in warning them of an upcoming drill – it's not as if the evacuation procedure was that complicated. All she had to do was turn left outside her door and walk straight out through the fire exit and then up the little staircase to the pavement.

"Did you have a nice weekend Jennifer?" Emma asked. They meant well of course, but it was getting a bit tiresome, the little visits to conservation and careful enquiries about her well-being.

"I went to visit my parents in Bristol, it was lovely."

Marie interrupted by shouting "Two minutes past one Theresa" and they watched as Theresa shot out of the door.

"You could have said something earlier, Marie." Emma sounded reproachful.

"How is she ever going to learn if we keep warning her?" Marie asked, "Besides, she's a tough girl, she can handle our Dr Dunstable's tantrums."

Tim took his mug and plate over to the kitchen and started washing up; Marie followed him and asked him what he thought about 'that' penalty. Jennifer and Emma waited their turn, before leaving the staff room and walking back down the hallway. Jennifer had just reached the stairs when she heard angry voices coming from Richard's office. Both male – funny, Richard and Frederick didn't usually have shouting matches. On the first floor Marie was dusting shelves and Tim seemed to be looking for a book; the football conversation would be continuing for a while yet. Jennifer made her way through the foyer and could see Theresa beyond the big glass search room doors, lost in thought behind her computer screen. Further down she went, down the stairs beyond the staff only door, down to her cosy studio. The boxes full of disaster supplies – plastic sheeting, disposable aprons, gloves, overshoes, torches, large sheets of extra absorbent blotting paper, absorbent water cushions, mops, even two free standing electric fans – were standing there invitingly, waiting to be unpacked. But no, they would have to wait till tomorrow; she'd prepared some wheat starch paste just before lunch which would have cooled off enough now to repair those poor documents that had been plastered with sellotape. Jennifer was searching through her drawer of off-cuts for some nice Japanese tissue of the right weight and tone, when Olivia barged in. She never bothered with knocking; everyone assumed she was hoping to catch them not doing any work, but Jennifer thought it more likely it just didn't occur to her to show any form of politeness towards her underlings.

"I just got this manuscript out of the store Jennifer and it's rather brittle – see, bits are falling off." Jennifer took the proffered manuscript and examined the yellowing, acidic paper. Early twentieth century, worst quality paper imaginable.

"I can deacidify and repair the pages Olivia, but that will take a few weeks to complete."

"That's far too long, I need to be able to answer this enquiry within the next few days." Olivia looked impatient and was not going to be willing to compromise. "Isn't there something else you can do?"

"If we had a scanner I could scan it for you, but as we don't..." Jennifer continued not wanting to have the same argument again "...why don't I photograph all the pages tomorrow so you can look at the images and find the information that way?"

"Fine" Olivia replied rather curtly and left the room.

Jennifer delicately put the manuscript in an acid-free folder and went back on the hunt for that piece of Japanese repair tissue she knew was somewhere in the drawer.

"Emma popped in a little later, but she only stayed a couple of minutes. I spent the rest of the afternoon in my studio, carrying out repairs."

Her voice was a little steadier now, her eyes clearer.

"When did you leave?"

"A few minutes after five, as always. I met Emma and Theresa in the foyer and we all left together."

Lucas got up again.

"Thank you Mrs Marr, that's all for now."

"She looked dreadful."

"Memories can do that to you, Nick." Lucas sighed. "They can be utterly overwhelming, leaving you lost in the past, unconnected to the present."

Nick gave his boss a disconcerted look.

"I think I'd better get our last witness."

Lucas could feel himself being tugged by a sadness he thought he'd overcome. No, he told himself and he physically shook his head, refusing to let the past seep into his mind and colour the present. He took a deep breath and started looking through Nick's notes, filling his thoughts with the events of the previous day.

Tim Edwards hesitated as he entered the room, looking at Lucas as if to ask permission to enter.

"Do come in Mr Edwards, and sit down. Sorry to have you kept waiting so long."

He'd seemed tall when seated on the sofa, but now it was he clear that he wasn't that much taller than Nick. A lot skinnier though. That combined with his thin short brown hair, thick black spectacles and rather pallid complexion, made him look decidedly unhealthy.

"I'm used to being last in the queue, inspector."

Lucas looked at him more closely; a remark like that could have easily sounded bitter, but there was a playfulness in the eyes and a gentleness in his face that was easy to warm to. Maybe not so unhealthy after all. Just tired?

"What do you do here, Mr Edwards?"

"Ah. Officially I am assistant to both Frederick and Olivia, helping them organise the collections, carrying out research, answering complex enquiries...that sort of thing."

"And unofficially?"

"Frederick doesn't like to delegate and Olivia wants a qualified archivist for an assistant." A faint smile hovered over his face. "Not always an easy situation."

Not tiredness, Lucas decided. Stress.

"Do you know Mr Hugo Bonner?"

Tim took his time before answering, tapping his fingers on the table while gathering his thoughts.

"I take it that means he's our dead body?"

"It looks that way."

"I've met Mr Bonner several times on his visits here and at fundraising events, but I never spoke to him much." That wry smile again. "I'm not quite important or rich enough and the wrong sex to flirt with."

Lucas looked up.

"Mr Bonner liked to flirt?"

"Oh, constantly. He was extremely good at it too – we always seem to get much bigger contributions from female patrons."

"Did he flirt with any of the staff here?"

Tim blushed and cleared his throat.

"Look, inspector, I didn't mean to imply anything. I don't think Hugo Bonner knew how to speak to women without flirting. And no, he never flirted more with any of my female colleagues than he did with anyone else." He paused. "At least not as far as I'm aware."

Lucas decided to drop the subject for now.

"Tell us about yesterday, Mr Edwards. I believe you had a meeting with Dr Dunstable?"

37

That wry smile again.

"I suppose you could call it that."

The brief walk to Olivia's office was over far too soon for Tim's liking. He hesitated outside her door, gingerly knocked and entered upon hearing the dreaded "come". As usual, Olivia was staring at her computer screen and didn't look up as he came in.

"Um...You wanted to see me Olivia?"

"Sit down Tim" Olivia said still concentrating on her emails.

The frosty tone made Tim's heart sink as he slid onto the chair. He'd managed to stay out of the doghouse for nearly a year now – what had happened?

"The Whitten collection" Olivia said in that special calm voice of hers. "How did you get on with that?"

She still hadn't looked at him. Confused Tim went over the few conversations they'd had about that collection; surely he'd done what she'd asked?

"I made a list of the contents and described each item – there were nearly two hundred letters, five manuscripts and nineteen notebooks. I sent it you on Wednesday."

She was looking at him intently now.

"And you're happy with what you've done?"

That same icy tone; there would be no right answer.

"I did everything you asked me to..."

"I'm very disappointed in you Tim."

Tim wished the floor would just open up right now, before she could go any further.

"You have a decent degree, you're supposed to be intelligent. I had high hopes for you, I thought you might manage to become an archivist. Clearly I was wrong – no archivist would just write out a list like that. There was no context, no..."

As Olivia went on, Tim stopped listening. She hadn't just wanted him to make a list, she'd set him a test and he'd failed. It didn't matter that she hadn't given clear instructions or that she'd always been happy with his lists in the past. She would have dropped hints and he hadn't noticed them and now it was too late. He realised she'd stopped talking and was staring right at him.

"I'll do it again and this time..."

"Don't bother," came the sharp reply "I'll do it myself." And with that she turned her attention back to the computer screen. Tim knew he'd been dismissed and left that cold room – why was it always so much colder in there than anywhere else in the building? – to return to the safety of his office. Emma gave him a sympathetic look as he came in.

"Doghouse?" she asked. He just nodded, too angry and embarrassed to say anything.

Emma checked the corridor behind him and whispered just about loud enough

"She's a horrid bully and a total cow – don't let her get to you."

Trying to find his composure Tim replied: "That's a whole lot easier said than done."

"I cried last time, so you're still coping better than me."

He managed to give her a smile.

"She's not going to be here forever is she?"

"Who is?"

Marie's question made them both jump.

"Marie!" Emma exclaimed "we didn't spot you coming in."

"Had a ticking off, did we?" Marie asked looking at Tim, who shrugged his shoulders. "Good thing it's tea time, then, a decent cuppa is just what you need."

"I'll be there in a minute" Tim said, still shaking slightly.

"Don't wait too long" Emma smiled "I've already promised Jennifer I'd save her a muffin, I'm not sure I can hide two."

"I take it Dr Dunstable often upsets people?"

"Let's just say you'd have plenty of suspects if it had been her body Emma found."

Lucas couldn't help but smile.

"How about the rest of your day?"

"I'm sure you've heard about the argument between Richard and Frederick around one o'clock?"

Lucas nodded.

"I tried to talk to Richard afterwards, to see what had happened, but he wasn't in a talkative mood." Tim sighed. "Catching people in bad moods is one of my specialties."

"I assume you didn't notice Mr Bonner around that time?"

"I didn't see him at all yesterday, I had no idea he'd been here. I was in my office all afternoon, working on the catalogue – I didn't see anyone, except at tea break."

"When did you go home?"

A genuine, warm smile now.

"Just after five, as always. Emma and I went downstairs together; she stayed chatting to Jennifer, I just said goodnight and made my way to the Tube."

Lucas rose from his seat.

"Thank you, Mr Edwards, that's all for now."

Seven

Emma still felt a bit shaky and was glad the police inspector had suggested they all go home. Well, it hadn't really been a suggestion, had it? More of a quiet command – he seemed to be good at those. She opened the door to her flat and was greeted by a blood curdling scream. An oddly deep voice proclaimed:

"I am the one true Dracula and you WILL join me."

"No, please, stay away, don't bite me," a very shrill voice shrieked.

Emma opened the door to the living room.

"Hey Jess."

"Em, what are you doing home? Are you sick?"

"I found a body at work. His head had been bashed in. The police questioned us and then sent us home."

Jessica dropped her script and threw herself on to the sofa.

"How ghastly!"

"It's not a joke, Jess."

Emma dumped her coat on a chair and went through to the kitchen; Jessica jumped up and followed.

"Seriously? That really happened? Are you ok?"

Emma was fighting back the tears that were welling up in her eyes.

"I don't know, I've never seen a man with a bloody mess where his head ought to be before." She knew she was sounding tetchy, but she just couldn't help it. Damn, why did she start crying?

Jessica gave her best friend a tight hug.

"It's ok Em, it must have been a terrible shock."

"I think I'll give mum a call," Emma sniffed.

"I'll get the sheets out."

"I'm not going to ask her to come down."

"You won't need to. Besides it's always fun to see aunt Elise. Can you imagine my mother being willing to sleep on our sofa?"

The image of Jessica's always perfect looking mother camping on their couch flitted before Emma's eyes and she burst out laughing. Trust Jess to find a way to cheer her up. She snuggled into the cushions, mug of tea and packet of chocolate digestives on the little table in front of her, and took her phone out of her bag.

Elise was bored. So horribly bored. Early retirement had seemed a good idea when she'd been offered such a generous package by an employer keen to shed permanent staff and work with free-lancers instead. After all, this way she'd be able to go after the stories she cared about, pursuing them whatever direction they took her in. But it had soon become clear that no one was interested in hiring her; since reaching sixty she had become invisible, her forty years of experience counting for nothing. After a very frustrating couple of years she'd given up and had decided to write her memoirs instead. The view from her study showed dark green Derbyshire hills, fields dotted with sheep and sharp bits of ancient rock jutting out at improbable angles. The view on her computer screen was rather more depressing: deciding to write a witty book about your experiences as an investigative journalist was easy - actually writing it not quite so. She didn't want to be stuck in the past, surrounded by ghosts all day. Elise sighed as her phone went - yet someone else desperate to sell her car insurance or loft insulation...

Thirty minutes later, bag packed and with a spring in her step, she jumped in her car and headed down to London.

The bright, spacious room reminded Lucas of old photographs of libraries, except that the sleek computer monitors looked totally out of place amongst the extra wide oak tables, leather backed chairs and enormous glass-fronted bookcases. He had to admit it felt like a very pleasant room to sit for a few hours and pore over ancient writings. Were those grey cushions that were strewn all over the tables for elderly customers or even older books, he wondered.

"Here we are boss."

Nick entered the room clutching a file full of papers, which he spread out all over the nearest table.

"All their statements about yesterday."

"Good. Flo said one till six, but as the alarm was set at five thirty, we'll assume our victim was dead by then."

Lucas divided the statements into two piles.

"You take the men, I'll take the women. We'll walk round the building, re-tracing their steps from one o'clock onwards." He scanned through the statements he was holding. "Probably best to start up in the staff room."

An hour later they felt as it they'd know the building for years and sat back down again in the searchroom.

"Well, that proves it," Nick said, "they all had enough time."

"And that's not even considering that our mystery man could have been let into the building in the morning."

Nick looked surprised.

"You don't think he came in through the front door?"

"You said it yourself Nick, it would be a very risky thing to do if you didn't want to be seen. But if someone opened either the fire door at the back of the ground floor just next to our Mrs Thorpe's cubby-hole, or the fire door in the basement, you could easily stay hidden."

Nick had to agree.

"A pity about the rain – no chance of finding footprints near any of those doors. And once you were in you wouldn't need to know a code to get into that storage room in the basement either – a perfect place for a clandestine meeting."

"I don't think we can get much more out of being here." Lucas decided. "Better give our friend a call as she was so keen to come back to set the alarm and then we can visit Mrs Bonner."

Lucas couldn't stop his eyes darting round from one beautiful art deco object to another– there was a seemingly never ending supply of them in this high-ceilinged room. Just to have one of this quality in his flat; maybe he ought to start visiting boot sales and hope for a miracle find. He dragged himself back from his surroundings and concentrated on the woman sitting down on the chair opposite: Helen Bonner. They'd arrived at the large Georgian house at the same time as she had and had watched her get out of her black Porsche - a short, elegantly dressed forty-something woman, with her shoulder length black hair expensively cut, wearing high heeled shoes which no doubt cost more than he earned in a month. She'd been surprised to see them and had seemingly no idea why they were there. They'd been ushered into this impressive room, invited to sit down on a chaise longue that looked like it belonged in an episode of Poirot and had been brought tea by a stern looking housekeeper. Now, ten minutes later, Mrs Bonner had deigned to join them and had already very deliberately looked at her watch twice. Lucas had very little sympathy left.

"Can you tell me where your husband is, Mrs Bonner?"

The widening of her eyes showed this wasn't the question she'd been expecting.

"My husband? Why on earth do you want to know that?"

"Please humour me, Mrs Bonner. When did you last see him?"

"Yesterday morning, around eleven." Her eyes darted from Lucas to Nick and back to Lucas again. "Has something happened?"

"You weren't worried when he didn't come home last night?"

She was breathing faster now.

"He said he would be late back...he was going to have dinner with Sam Ripley."

"Who is that, madam?" Nick asked.

"Hugo's business partner. They often meet over dinner...and a few drinks. I don't like Hugo coming home when he's drunk...not a very good example for Matthew. Our son. So he tends to spend the night at Sam's. But he's always home by the time Matthew comes back from school." Her voice was steadier now. "Has there been an accident?"

Lucas met her gaze and lowered his voice.

"I'm very sorry to have to tell you this, Mrs Bonner, but the body of a man was discovered in the Literally London building this morning. The general description fits your husband and we found his wallet in the jacket pocket."

"He died at the archive?" She paused a moment, looking around the room, trying to make sense of what she'd just heard. "But then why aren't you sure it's Hugo? Anyone there would be able to tell you..."

"I'm afraid it's not that straightforward." Lucas hesitated – exactly how much detail did he want to put her through? "The manner of his death left the face unrecognisable."

All colour drained out of Helen Bonner's face.

"We're still investigating, of course, but it looks like he was murdered."

There were still no tears, no signs of grief, just shock.

"Is there someone we can call?" Nick asked. "A family member or friend perhaps?"

Helen gave him a contemptuous look, rose from her chair, and straightened herself to her full 1m60 height.

"I am not a child, sergeant." She was back in control, of both her voice and emotions, and turned to Lucas. "If you will excuse me, my son will be home from school soon and I will have to explain to him what has happened. Then I will come to identify my husband's body."

"Thank you Mrs Bonner. We will send a car over later to take you to the mortuary."

Elise still didn't really like London. Great to visit, obviously, but horrible to live in, just as it had been thirty years ago: too big, too many people, too much concrete. And far too many cars, she added, as yet someone else tried to undertake her. The cyclists were a new phenomenon and added even more confusion to the roads; no wonder Emma preferred an Oyster card to a car. Road works up ahead meant she had to follow a diversion and she suddenly realised she was only a few streets away from the flat where she and Daniel had lived for nearly five years. On an impulse she changed lanes – causing wild tooting behind her – and drove into the street. Yes, it was still there, the little Victorian terrace with the tiny front garden; if she half closed her eyes those curtains on the second floor looked exactly like theirs had. She parked the car and was about to get out, when she stopped herself – what on earth was she doing? What was she hoping to find here? All the wonderful memories were part of her, not hiding in that little flat up there. And Daniel certainly wouldn't be there. Funny how his name could still overwhelm her with so much joy and so much pain all rolled up in to one. Come on Elise, she reprimanded herself, not like you to get all maudlin like this. Pull yourself together, woman! She started the car, almost hit a cyclist as she pulled out – seriously! who expects cyclists in London! – and extra carefully re-joined the traffic on the main road.

"Mum." Emma gave her mother a hug and was surprised at the depth of relief she felt.
"Sweetheart, next time you're desperate to see me, just call," Elise whispered. "No need to be quite so dramatic about it."
"I'll try to remember."
Emma let go, dried her eyes and closed the door.
"Now where's my other favourite girl?" Elise called.
Jessica came out of the kitchen.
"Aunt Elise! I haven't been traumatised today, but do I still get a hug?"
Elise looked thoughtful for a moment.
"Were you making me a cup of tea in there?"
"Of course."
"Then come over here darling!"
Emma put Elise's case in her bedroom, then realised just what kind of state the room was in and hastily did some tidying. When she walked back into the main living area, Jess and Elise were chatting away on the lush dark blue three-seater sofa, drinking tea and nibbling biscuits. Emma glanced round the rest of the room: the small pine dining table with its four chairs had a lovely bowl of fruit on it and nothing else – well done Jess. The Ikea bookshelves that lined the expanse of wall behind the sofa weren't looking any more disorganised than usual and although the two cream rugs sprawling over the wooden floorboards could do with being hoovered, overall the space wasn't in too chaotic a state. Certainly good enough to pass her mother's – admittedly low – expectations. Emma sat down on the equally dark blue armchair and grabbed a chocolate digestive.
"So sweetheart," Elise began, "how are you holding up?"
Emma grimaced.

"Not too bad. There are now actual moments I'm able not to think about what's happened." She closed her eyes. "Although not seeing it is a different matter."

"Tell me about Hugo Bonner. What kind of a man was he?"

"Distraction. Good idea mum. Let me see...he was very charming. The kind of man everyone notices when he walks into a room and who everyone hopes will join them." She sighed. "When he was talking to you he made you feel as if you were the only person around, or at least the only one interesting enough for him to want to be with."

"Emma," Elise said trying not to sound too worried, "just how well did you know him?"

"Honestly mum! He must have been at least fifty!"

"That's not really an answer sweetheart. Catching an older man's attention can be very flattering."

"Anything you'd like to share with us, Aunt Elise?" Jessica innocently asked.

"No thank you dear, we're talking about Emma and Hugo Bonner at the moment."

"There is nothing to talk about." Emma had emphasized each word clearly and deliberately. "I only met him a few times – mostly at work and once at a big fundraiser. And yes he was charming, but in a very obvious, overly confident way. *Not* in an attractive way. At least not to me."

"But to other women?"

"All the old ladies at the fundraiser drooled over him."

"Well I'm glad to hear *you* didn't fall for his charms, anyway." Elise gave Jess a wink. "And now that you've met yet another man you've decided you weren't attracted to, perhaps you'll finally meet one who does pass muster."

Oh no, Emma thought, not my love life again.

"It's terrible Aunt Elise, I keep introducing her to perfectly nice guys, but she's so fussy and just won't..."

Emma grabbed the cushion that was lying next to her and hurled it at Jess, who managed to duck just in time, while snatching a different one from the sofa and hurling it in Emma's direction. Emma expertly caught it, feigned a throw at Jess and managed to hit a startled Elise instead.

"Pillow fight" they all yelled together, grabbing whichever cushion they could find.

Eight

The large open plan office space on the second floor of the police station had been designed to facilitate communication and encourage cooperation between the various detective sergeants and inspectors. In other words, everyone could see what everyone else was doing and - even worse as far as Lucas was concerned - could hear what everyone else was saying. The constant background noise of conversations on the phones and between colleagues, not to mention the animated banter that continually floated round the office, made it practically impossible to really, seriously, think. Perhaps the architects had not considered thinking to be an activity police officers ever needed to indulge in. Lucas switched on his computer, ignored the warning that his inbox was almost full and clicked on the report containing background checks on all the staff at Literally London. Nick wheeled his chair round to face his boss.

"Anything interesting?"

"Let's see. Richard Owen, doctor in English literature, worked at various universities, has been in charge at our archive for nearly ten years, nearing retirement age, married, grandchildren – nothing out of the ordinary there."

"How about the scary woman?"

"Scary?"

"They're all scared of her, that was obvious."

"Olivia Dunstable, archivist, history degree, not quite sixty yet, widow..."

"Someone married her?" Nick sounded quite incredulous.

Lucas gave him a warning look.

"No children and despite your dislike of her, nothing out of the ordinary."

"I bet she's waiting for Owen to retire, so she can take over. They must all be shitting bricks about that."

"Stay focussed Nick, she's not our victim. Right, Frederick Samuels, parents emigrated from Jamaica when he was two, went to a minor public school, chartered librarian, recently divorced, two grown-up kids. Nothing again."

Nick had wheeled round to the other side of the desk now.

"What about the woman who found the body, Emma Baines?"

"Degree in English literature, has worked in the place for four years, single, shares a flat with an actress – both are from Derbyshire, so presumably childhood friends."

Nick sighed.

"This is getting boring."

"Jennifer Marr, degree in art history and in paper conservation..." Lucas stopped suddenly.

"Something interesting?"

"No, just how her husband died. He suffered from depression and killed himself just over two years ago. An overdose of prescription drugs."

"Tragic, but unlikely to have anything to do with this. Is there no one in this place with any kind of criminal record?"

"Our very talkative Mrs Thorpe wasn't exactly forthcoming about her troubled past." Nick sat up straight; this sounded more like it.

"Marie Thorpe used to be a cabbie, but lost her driving licence after a conviction for dangerous driving. Looks like she caused quite a pile-up; very lucky no one died or she would have ended up in prison. She was in and out of jobs for a few years after that."

"No suspected drug dealing or fencing in that time? It could explain the secret meeting."

"No, no hint of anything untoward. She may not be the brightest person in that place, but I doubt she'd be stupid enough to risk a perfectly good job by letting dubious characters into the building."

"Who does that leave?"

"The other researcher, Tim Edwards. Degree in English, was a teaching assistant for a while, but then joined this place nearly five years ago. Lives with his girlfriend, a primary school teacher."

"Nothing there either then."

"One more to go, the very young Miss Theresa Woodward. Various office temping jobs since passing her A-levels, started at the archive six months ago."

"Seems odd she got the job, it doesn't look like her kind of environment."

"She's had a caution for cannabis use, but nothing worse than that."

Lucas' phone rang.

"What have you found Flo?"

"I haven't got much for you, I'm afraid. Cause of death was having his head bashed in, but whether that happened because of the racking or not is impossible to tell. That store is temperature controlled, which messes up my ability to give you an accurate time of death – I'm afraid I've had to extend it to any time between noon and seven pm."

"Thanks Flo." Lucas turned to Nick. "Have we tracked down this Sam Ripley yet?" Nick nodded.

"Bonner and Ripley own a chain of bookshops called *Books Galore!*; the head office is in Fleet Street. I made some discrete enquiries – he hasn't been seen there since Friday."

"See if you can find out a bit more about the company; it can't be an easy time for bookshops with all this internet competition. I'll continue digging into the archive."

The website of Literally London had a very professional look to it; either someone there had unexpected computer skills, or it had been set up by a specialist firm. The latter seemed more likely, Lucas thought. There were gleaming images of the interior of the building, a searchable database for the collections, an appeal for volunteers, fundraising information and of course a history of the archive itself. The Bonner name featured prominently throughout, finishing with Hugo, the current head of trustees. There seemed to be another five, with a Mrs Amanda Beecher as deputy. She'd presumably be in charge now. They'd need to talk to her tomorrow as well.

Helen Bonner stood in the cold sterile room and looked down on the lifeless body of her husband. After positively identifying both the suit and his wedding ring, she'd insisted on seeing him, even though she'd been warned the face was still harrowing to look at. Flo replaced the pristine sheet over the body, having only allowed her a brief glance. Helen stared at the contours of the sheet for a little longer, before dragging herself back to the present. In the little bare waiting room she sat down next to her son and pulled him close as tears started streaming down his face. Hugo always had been a far better father than husband, she had to admit.

"This is a lovely place, sweetheart."
Elise smiled approvingly at the abstract art on the walls, the minimalist look of the furniture and the discreet music gently blending in to the background. Emma took a sip of her vodka and tonic and smiled back.
"We discovered it a couple of months ago. Wonderfully peaceful and great food too."
Jessica raised her glass of rosé and chimed it loudly against Elise's dry sherry.
"To unexpected events and welcome guests!"
Emma sighed.
"That's one way of phrasing it."
Elise opened up her menu and scanned the contents expectantly.
"So girls, what's good to eat in here?"

Lucas preferred being in the office in the evening; the day shift had all gone now and the night shift were always much quieter. Nick had stayed late tonight as well and was opening up several cartons of Chinese food.

"We know they all had the opportunity to let him in, kill him and hide him in that strongroom."

Lucas nodded, grabbed some special fried rice and took a fork out of his desk drawer.

"We'll need to concentrate on motive. Who benefits from Hugo Bonner's death?"

"Assum..." Nick swallowed and started again. "Assuming it is Bonner." After another mouthful he added. "You were right about those bookshops – they closed down two last year."

Lucas dropped his spring roll in the carton and answered his phone.

"Bohr."

"Hello Lucas."

"What's the verdict Flo?"

"Positive ID from the wife, in as much as anyone could be positive in these circumstances. I should get his dental records tomorrow and the son has given a DNA sample for comparison."

"Great, thanks. Let me know as...."

"...soon as. I know. Good night, Lucas."

"Good night."

Lucas out his phone down and looked at the clock – nearly eight.

"There's not much more we can do today, Nick. Let's call it a night; go home before Karen stops talking to me."

"Ok boss, see you tomorrow."

Lucas sent a few more emails, spent another ten minutes on the web and then told himself in no uncertain terms to go home.

The waiter placed a plate of gorgeous looking food in front of Elise: succulent rack of lamb, creamy mash and delicately minty petit-pois. Jess was already tucking in to her steaming bowl of onion soup, while Emma gleefully dissected her fish pie to discover what delights awaited her. The conversation, which had so far covered Jess'

most recent auditions and Elise's writing attempts, halted momentarily to allow full appreciation of the morsels laid before them. Satisfied that everything tasted at least as good as it looked, Elise took a sip of the house red - smooth and velvet - and turned her attention back to the burning issue of the day.

"Sweetheart, are you sure you've no idea who the murderer might be? After all, Hugo Bonner must have been killed inside the building."

Emma stared dolefully at the pink piece of salmon skewered to her fork.

"Thank you mother, that's just what I wanted to hear."

"She's right though, Em," added Jess as she tore a piece off her chunk of artisan bread. "He can't have been killed somewhere else - how on earth could someone have brought a dead body into the building without being seen?"

"I don't know how! How on earth did someone get killed in our building without anyone noticing!"

Emma's raised voice caused quite a stir at the nearby tables; she gulped down the remaining wine in her glass and reached for the bottle as Elise put her hand lightly on her arm.

"I'm sorry darling, I forgot how upsetting the whole experience must have been for you. Let's talk about something else."

Elise shot Jess a pleading glance; she happily obliged and started to recount her disastrous experiences when she'd auditioned for a revival of The Importance of Being Earnest.

"You can see why I'm not expecting a call-back", she dryly said a few minutes later, as Elise was trying to recover from the image of Jess falling down the stage and practically landing in the director's lap. Emma hadn't really been listening though and was staring at her half empty plate.

"It can't be true," she almost whispered, "none of them would kill anyone. Surely."

"Granddad, granddad, Ollie hit me!"

"Not true, granddad, I didn't, I didn't! Alex was mean to me!"

Richard sat in his brown leather armchair, evening paper in his hands, large glass of whiskey by his side. No lurid headlines about the archive; nothing at all yet about Hugo's death as far as he could see.

"Granddad!"

Six year old Oliver was tugging at his arm, trying to look round the newspaper.

"What is it Ollie?"

Before he could answer his older brother was there, eager to give his version of events first.

"Boys, boys, how am I supposed to understand anything you say when you're both talking at once. Run along now, please, and stop making so much noise."

"But granddad..."

The pleading didn't help; Richard ignored them and went back to his newspaper.

The two boys shuffled out of the room, all animosity forgotten.

"Grandma," Alex asked, "why won't granddad play with us?"

"Granddad's had a difficult day at work, dears," Rose explained. "Don't worry, he'll play again next week." She glanced at the clock. "Daddy will be here soon to pick you up – who'd like an extra pudding today?"

With shrieks of joy the boys ran ahead into the kitchen, sat down at the table and devoured the extra helping of custard Rose ladled out. They'd just finished when the doorbell went and five minutes later they were in the car, waving a frantic goodbye.

"Richard?"

Rose walked further into the room.

"Richard! You missed the boys going home. And you didn't even say hello to Thomas."

"What dear?"

Richard dragged himself away from the thoughts that had been whirling round his head and tried to focus on the here and now.

"Oh Richard. I never realised Hugo was such a close friend."

Rose knelt down beside him, spotted the empty glass and sighed.

"You know you're not supposed to drink anymore, not with your blood pressure. I'll make you a nice herbal tea."

Before she could straighten, Richard put his trembling hand on her shoulder.

"I didn't...I mean I never meant to...it was never supposed to..."

With raised eyebrows Rose leant in a little closer.

"What *are* you talking about, dear?"

But Richard had retreated back into the maelstrom of his mind.

Theresa looked round her tiny flat – she was used to having friends round, but this evening you couldn't have crammed a single other person into the space. Her iPod, docked in the speaker, was blearing out the latest hits, and there was a satisfying buzz of conversation competing with the music. They'd all followed the morning's events via her updates on instagram and WhatsApp and had started trickling into the flat during the afternoon. She'd recounted the story dozens of times by now and wasn't that sure anymore whether all of it was still exactly what had happened, but who cared – she certainly didn't. A rap on the door was followed by two more guys trying to squeeze in. She squealed in delight as she recognised super cool Justin; this was now officially the best night of her life. Ever!

"Now that we've got our potatoes going, we'll start chopping the vegetables." Melanie's clear voice effortlessly reached every corner of the room, allowing all her students to follow her instructions to the letter. Not that that mattered to Frederick – he always made sure he was there early enough to have *his* bench, right at the front. It took him ten minutes or so to make sure the pots, pans, cutlery, appliances and ingredients were in their correct places; then he could relax and chat to his fellow cooks-in-waiting. The small class had a good mix of men and women of different ages, all keen to improve their culinary skills. Most were single and, just like Frederick, hoping to find their next someone. Two ladies in particular were always keen to talk to him, but Frederick had his sights firmly set on Melanie herself: she was pretty, funny, petite and a fantastic cook – everything he wished for in a woman.

"Time to fry off the mince," Melanie instructed.

Frederick obliged and took the packet of mince out of the fridge. As he added the red meat to the sizzling pan, he remembered Emma's description of the bloody mess she'd found – not the most appetising thought. He'd always thought of Hugo as a posh version of a slightly dodgy second-hand car dealer: full of charm but you wouldn't trust him with your hard-earned cash. Richard looked very upset about it all – of course Hugo had always backed him up with everything. Or had that been the other way round?

"Careful, Frederick, your mince is about to burn."

Melanie was standing at his side, just that little bit closer than usual. He gave her a big smile.

"Apologies, dear teacher. My thoughts had strayed."

"I'll forgive you if you keep them firmly in this room for the rest of the evening."

Frederick tipped the fried mince swiftly into the shepherd's pie bowl, then turned towards her and met her gaze.

"I promise to not think of anything but your commands."

She twirled a stray lock of her long black hair.

"*All* evening?"

Absolutely, Frederick mused, as he watched her move on to the next bench.

"Oh Beth, that's a lovely place."

Marie and her daughter were sitting at the kitchen table, leafing through wedding magazines.

"And this dress, just gorgeous."

Beth leant in to have a closer look.

"I can just picture you in it, love, all that lace and the pink flowers. You'd look ever so pretty."

"I'm not..." Beth started, when her father walked in.

"Are you making a cup of coffee, Bob?" Marie asked. "You couldn't make me a cup of tea, could you? I'm still all in a jitter from work."

Bob filled the kettle as Marie went on.

"I just can't believe it, Hugo Bonner murdered in my building. The poor dear, he must have been lying there when I locked up last night and I never saw anything. " She had to raise her voice now to be heard over the nearly boiling water. "You don't think they'll blame me, do you? For not findin' him, I mean. What if he were still alive last night and I could've saved him? They can't arrest me for that, can they?"

The kitchen suddenly fell silent as the kettle stopped.

"I did the same rounds I always do; I can't go into every nook and cranny of that place when I lock up, it would take forever."

Bob placed two cups of tea on the table, one next to Marie, one next to Rose.

"No, Richard'll tell'm I always do my job properly. And what was he sneaking about for, anyway? I can't be held responsible if I didn't even know he was there."

Marie slurped some tea as Bob took his coffee, winked at Beth and headed back to the television.

"Oh look Beth, how about this dress?

A different magazine was lying open on the table now.

"That's a lovely colour, that is, ivory instead of white. Nice length too, you wouldn't have to worry about it being muddy..."

Beth smiled and sipped her tea.

Olivia re-read her report – yes, that would do. Academics could be quite picky, but this covered everything he'd asked for. She emailed it to herself at work and opened up the next research request. Being sent home by the police hadn't been such a nuisance as she'd feared; at least here she could guarantee there would be no interruptions. Typical of Hugo to be so disruptive, even in death. Of course, with him gone, Richard's position was considerably weakened. Changes should be possible now. A tiny smile appeared on her face; it should all work out nicely.

"Yes mother....that's nice...did he really?" Jennifer took a large sip from her gin and tonic and gripped the phone a little tighter. "Here? Well, someone died at the archive today and...yes mother...yes they do tend to be elderly...did you?...how exciting...well, I should go...yes mother...I'll call again next week...give my love to Dad...yes mother...bye mother."

Jennifer put the phone down, topped up her drink and reached for the remote control. The television flickered into action – it looked like something to do with antiques. Or perhaps cookery? It usually was one of those. Not that it mattered, any mindless drivel would do. Anything to distract her, anything to stop remembering, to stop thinking, to stop hearing. She cranked the volume up another notch and willed herself to concentrate on the screen.

Isobel hung her dressing gown over the bedside chair and slipped into bed, snuggling up close to Tim. She could tell from the look in his eyes which question he was about to ask and placed her finger on his lips.

"No it hasn't. But that doesn't mean anything yet."

He kissed her finger away and caressed her cheek.

"Three days late, though."

"Three days is nothing, Tim, you know that."

She fluffed up her pillows, sat up against them, and took her tablet from the bedside table.

"It's on the local news website now: 'Man found dead in archive'."

Tim looked up from his book.

"Does it mention Hugo Bonner?"

Izzy scrolled down.

"No, it's all very vague." She closed down the website and put the tablet down. "It's not really going to make any difference for you, is it?"

Tim placed his hand on top of hers and squeezed gently.

"None whatsoever."

"It's just that it would be a bad time to look for somewhere else again..."

"Izzy, I promise." He pulled her close and kissed her gently on the lips.

"Everything's going to be all right."

It was long after midnight when Helen tiptoed out of her son's room. He'd finally nodded off, exhausted from crying. She felt a twinge of guilt at the lack of tears of her own, but wasn't going to pretend to be heartbroken about the death of someone she'd stopped caring about a long time ago. She poured herself a gin, decided against tonic, and reached for her phone again.

"Helen?"

"At last! I've been trying to get hold of you for the past hour. Hugo's dead."

There was a moment of stunned silence on the other end.

"What do you mean?"

"He's dead. Someone killed him in that archive of his. The police have been asking all kinds of questions and I had to identify his body." Her voice broke slightly. "Matthew came with me, poor boy."

"Shit."

"Is that all you can say?"

"Well, I'm sorry of course." A slight pause. "Did you mention me?"

"How stupid do you think I am?" She sounded angry. "Really officer, my husband's been murdered? I'd better tell you all about the affair I've been having then, so we can be your prime suspects."

"All right, all right, no need to get like that. It's just all a bit of a shock, that's all...I guess we'd better not be in touch for a while."

"I had realised that, yes."

"Helen...you didn't actually...I mean...you know..."

"No I didn't. I'd ask you the same question, but there's no need – you'd never have had the nerve."

She pressed the 'end call' button, wishing it was still possible to slam a phone down to end a conversation; that would have been much more satisfying.

WEDNESDAY 10 APRIL

Nine

Emma woke with a jolt to the joyful sounds of Mendelssohn's Italian symphony, pouring out of her radio courtesy of Classic FM. She slammed down the snooze button and dozed back off, until the memories of the previous day came flooding back and she had to switch on the lights to get rid of *that* image. No need to wonder whether it had really happened, not even her imagination was that crazy. She snuggled deeper into the duvet and tried to remember whether Hugo had had a family. Wasn't there a wife? Maybe even a child? Those poor people must be absolutely devastated. She'd only been eight when her father had died, but could still remember the shock and the sense of loss. The most upsetting thing of all had been her mother's crying – mums just weren't supposed to get that distraught. She peeled off the duvet, grabbed her dressing gown from the chair and sauntered into the bathroom. The face that stared back at her from the mirror was still a bit pale; even the eyes seemed a more subdued green than usual. Then again, she had had a lot more wine than she was used to. She dragged herself under the shower and slowly began to wake up. By the time she was dressed and in the kitchen, she felt she probably would be able to cope with the day ahead after all. Even if the ping of the microwave was ridiculously loud this morning. She sliced a kiwi into her porridge and began to imagine how the day would play out. Would they be allowed back into the store? Would she *want* to go back into the store? Would there be more questions from the police? Her spoon hovered in the air as the smiling image of inspector Bohr popped into her head. Very unusual name that, Bohr. He looked a bit Scandinavian, with that amazing mop of blond curls – of course, that's where she knew the name from, the Danish physicist! Dare she ask him if they were related?

"Good morning sweetheart."

Emma nearly fell off her chair.

"Mum! You startled me, I didn't hear you get up."

Elise laughed and gave her daughter a big hug.

"Did you manage to sleep all right?"

"I should ask you that, the sofa is far from ideal."

Elise took a mug and teabag and walked over to the kettle.

"I slept wonderfully, sweetheart. I am surprised you're still here though or aren't you going to work today?"

Emma looked at the clock: half past eight, how had that happened? She grabbed her bag and coat, ran out of the kitchen, stopped, ran back in again and gave her mum a hug, ran out of the flat, down the stairs, along the street and was just in time to watch her bus disappear in the distance.

Nick rushed up the stairs, taking them two at a time. He'd grown so used to Alfie waking him up before six o'clock every morning, that he hadn't bothered to set his alarm and of course, for the first time ever, Alfie had slept in. When Karen had roused him at half past seven, he'd been certain something terrible must have happened to his son – that he'd been kidnapped or was deadly ill. But no, Alfie had just been fast asleep in his racing car bed, looking as angelic as only three-year old boys can. He reached his desk just as Lucas put down the phone.

"That was Sam Ripley, Bonner's business partner. He's agreed to meet us in an hour at their office on Fleet Street."

"How did he sound?"

"Shocked, annoyed, worried – take your pick."

"Not particularly upset though?"

"Not exactly grief-stricken, no. We'll need to talk to Mrs Bonner again as well, of course. Call her, will you Nick, and see if she can meet us some time this afternoon."

Lucas tried to decide what he thought of Helen Bonner. She hadn't seemed as distressed as most wives tended to when they were told their husband had been murdered, but then again, she came across as someone who would always hide her feelings as much as possible. Not at all like Emma Baines, whose sparkling eyes betrayed every emotion she felt.

"Mrs Bonner will see us at half past two. She clearly doesn't doubt that the body is that of her husband."

"She must know she'd have heard from him by now if he were still alive. Unless he's doing a runner – is the missing person call still active?"

Nick checked the database.

"Yes, his description's still on there."

"Up the urgency – add he's a person of interest in a murder investigation. He wouldn't be the first to fake his own death before leaving the country."

"She wouldn't be the first woman to murder her husband," Nick grumbled.

"Have I missed something?" Lucas asked. "A vital clue that makes her our prime suspect?"

Nick blushed.

"I just don't like her much."

"If we arrested everyone we didn't like..."

"The world would be a much nicer place!"

No Marie this morning to greet her as she came in. Odd how she could miss something that annoyed her every day. Emma rushed upstairs and dashed into the office. Tim looked surprised.

"Twenty past nine, that's not like you Emma; we thought you might not come in today after what happened yesterday."

"I missed the bus. So I had to get the Tube. The very overcrowded, pack in as many as you possibly can Tube. Standing next to some middle aged guy who couldn't be bothered to put his hand in front of his mouth when he sneezed. Every time he sneezed."

"Ok, ok, tell you what, you sit down and I'll get you a cup of tea."

Emma plonked down on her chair and angrily turned on her computer. Rush hour Tube - guaranteed to put anyone in a bad mood.

"Ah Emma, you *are* here."

Richard appeared through the door.

"I'm sorry I was late, it's just..."

"No need to explain my dear. "

He moved the spare chair from its place against the wall and sat down opposite her.

"How are you coping Emma?" he asked. "Discovering a body like that, being questioned by the police...not exactly everyday things to deal with."

Emma felt a surge of affection for her boss, who was always so gentle, always so concerned for their wellbeing, always wanting everyone to be happy. If it hadn't been for Richard's fatherly presence the mere existence of Olivia would have sent them all scurrying off years ago.

"I'm fine, Richard, really. My mother's come down to stay for a few days, so I'm being well looked after. And the police were actually very friendly."

"That's good."

Richard looked rather pale himself and the bags under his eyes showed he couldn't have had much sleep.

"Did you know Mr Bonner well?"

"Hugo and I first met when I was working at the Bodleian and he came round for a visit. That's nearly fifteen years ago now." He gazed into the distance, reliving the memories of those days in Oxford. "Then when the job of director came up here, he offered it to me." He sighed. "We've been through a lot together."

"Can you think of a reason why he would have come here without telling anyone?" Emma asked.

"Maybe he was spying on us."

Tim had re-appeared with two mugs of tea, one of which he handed to Emma.

"Nonsense." Richard was clearly annoyed at the suggestion and raised his voice. "If Hugo thought there was a problem he wouldn't have skulked around the place, he would have come to me."

"Then why did he..." Tim insisted.

"I don't know." Richard grabbed his chair and put it back against the wall. "I DON'T KNOW!" he repeated as he strode out of the room.

Tim's face had gone bright red and he sat down.

"That wasn't such an odd thing to ask, was it Em?"

"Of course not." Emma though for a moment. "I'm not sure it's the main question though. I mean, how did he get into the building? How did his murderer get in? Why was he killed? And why here?"

"You don't think it was one of us then?"

Emma stared at him in disbelief.

"You think it is?"

Tim shrugged his shoulders.

"I can think of one person who's certainly capable of murder."

"No," Emma said, shaking her head. "Not even Olivia would go that far."

Lucas had given in to Nick's pleading looks and was letting him drive the Golf today. The only reason he didn't let Nick drive all the time was because he knew if he didn't keep forcing himself he'd just give up driving altogether, which wouldn't be any good in the long run. They managed to find a space on Fleet Street itself, not too far away from the building that housed the headquarters of 'Books Galore!', Sam

Ripley's and Hugo Bonner's business venture. The office was on the third floor and consisted of one large room, which could easily accommodate the four people who were busily tapping away at their computers, and one slightly smaller room with two large desks. Sam Ripley had come to meet them as soon as he'd seen them arrive and had ushered them straight into his office, where tea and coffee were already waiting. He must be around fifty, Lucas thought, a cuddly bear type of person – big, but with an even bigger smile. Except that he definitely wasn't smiling today.

"So, Mr Ripley, what exactly is your business?"

"Hugo Bonner and I own a small chain of bookshops. Do you seriously think he's dead?"

"It does look that way. How did you meet?"

"He came into my bookshop on Shaftsbury Avenue about eight years ago. Said he was looking for a business to invest in and would I be interested in expanding. We met a few times, he had big plans and the money to back them up, so we went in business together. We now own three bookshops in London, two in Birmingham and one in Leeds."

"Was he more of a silent partner?"

"Oh no, he is...was great at dealing with banks, suppliers, estate agents. I basically run the shops, but he does...did all the bigger business stuff."

"And how is the business doing?"

"It's a difficult time for bookshops; the internet is fierce competition. We had to let a few people go last year and our expansion plans have halted. To be honest, we may have to close one of the London shops to keep the others open. I really don't know how I'm going to do all that on my own – Hugo had the business brain, he dealt with all that sort of stuff."

"We'll need to have a look at your accounts."

"I'll get Martin, our accountant, to make you a copy."

"When did you see Mr Bonner last, Mr Ripley?"

"Friday. He left the office around three o'clock as usual."

"You didn't make plans to meet him for dinner on Monday evening?"

Sam hesitated and looked rather embarrassed.

"Look, Hugo is...was a great guy in many ways, but he liked women and they most definitely liked him. He'd tell Helen he was meeting me for dinner and 'sleeping off the alcohol' in my flat, when actually he'd be with some woman somewhere."

"And you were happy to lie for him?"

"He was my partner, what was I supposed to do? I felt for Helen, of course, but it's hard to believe she didn't know what was going on and I wasn't going to interfere in their marital arrangements."

"And you weren't surprised when he didn't come to the office on Tuesday?" Nick asked.

"It wasn't unusual for Hugo not to be in every day." Sam hesitated. "You'll find out anyway – we had a bit of a row on Friday. You have to understand, Hugo was a very charming man, used to getting his own way. Always. The fact that I didn't agree with his plans for the business and wasn't just lying down about it, caused some friction."

"What didn't you agree about?"

"Hugo wanted to keep expanding – go bigger, more shops, more staff, bigger turnover. I thought that was insane, the way to lose everything. Of course he would have still been ok if the business went under, but I'd have been left with nothing."

"And where were you on Monday, Mr Ripley?" Nick asked.

"I'd stayed with a friend in Leeds for the weekend and visited our shop there in the morning. Marion, the shop manager, can feel a bit left out being so far away from the rest of us, so I pop in whenever I can."

"When did you get back to London?"

"About five o'clock. I went straight home and stayed there all evening."

"Can anyone vouch for that?"

"Afraid not, I live on my own. A confirmed bachelor, as they used to say."

"Do you know anything about the organisation called Literally London?"

"Hugo's baby? Of course, he loves...loved that place. Why do you ask?"

"Did he mention any problems regarding the archive? Conflicts with anyone?"

Sam thought for a moment, but shook his head.

"He only ever mentioned the director, Richard I think? He clearly liked him. If he was worried about anything to do with that place, he never mentioned it to me."

"What about your business, sir? Does Mr Bonner's wife inherit her husband's stake?"

"Yes, as far as I'm aware she gets his 51 percent."

"So Bonner had control of the business?"

"Yes inspector, I'm the junior partner."

"That must have been difficult at times."

"As I said, we had our differences."

"Will you have the same differences with Mrs Bonner?"

"I have no idea inspector. I'm sure Mrs Bonner has other things to worry about right now."

Sam stood at the side of the window, hoping he couldn't be seen, and watched the two policemen get into their car. The meeting hadn't been nearly as bad as he'd feared, only questions that were easily answered. Of course they might well come back if they didn't find any more likely candidates. He waited for the car to drive off before turning away from the window; the archive place would keep them busy for a while though, surely? He took a deep breath and walked into the main office.

"Can I have your attention please, everyone?"

Four anxious faces stared at him, all clearly wondering why the police had been visiting.

"I have some bad news, I'm afraid. Hugo Bonner is dead. Apparently he was murdered on Monday." He hesitated, not quite knowing what the right thing to say would be. "I'm sure we're all shocked and saddened by this news. He was a good boss to work for and certainly never boring to work with." To Sam's relief none of the staff showed signs of an imminent breakdown. "I will send our condolences to Mrs Bonner – Melissa, could you organise a suitable bouquet?" As she nodded he could see that there were tears in her eyes; he'd always wondered whether there might have been something going on there, although to be fair Daisy looked quite upset as well and even Hugo wouldn't have seduced someone that young. "And Martin, the police would like to see a copy of our accounts – could you sort that out?" No tears there at least, or from Mike who had already turned back to his computer.

Ten

Marie still couldn't believe it – Hugo Bonner dead. Killed in her building and she didn't see anything; the shame of it. She picked up a duster from the cleaning cupboard and headed for the basement, where she found Jennifer in her studio unpacking the disaster supplies. At least, she found her in tears in amongst a mass of plastic sheeting, Tyvek overshoes, mops, torches and disposable aprons.

"Jennifer dear, what's the matter?"

"I thought unpacking all this stuff would be a good distraction," Jennifer whispered, "but it's not really working." She gave Marie a watery smile. "All this has brought back a lot of memories."

Marie put her arm round her and give her a big squeeze; she could feel just how badly she was shaking.

"You poor thing, I'm sure it has. Don't you worry about all this stuff, I'll put that away next door. You go on upstairs and have an extra cup of tea. I'm sure Tim and Emma could be persuaded to have an early break as well."

Jennifer took a deep breath.

"Thanks Marie, you're a good friend. I'll see you upstairs."

It only took her about fifteen minutes to move everything on to some empty shelves in the store next door; Jennifer would still have to sort through it all, but at least it wasn't in her way now. She started to open the door of the store and was surprised to hear Olivia's voice; carefully she glanced out through a small gap to see Frederick and Olivia walking as far as the door to the strongroom.

"Really Olivia, is all this necessary?" Frederick sounded extremely annoyed.

"Yes, Frederick, I do think it's very necessary for us to have a private conversation." She was using her calm, rational voice.

"You know as well as I do that Hugo always supported Richard in everything; without Hugo on the board we can finally run this place properly."

"The poor man has only just died, Olivia, couldn't you wait a while to start scheming?"

"No Frederick, we must act now. I have friends on the board; if you back me up, they will agree with us and Richard will be isolated."

"But what are these changes you keep going on about?"

"Turn this place into a serious research facility. No more brainless girl in the searchroom, but a qualified archivist. No more wasting money on conservation, when we could have an assistant librarian instead. No more opening the doors to all and sundry; if we're by appointment only we'll only get the genuine researchers in. Think of all the work we could get through, the articles we could publish."

Frederick hesitated.

"Perhaps some changes would be useful, but I'm not sure I could agree with all of that. And why would we need to go behind Richard's back? I'm sure if we talk this through sensibly..."

"Think carefully about this Frederick. I told you, I have friends on the board now, not Richard."

With that Olivia turned round and went back upstairs. Marie watched on as Frederick stood in deep thought for a minute, before heading upstairs himself.

Well, well, Marie thought, time I joined the tea break.

"Hey mum," Emma said as she answered her phone. "Having a nice morning?"

"A rather exhausting one actually; Jessica has roped me into practising with her for her audition again. I'm getting rather fed up with being Dracula!"

"Oh dear, you sound like you could do with a break."

"That's why I'm calling you sweetheart – I thought we could meet up for lunch?"

"Great idea. I'll meet you at the coffee shop opposite the building just after twelve. But I'd better get to the staff room now or I won't have time for a cup of tea."

"Oh dear darling, that would be a disaster!" Elise laughed, "See you soon."

Emma cheerfully walked into the staff room to be met by a group of sombre faces. Strange, she hadn't thought everyone would have been so upset about Hugo Bonner. Theresa ran up to her, looking furious.

"Do you know what Marie overheard?"

Emma looked confused, so Theresa continued, talking quickly and rather incoherently.

"Olivia. Wants to sack me. And Jennifer. Plotting against Richard. With Frederick."

Emma was still confused and looked over towards Tim and Jennifer.

"It's true," Jennifer said, "Marie overheard her trying to convince Frederick to get rid of Theresa and conservation. Apparently she now has friends on the board and with Hugo gone..." Her voice trailed off.

Tim looked nervous.

"Marie's just gone to tell Richard."

Emma gave Theresa a hug and looked at the clock.

"No one's getting rid of you. Or you," she said looking at Jennifer. "She'll expect you back down there in three minutes. Just pretend you don't know anything and let Richard surprise her, that'll give him the edge."

Theresa looked a lot calmer now.

"It's not as if I even care about this crummy job." She looked up at Emma. "She called me brainless."

"She's an evil cow." Emma surprised herself at how venomous she sounded. "Richard won't let her get away with it."

"No, he most definitely won't."

They all looked at the door, where Richard had just come in, followed by Marie. He looked rather pale, but very determined.

"I suggest you all go back to your offices and let us have an extra management meeting."

As soon as Lucas and Nick were through the sliding door, Marie Thorpe darted out of her cubby hole and was there to greet them.

"Did you hear us come in just then, Mrs Thorpe?" Nick asked.

"Yes, I can always hear those doors if I'm down here."

Lucas and Nick exchanged a quick glance – another reason to avoid the front door if you didn't want to be seen.

"Is Dr Owen in his office?" Lucas asked.

Marie hesitated.

"They're having a bit of an emergency management meeting up there at the moment. I'm not sure..."

For Marie Thorpe to be lost for words something quite extraordinary must be going on, Lucas thought. The demise of Hugo Bonner seemed to be creating tension already. Tempting as it was to interrupt the meeting and see what was happening, he felt that would probably be counterproductive; besides there were other people he wanted to talk to as well.

"Perhaps we could start with Miss Baines, then?"

Marie looked relieved.

"Yes of course, do come up. You could use the staff room if you like; I'll make some teas."

On the second floor the tension was impossible to ignore; Emma Baines, Tim Edwards and Jennifer Marr were deep in discussion in the general office and looked surprised to see them.

"Could we have another word please, Miss Baines? In the staff room perhaps?"

Lucas felt a tingle of pleasure as she smiled at him; when she walked past it became obvious that she was nearly as tall as he was and that her eyes were a marvellous mixture of blue and green. Only when he noticed Nick looking back at him in an odd way did he manage to re-focus and follow them to the staff room.

Lucas listened as Emma went over the events from Monday morning yet again.
"Wait," he suddenly said, "you rolled that racking against the body? And tightened it further when it stopped?"
She was losing patience now.
"How many times do I..."
Lucas watched all the colour drain out of her face as the implication slowly dawned on her.
"I...I squashed his face? That was all my fault?"
Emma looked as if she was about to be sick.
"We can't know that for certain," Lucas replied, "it's perfectly possible that the murderer rolled the racking back after destroying the face."
"Absolutely," Nick added, "if they wanted to hide his identity, they wouldn't have left that to chance."
Lucas took the yellow mug from the table and gently handed it to Emma.
"Deep breaths and drink up."
As Emma took the mug from his hand, their fingers briefly touched and she gave him such a warm smile, he momentarily forgot where he was.
A loud bang made Lucas jump up and he ran to the corridor as Nick and Emma practically fell off their seats. As he stood there trying to work out what had happened, Frederick came out of Richard's office.
"What on earth was that?" Lucas asked.
"Olivia in a bad mood," came the answer. Lucas still looked bewildered.
"She slammed the door," Frederick added, "rather forcefully."
Lucas turned to Nick.
"Definitely time for another chat with Dr Owen."

There were still two chairs facing the large mahogany desk, so Nick and Lucas sat down and waited for Richard to return with his cup of tea. He'd looked so agitated when they went in, Lucas had suggested he get some refreshments before they talked. It was a nice office, Lucas thought, if a bit old fashioned with the large framed prints on the walls.
"Here we are then," Richard said as he came in carrying a tray with three mugs of tea. "Milk no sugar for you inspector, milk and sugar for you sergeant."

Richard's hands were still trembling slightly as he handed out the teas.

"Thank you Dr Owen. Not a good morning so far?"

"Just a few differences of opinion, inspector. After what's happened we're all rather on edge." He sighed and sat down. "Hugo was a dear friend of mine, it's all been rather too much to take in."

"How long had you known Mr Bonner?"

Richard closed his eyes for a moment.

"Thirteen years. I was working in the Bodleian Library in Oxford; Hugo came for a visit and tried to persuade us to donate some books to Literally London."

"Did you?" Nick asked.

Richard gave him a pitying look.

"Apart from the fact that these were particularly valuable and unique books, libraries and archives tend to be very precious about their collections. Every Senior Librarian the Bodleian has ever had has considered the books to be 'theirs'. In the same way, I might add, that Hugo saw the collection here as his personal possession."

Richard took a sip of his tea and seemed momentarily lost in his memories.

"For some reason Hugo took to me that day, even though he went home empty-handed. Of course I was only one of the assistant librarians, but I was the one who'd been charged with giving him a tour of the building. He asked me to do some paid research for the trust and then kept in touch over the next couple of years. When the previous director here retired, Hugo offered me the job."

"If I've understood it correctly Mr Bonner was the chair of the trustees?"

"Yes. There are three others, but really it was Hugo who made all the decisions. As I said, he still firmly saw the collection as his property."

"And now that he's gone?"

"I assume the vice chair, Amanda Beecher, will take over. You would need to ask her."

"Could there be big consequences for the archive?"

"I couldn't possibly say, that will be for the trustees to decide."

"Not Dr Dunstable?"

Richard looked quite angry now.

"As I said, the trustees will decide what happens next."

"We will need to look at the finances of the archive and the trust as part of our routine enquiries."

"I have the accounts for the archive here – I'll copy them onto a CD for you. As for the trust..."

"We will talk to Mrs Beecher."

68

Marie watched the policemen leave and sank back down in her chair, quietly pondering the whole situation. Which way would it go? Richard wasn't going to stay on that much longer, surely. He must be in his mid-sixties already. Olivia would be a disaster, but could well get it; she knew how to behave in front of the right people. At least she'd never had any major falling outs with Olivia, she would be ok. Surely.

Brainless? Theresa was seething from the insult. So she hadn't gone to some posh school or college, she'd worked hard since she'd turned sixteen, never relying on any hand-outs. She'd earned the chance to have a go at this job and hadn't made many mistakes either. She'd even started thinking she might like to become an archivist – ha, not if it turned you into the mad woman! What if Olivia really did take over? She couldn't just fire her could she? Well, she probably could, they always seemed to find a way. Maybe she should start looking for a different job? But she liked it here. They'd all be so much happier without that vicious bully around.

Frederick kept pacing up and down his office, going over the morning's conversations. Hardly real conversations, the second had been more of a shouting match. Of course he'd known Olivia wanted the top spot, but he never considered she'd have been scheming so far in advance. Friends on the board. Maybe she was bluffing, getting him to support her rather than be a rival. If that had been her intention, she'd soon find that he was just as ambitious and equally keen to become the next director. But how could he convince Richard now to persuade the trustees to give the top job to him? Maybe he still would – lesser of two evils and all that. That damn woman.

The long needle delicately traced out an infill for the missing piece of the letter Jennifer was working on. Despite her fury she managed to keep her hand steady; she carefully tore out the infill from the special repair paper and pasted it into place. Another letter repaired, another little piece of history that could be safely held again. As she put the heavy weights on top to make sure the adhesive would stick and dry out evenly, she suddenly got the urge to chuck them through the window – a bit of mindless vandalism might make her feel better. But of course she didn't. She never did.

The computer was still showing the same page of the report Tim had been trying to write all morning. The letters were just a blur, a meaningless jumble; he was staring far beyond them. Richard had been so understanding, had trusted him, had given him this chance. If she took over, would she find out? She was bound to, wasn't she? Would she believe him? She might tell everyone. No, that wasn't her style. She was more likely to hold it over him, a grenade she could drop whenever she felt like it. He'd have to leave, start all over again. Even the computer was a blur now.

Richard sat down on his dark brown leather chair and looked round his office. HIS office. He'd just walked round the whole building, the searchroom, the stores, the library, the basement. Even the ghastly staffroom. It was HIS building. HIS staff. HIS little family. And there was no way he was going to let that woman destroy it all. Over his dead body.

Another email flashed on to Olivia's screen. She glanced at it, intending to ignore it for now, but it actually looked interesting. A request from a university professor in Moscow, written in delightfully formal English. Did the archive hold any manuscripts by an author called Janine Meadows, born in London in 1901? And if so, would it be possible to obtain copies? The kind of simple request even Theresa could answer. She clicked on forward and started to put Theresa's email address in the 'to' box, then changed her mind and pressed cancel. Having a contact at a university in Moscow could be useful. If she were invited over, she could make sure the trustees were invited as well. They were bound to appreciate a Russian jolly. She opened the database and typed in 'Meadows'.

Eleven

Emma had never been more relieved to have an excuse to go out to lunch; the atmosphere in the building was rather poisonous since the morning's revelations. Elise was already sitting down, sipping a steaming cappuccino, but got up to give Emma a big hug.

"Hello sweetheart."

"Hi mum."

Emma placed her order, then related the morning's events; Elise was quite astonished.

"You've told me odd things about that woman before, but this is just unbelievable. She doesn't seem to care at all that that poor man got killed."

"Maybe she killed him so she could take over the archive."

"I suppose it's possible, people have been killed for a lot less."

"Mother, I wasn't being serious! As much as I dislike Olivia, I really don't think she's a murderer."

"Who is then?"

Emma looked confused.

"Darling, it really does have to be one of your colleagues. It's odd enough Hugo Bonner managed to get in unseen, but for his murderer to have gotten in, committed murder and gotten out again without anyone seeing anything? That's quite preposterous."

Emma still wasn't convinced.

"These are people I talk to every day, mum. They're all really nice, except for Olivia, but even she wouldn't go that far. It just doesn't make any sense."

She took another bite out of her ham and cheese toastie and added:

"I'm sure inspector Bohr will find out what really happened."

Seeing the dreamy look in her daughter's eyes, Elise's curiosity was piqued.

"Is he Danish, this inspector?"

"You know, I thought that, Niels Bohr and everything. He is very blond, with amazing grey eyes. I really will have to ask him."

Her toastie finished, she looked thoughtfully at her soy latte.

"Why on earth did he sneak into the building – I just can't think of any reason."

"Oh my dear, don't be so naïve, I can think of plenty."

Emma looked surprised.

"Fraud, theft, drugs, planting something incriminating, meeting someone he shouldn't, plotting..."

"All right, mother, you've made your point." Emma hesitated before continuing. "Maybe Olivia asked to meet him, to see if she could turn him against Richard?"

"Or Richard to warn him about Olivia" Elise suggested. "There's definitely some major power struggle going on in that trust. Who's in charge of it now?"

"The vice chair, I suppose, Amanda Beecher."

"Amanda Beecher? The wife of Alexander Beecher, the banker?"

"I think her husband is a banker, yes. Why?"

"Oh, I've known Amanda for ever. Mind you, I haven't actually seen her in ages, but I bet she'd be happy to meet up with an old friend."

"I thought your investigating days were over?"

"So did I," Elise answered with a twinkle in her eyes.

"Have you found out yet what happened to my husband?" Helen Bonner had most definitely regained her composure.

"We're still in the early stages of our investigation, Mrs Bonner. I believe your husband told you he was meeting Mr. Ripley on Monday evening?"

Helen's cool stare was starting to make Lucas feel uncomfortable.

"No need to be coy, inspector, I realise Hugo lied. And yes, I know why."

"Perhaps you could enlighten us?"

"My husband liked to prove to himself that he was still young and charming, capable of seducing any woman he met. He had affairs; as long as he was discreet, I saw no need to deprive him of his hobby."

Lucas found this hard to believe.

"I've met women and men before who claimed not to mind their partner cheating on them; most of them are now in jail for assault or murder."

Helen looked at him with contempt.

"You can believe whatever you like, inspector, I loved my husband *with* his faults and he loved me. I knew what he was like when I married him and yes, I also knew he liked the fact that my family is wealthy."

Lucas was surprised.

"I though the Bonner family were wealthy in their own right?"

"Were, inspector, were. Of course Hugo still inherited quite a bit and easily had enough to indulge his hobbies, but this house is mine as are our others. I pay Matthew's school fees and I pay all the bills."

"And where were you on Monday, Mrs Bonner?"

"Indulging my own little hobby."

Lucas refused to take the bait and patiently waited for her to expand. She seemed disappointed – good, he thought.

"I also have a business, inspector, a chain of flower shops. Four to be precise, all in London. Every Monday I visit each shop and meet with each manager; they are in charge of day to day business, but I decide the longer term direction. I visited the first shop at eleven thirty and came back home at five. Matthew was busy revising for his A levels; I felt he could do with a break and as Hugo had said he wouldn't be home, we went out for an early supper, returning home around eight. Was there anything else?"

"We will need to look into your husband's financial affairs, bank accounts etcetera and it would be very useful if you would allow us access to yours as well."

Lucas had tried to phrase it carefully; he knew getting a warrant for Helen Bonner's financial transactions would be difficult.

"In case I hired someone to kill Hugo, you mean? Or in case I've just told you a whole load of lies?" She gave him a faint smile. "Or perhaps just out of curiosity? I will tell my bank and my accountant to give you anything you need."

Elise waited patiently outside the door to flat 3, having rung the rather ornate doorbell. Although in this building 'flat' didn't really seem to be the right word – miniature palace perhaps? Twenty years ago Amanda Beecher had been Amanda Wright, a bright Birmingham girl, just out of college and keen to make a splash as a journalist. They'd been paired up together and had spent a year or so travelling all over the Midlands, covering the stories deemed important enough for the national press. But then Amanda had met Alexander Beecher, the two had fallen in love and she'd moved to London with him. And had disappeared from the world of journalism.

"Elise!"

"Mandy – it's been far too long."

After half an hour of going over the good old times, Elise decided it was time to focus on the present. She took one more delicious biscuit and put her cup of tea down.

"You're probably wondering why I called you out of the blue like that."

"You mean on the day I find out a friend of mine has been killed?" Amanda replied rather ironically.

Elise smiled.

"Remember my daughter Emma?"

"Of course I do, a very sweet little girl."

"She's not so little now. She's here in London and works as a researcher at Literally London."

"Really? I never realised that was her. Emma Baines – of course, she has Daniel's name." The mood subtly changed as Amanda looked sorrowful. "I was so sorry to hear about what happened; he was a lovely man."

Elise suddenly found herself back in the newsroom, looking at the latest news reports flooding in and reading how a press convoy had been attacked in Congo, with one fatality. She'd known straight away it was him – why else would she have suddenly felt so numb. She hadn't wanted him to go, but of course he'd gone anyway. 'People are dying Elise, they're committing atrocities down there. Words alone aren't enough – no one will do anything if there aren't pictures for them to see.' They'd brought his camera back and the photographs had been so stunning they'd been used all over the world. And in his obituary. Elise mentally shook herself back to the present and saw the sudden concern in Amanda's eyes. She took a deep breath.

"Yes, well, that was a long time ago now. Emma was the one who found the body yesterday, so I came down to make sure she was all right."

"The Emma Baines I've met didn't strike me as a woman who needs her mummy around."

Elise was slightly annoyed.

"She's still my little girl. Besides, retirement isn't all it's cracked up to be."

"So you're going to investigate?"

"Well it is odd that he was sneaking around the building like that, don't you think?"

Amanda looked surprised.

"I didn't know that; all I've been told is that he was killed."

Elise related everything she knew and then sat back expectantly. Amanda still looked puzzled.

"It's difficult to imagine Hugo sneaking about anywhere; he is...was always the centre of attention. I don't understand why he'd do this."

"Any problems at the archive he might have been investigating?"

"I know how you think Elise, you're wondering about embezzlement, but I'm sure that can't be the case. We employ an accountant to oversee the finances of both the trust and the archive and we are audited annually by an independent company."

"Not embezzlement then. Any personnel issues?"

"As there are everywhere. Richard is getting close to retirement; he and Hugo were very close, Hugo always agreed with his decisions. Olivia has been smooching up to me and the other trustees, she's desperate to be next in charge and has some ideas about doing things differently. Nothing you would kill someone for."

Depends on how ambitious you are, thought Elise.

"Emma told me about all the security, key pad access to the stores. Seems a bit excessive for some old books and papers."

"Some old books and papers?? Do you have any idea how valuable these collections are Elise? The books on open shelving aren't totally irreplaceable, but the books and manuscripts in the stores are completely unique. We regularly get offers for items in the collection and we're talking thousands, even tens of thousands here. Of course they're not for sale, we'd never consider that."

The doorbell rang.

"I meant to tell you," Amanda said, "I had a phone call from an inspector Bohr earlier asking if he could come over to see me. I expect that's him now."

Elise hesitated.

"I haven't met the inspector yet; perhaps he doesn't need to know why I'm here?"

Amanda smiled.

"Don't worry, I still know how to be discreet."

Elise could hear voices in the hallway and got up as Amanda led two men into the sitting room.

"Inspector Bohr, sergeant Fletcher – my good friend Elise Horton."

"I'm sure you don't want me here for police business. I'll find my own way out Mandy; I'll call you soon."

Elise hastily left and walked back to her car. So that was the inspector Emma was getting all flustered about? She couldn't see it herself: he must already be forty and wasn't anything special to look at. Now that sergeant on the other hand...if she were thirty years younger. Or should that be forty? You're getting old Elise, she thought as she climbed into the car. But, she added after a quick look in the mirror, not too old yet.

Lucas found himself seated on a pale green soft-leather sofa in easily the most unobtrusively stylish room he'd ever been in. The lush cream carpet and cream curtains made the room feel even more spacious than it was, while the pale green and soft wood furnishings created a very calming feel. He normally didn't like fire places pretending to burn wood while actually running on gas, but this one had such a beautiful marble mantelpiece he forgave the deception. Either Mrs Beecher had a very strong sense of style or she'd employed a very expensive interior decorator.

"My husband and Hugo Bonner were school friends, inspector. Hugo and Helen are dear friends of ours. Poor Helen. And Matthew, of course. Losing his father at such a young age. Quite unimaginable."

"Is that how you became one of the trustees of Literally London?"

"Yes. About ten years ago Hugo was looking for someone to join the board and as he knew how much I love books, he asked me. Then when the previous vice chair decided to retire a few years ago, I took up the post."

"Do you now become chair?" Lucas asked, putting his delicate tea cup carefully back on the saucer. He couldn't remember the last time he'd drunk out of an actual cup, rather than a mug.

"Oh dear no, I imagine Helen or even Matthew will take that on. But I'll hold the fort until they've had a chance to recover." Amanda suddenly looked very serious. "You must understand, inspector, that the Bonner family still very much sees the archive as 'theirs'. And although technically it is now owned by the Trust, the Trust's charter stipulates that the position of chair must always be offered to a member of the Bonner family. And as the chair is entitled to push through decisions and has the only veto...well, you can see it's still very much a family thing."

"Then what does the board actually do?"

"Fundraising, mainly. Keeping an eye on the accounts. Persuading people to make donations."

"About the accounts..."

Amanda immediately interrupted.

"They are annually audited by a very reputable firm – you won't find any discrepancies there."

"Under the circumstances, I'm afraid we'll still need to have a look."

Amanda relented.

"Fine. I'll ask our accountant to provide you with copies of everything you'd like to see."

"Thank you." Lucas picked up his tea cup once more and finished the contents.

"Can you think of any reason why Mr Bonner would have visited the archive secretly?"

"None whatsoever. If Hugo was concerned about anything or anyone there, he didn't confide in me."

Emma wasn't used to such quiet tea breaks. Tim seemed to be in a world of his own, Jennifer was looking pale and being very monosyllabic, even Theresa was looking rather glum. Marie had tried to get a conversation going three times now, without much response. She desperately tried to think of something to say.

"Why don't we invite the other trustees over?"

Blank faces stared back at her.

"Why not? When you think about it it's ridiculous they don't come and visit more often. I can't remember the last time any of them apart from Hugo Bonner actually came here."

They still looked doubtful, but at least she'd got their attention.

"Why would they listen to us?" Theresa asked, sounding quite sullen.

"They don't need to." Emma was getting quite excited about the idea now. "We ask Richard to invite them – they can hardly say no, not in the circumstances. Then we show them the work we do..."

Theresa sat up straighter.

"I could show them the searchroom, explain everything I do, show them I belong there."

"Good thinking," Marie added, "I could tell them about the amount of cleaning and monitoring a building this size requires."

Tim had returned from wherever his mind had been and joined in.

"If they got to know us it would make it much more difficult for Olivia to persuade them to get rid of us, no matter what she'd say."

"Exactly." Emma looked at Jennifer, who still hadn't responded. "They could visit conservation as well Jennifer, see the great work you do. If we can just get them a bit more interested in the place and in us, it'll be all right, whoever's in charge."

Jennifer still didn't look convinced, but at least she wasn't as pale any more.

"Better go dear."

Marie gave Theresa a nudge, who checked the time and left the room. Forty-five seconds later Olivia came in, ignored them all, switched on the kettle, put two heaped teaspoons of instant coffee in her mug and disappeared again.

"Mr Ripley?"

Sam looked up from his computer.

"Yes Melissa?"

"It's nearly six o'clock, sir, the others have all gone."

Sam looked at the clock on the wall opposite.

"Good heavens, that late already! I had no idea." He smiled ruefully. "Bit of an unusual day, wouldn't you say?"

Melissa stifled a sob.

"Like you said, sir, he was a good man. It's very hard to believe he's gone; murdered, even."

Sam got up from behind his desk and walked a bit closer to her, putting his hand lightly on her arm.

"Terrible business, I know. You go home now Melissa and if you feel the need tomorrow to have a day off to recover from the shock, then you just do that."

He waited another ten minutes after Melissa left the room – just in case she'd forgotten something – and then locked both the main door into the office and the door to his own office. He unlocked the filing cabinet and took out several bundles; next he unlocked the large corner cabinet and took out the shredder.

Emma decanted the pizzas out of their boxes and slid them on to the plates; her mother never objected to take-aways, but drew the line at eating out of the packaging. She took the plates through to the living room and put them down on the dining table. Jess had already opened a bottle of red, while Elise had set the table.

"There...much nicer than eating out of cardboard, don't you agree?"

The conversation returned to the events at the archive and Elise recounted her meeting with Amanda Beecher.

"So you see, Mandy is quite certain there can't be any embezzlement going on."

"I never thought there was, mother, that was purely in your imagination."

"She did mention some of the items in your collection are very valuable – is that true?"

"Of course they are, they are completely unique."

"So does that mean there are collectors who would pay a lot to get hold of them?"

"No mother, it's not possible that someone is selling our documents. They're all listed in our catalogue, it would be impossible to sell them on."

"Darling, there are always people willing to sell and buy stolen goods. Would you actually know if something went missing?"

Emma gave this some thought.

"Perhaps not immediately, but the world of literary manuscripts is quite small. Someone would notice that the document was listed in our catalogue. Especially the really valuable ones, you just couldn't get away with that."

"Besides," Jess added, "why on earth would Hugo Bonner be stealing documents? He's loaded."

"He could have suspected someone else of stealing." Elise got quite excited now. "That would explain why he was snooping around and would give someone a motive to kill him. Except of course," she added disappointedly, "according to Emma it wouldn't really be possible to sell anything you stole."

"Actually," Emma began, "there would be a way."

Elise and Jess looked at her expectantly.

"We don't have the staff to catalogue everything that comes into the collections."

Blank faces showed she had to expound.

"Say three boxes full of manuscripts arrive. We don't have anyone to list everything that's in them, so the catalogue would just say the name of the author and 'three boxes, unlisted'. One of Tim's jobs is to box list collections – going through each box and just writing out a list of what there's in there – but until he's done that we don't really know what there is. There's still quite a lot of unlisted boxes dotted around."

"So if someone went through those and stole the most valuable documents, you'd never know they'd been taken?"

"No, we wouldn't."

"That must be it then," Elise said triumphantly. "You'd better tell your inspector."

Emma gave her a withering look.

"What exactly am I supposed to tell him? That it theoretically might be possible to steal documents from the collection and sell them? Without any proof that anything is missing or has been sold? I'm sure he can come up with all kinds of theories himself – it's finding proof that's the hard bit."

The voice of Kylie Minogue suddenly filled the room; Jess grabbed her phone, pressed the green button and disappeared into her room. About thirty seconds later an almighty scream emanated from the bedroom, after which Jess ran back into the front room, started jumping up and down and waving her phone around.

"I got it, I got it, I got it!!!!!"

"You're very excited for a part in a two-bit Dracula movie."

"Noooooooo, not that part, I couldn't give a toss about that part. I'm going to be in the Importance of Being Earnest!"

THURSDAY 11 APRIL

Twelve

Lucas fastened his seatbelt, steeled himself, and switched on the engine. He reached to turn on the indicator, when he heard his phone. Any excuse would do, so he switched the engine back off and answered.

"Bohr."

"Good morning Lucas."

"Good morning Flo. You sound very cheerful."

"Always feels good to have some news."

"Positive ID?"

"Dental records check out. However…"

"However?"

"The DNA from the son isn't a match."

Another man? Jealous maybe? Revenge after all these years? The possibilities this news brought swirled through Lucas' mind.

"Lucas?"

"Sorry, yes I heard. So it *is* Bonner, but he's not Matthew's father?"

"That is the most likely explanation. Although it would be best if we could have a DNA confirmation of the actual father, so we can rule out that someone went to a lot of trouble to match dental records."

"Thanks Flo, I'll see what I can do."

That was going to be another interesting chat with Helen Bonner, Lucas thought as he carefully joined the queue of traffic.

"Morning Marie."

"Morning Emma."

The excited tone of her voice made Emma slow down – what had happened now?

"Richard's got an announcement to make. He wants all of us to gather in the staffroom."

Emma saw the glint in Marie's eyes, the willingness to say more if asked.

"That sounds very mysterious. I bet you know what it's about though?"

Marie lowered her voice to a loud whisper.

"I shouldn't really say, but he has asked me to get some nice cakes and he's wearing his best suit. I think we can expect a special visitor. Or visitors."

"Interesting. I'd better get to the staffroom then."

Who could this mysterious visitor be, Emma wondered as she wound her way up the stairs. Some wealthy donor perhaps, or someone considering adding their precious collection to the archive's? They did sometimes receive free gifts, although usually the trustees had to find the money to pay for the offered manuscripts and first editions. Emma was nearly the last to arrive and sat down on the sofa in between Tim and Jennifer. A few minutes later Theresa burst in, closely followed by Marie. Richard didn't waste any time.

"Mrs Beecher, the acting Chair of the Literally London Trust, will be visiting us this morning. I imagine she will want to talk to everyone, but I will see her in my office first. I'm sure Marie will let you all know when she's arrived."

With that Richard walked back to his office; the others all followed him out of the room, carefully avoiding looking at Olivia who was still sitting statue like on her straight-backed chair.

"Thank you for seeing me again Mrs Bonner."

The art deco room was less of a surprise this time; Lucas almost managed to ignore the beauty of his surroundings and concentrate fully on the conversation.

"I didn't get the impression I had a choice."

"The dental records have confirmed that the body is that of your husband. However...this is a little delicate I'm afraid."

Helen gave him a cold look.

"The DNA sample your son gave doesn't match. Is there any chance Hugo wasn't Matthew's father?"

Helen's face remained calm, but the sudden whiteness of her hands betrayed her emotions.

"I always wondered." She hesitated. "Could never be really sure." She looked straight at Lucas now. "You must think me a very cold bitch."

Lucas managed to look sympathetic.

"Most families have their secrets."

"I found out very early in our marriage that Hugo wasn't the faithful type. Of course I thought I could change him; when it dawned on me that I would never be able to, I decided to have a fling myself. When I got pregnant I just hoped for the best. Hugo never doubted Matthew was his son and he genuinely was a very good father. Just a rather lousy husband; I would have left him by now if it wasn't for Matthew."

"I'm afraid we'll need to talk to Matthew's biological father."

For the first time since he'd met her, Helen lost her ice queen persona.

"Are you insane? He has no idea... Matthew might find out... No, I can't possibly allow that."

"If you don't give me a name, I'm afraid we'll have to start digging ourselves. The time frame is easy to determine; we'd have to start talking to relatives, friends, see who remembers what about that period." Helen looked at him in total disgust. "Of course, if you tell us who the father is, we can be very discreet about it. You would still need to talk to him of course, but no one else need find out."

Helen sat in silence for a few minutes, weighing up the various options. In the end she relented.

"Someone would be bound to remember we spent a lot of time together back then. At least this way I can talk to him first."

"Who?"

"Alexander Beecher."

Amanda Beecher smiled graciously as Marie handed her a cup of tea. Richard had just been called away by a phone call, so she'd sat down on the amazingly orange sofa while Marie made her a drink. The meeting with Richard had been quite formal; she still wondered why he was so uneasy. And it wasn't just him; as they'd walked around the building all the staff had been on edge. Surely she wasn't that scary? She'd been genuinely interested in the work that was being done and she hadn't come to enforce budget cuts or brought other bad news. Were they all this upset about Hugo's death?

"A slice of cake Mrs Beecher?"

"Thank you Marie. And my name is Amanda."

"I'm sure you have more important things to do than gossip with Mrs Beecher, Marie."

The unexpected voice cut through the room and almost physically slapped Marie in the face.

"If you'll excuse me Amanda, I'd better get back to my duties."

Amanda got up, smiled at the short, stout woman who'd just entered the room and held out her hand.

"Amanda Beecher."

"Dr Olivia Dunstable. Archivist."

A rather limp handshake followed, after which Olivia sat down on her usual chair.

"I'd hoped to have a word with you Mrs Beecher. It's always a pleasure to meet such a cultured, intelligent lady as yourself. I'm sure you've realised by now that there is a lot of waste going on in this building. I have several ideas to improve the way our resources are spent, which I'm sure you'll find very interesting. My dear friend Arthur Wells certainly does."

The mention of her fellow trustee's name clarified the situation: clearly some kind of power struggle was going on and Dr Dunstable had already ensured the backing of one trustee.

"Of course we can always look at ways to improve the service the archive provides, but it does seem a bit soon..."

"Believe me, there's no time to waste. Did you realise we have a member of staff with no qualifications at all helping our researchers in the searchroom?"

Amanda tried not to smile at the memory of enthusiastic, bundle of energy Theresa showing her round the searchroom. She could well imagine Dr Dunstable wouldn't approve.

"And who needs a conservation studio? A waste of money if you ask me."

"Really? It seemed like highly skilled work to me."

"Oh I'm sure Jennifer does her best, but she's so very, very slow. Far more sensible to get funding on a project by project basis and let someone in private practice do the work. They're bound to be a lot cheaper. But another archivist, now that would be really useful."

No wonder everyone had been walking on eggshells if they thought she might agree with all these ideas.

"I can assure you I will call a meeting of the trustees at an appropriate time, where we'll discuss the future direction of the archive. And of course we'll be happy to receive written suggestions from members of staff and will examine them all diligently."

Olivia Dunstable looked very unimpressed, but Amanda knew Marie had heard every word and was now rushing round the building encouraging everyone to write down their own suggestions.

"Olivia. How kind of you to keep Amanda company."

"Not everyone abandons an important guest to the caretaker, Richard. "

Olivia stood up, said her farewells to Amanda, and left the room.

Back at his office, Lucas related the morning's events to Nick.

"I promised Mrs Bonner I'd wait an hour before getting in touch with Beecher."

"Odd that it's Amanda Beecher's husband."

"We already knew the couples were friends, so I wouldn't say it's that odd. Have you found out anything more this morning?"

"I've tried to dig a bit deeper in the backgrounds of everyone at the archive – there must be a few skeletons lurking there. And I've started going through Bonner's financial statements; nothing unusual yet, but there's still a lot to check."

Lucas was about to reply when his phone went.

"Bohr."

"This is Alexander Beecher, inspector Bohr. I've just had a very...interesting conversation with Helen Bonner."

"I appreciate you calling me, Mr Beecher. Can we talk somewhere?"

"I'd rather avoid speculation at the office, I'm sure you understand. My wife has gone out for the morning, so I could meet you at home in about twenty minutes?"

"Excellent, I'll be there."

Nick had gone back to the financial statements, but looked up when the call finished. "We'd better go together to meet Mr Beecher; it's going to be the kind of conversation that is vastly improved by having a witness."

The first thing Lucas noticed about Alexander Beecher was the slight tremor in his hand as he held it out to greet him; the second was the distinctive smell of very good whiskey. He must have had a couple of drinks as soon as he got home. Quite forgivable under the circumstances. Lucas wasn't sure how he'd react if he were told he had a teenage son, but he imagined there would be alcohol involved.

"My apologies for having to rake up the past, sir, but under the circumstances..."

Alexander nodded.

"Although I'm still not entirely sure why my being Matthew's father is relevant?"

"We need to be sure the body found at the archive is that of Hugo Bonner. Since there is no paternal DNA match with Matthew, we have to be certain Matthew isn't his son."

Nick took a DNA sampling kit from his pocket, unscrewed the lid and handed Alexander what looked like a small stick with some cotton wool stuck to it.

"If you wouldn't mind, sir. The inside of your cheek."

Alexander snatched the small rod out of Nick's hand, stared at him as he very deliberately stuck it in his mouth and then thrust it back in his fingers.

"Satisfied?"

"You had no idea he is your son?" Lucas asked.

Alexander poured himself another drink.

"None whatsoever. Helen and I had a little fling; it wasn't serious and it didn't last long. I always saw her pregnancy as a sign that she and Hugo had settled their differences."

"You never saw any kind of family resemblance?" Nick sounded surprised. "You never wondered?"

"I just bloody said so, didn't I?"

Alexander emptied his glass and poured another.

"She doesn't want him to know. I have a son and I can't talk to him. How do you think that feels?"

"It's obviously been a shock to both of you." Lucas tried to sound sympathetic. "Given some time I'm sure..."

"Oh, you're sure are you? If you hadn't been ferreting around in other's people's business...if that idiot Hugo hadn't got himself killed..."

His eyes started welling up and he reached for the bottle again.

"We'll let ourselves out, Mr Bonner. Thank you for seeing us."

"What do you think?" Nick asked as he was getting in to the car.

"If he knew and killed Bonner out of jealousy, he's hiding it very well."

"He wouldn't risk getting drunk in front of us if had something to hide, would he?"

"Very unlikely, I agree."

"Inspector Bohr?"

Lucas turned round and watched Amanda Beecher walk up to him.

"Did you come to see me? I've just been to the archive, to re-assure everyone there."

"I'm sure they appreciated it, Mrs Beecher. We've actually just had a brief chat with you husband."

"Alex? Surely he's at work?"

"He suggested we meet him here." Lucas tried to look reassuringly himself. "It's always a bit awkward if the police turn up at your workplace."

"Why did you want to see him?"

"Just following lines of enquiries." Was that diplomacy or cowardice – Lucas wasn't sure. "Good day, Mrs Beecher."

He quickly got into the car and drove off.

Amanda stared at the Golf, watching it disappear amongst the traffic. Why on earth had they wanted to talk to Alex? Yes, he and Hugo had been friends, but if they were going to talk to all of Hugo's friends they were going to be wasting an awful lot of time. She opened the front door feeling slightly apprehensive. 'Come on Amanda' she told herself, 'don't be silly.' As she walked in to the front room, a waft of alcohol reached her all the way from the sofa.

"Alex? What's going on?"

Thirteen

Emma was really getting worried about Tim now. He'd sat motionless at his desk since Amanda Beecher had left and it was now nearly lunchtime.

"Tim?" she tried again. Still no response. Desperate times called for desperate actions; she opened the locked bottom drawer of her desk, took out the unassuming plastic container that was always hiding down there, opened the lid and took out her emergency bar of dark, beautiful chocolate. Breaking it in two she walked over to Tim and gently gave him a nudge.

"I don't know about you, but I need this today."

It took a few seconds for Tim to return from wherever he'd been; as he slowly focussed on her outstretched hand and the gleaming piece of chocolate he stopped looking quite so pale and managed to give her a warm smile. They both ate slowly, enjoying the crunchy first bite, savouring the slow melt, relishing the release of its delicate velvety taste before allowing it to go down, covering their throats in a warm embrace. They sighed in unison.

"What's the matter Tim?"

"Bad memories." He looked at her anxiously. "We'll always be friends won't we? No matter what?"

"Of course" Emma said surprised. "You know you can tell me, whatever it is."

"Maybe one day." He seemed a lot more himself now and sat up straight. "I think I know what I need to do." He gave her a big smile. "Thanks for the chocolate."

Emma smiled back.

"Come on, let's go out for lunch."

Lucas finished off his cheese and tomato sandwich, while staring at his inbox. How could there be this many unread emails again? Nearly fifty since yesterday! A lot of them seemed to have emanated from Human Resources; some of these might well be important, but, he conceded as he pressed the delete button again, he would never know.

"Wow."

Lucas glanced over at Nick.

"Find something?"

"I've been going through the correspondence we found in Bonner's office. You should read this."

He handed Lucas a letter, printed on very good quality, thick paper.

Dear Mr Bonner

A friend of mine who attended your recent fund raising event for Literally London mentioned this fascinating archive to me, as he knows how much I love books. As I also used to work in an archive, before inheriting quite a substantial amount of money, he felt I might like to contribute. I had a look on your website and to my surprise saw you are employing an ex-colleague of mine, Dr Olivia Dunstable. I can only assume you are unaware of the controversy surrounding Dr Dunstable's 'career' as I am sure you would not have employed her otherwise. I would be happy to discuss making a very generous donation to the archive, but only if Dr Dunstable ceases to work there.

"Well, well," Lucas said, looking at the top of the letter. "Dated a week ago, from a Ms Patricia Hale. Give her a call will you, Nick, and see if she can tell us what this is all about."

Nick took the letter back to his desk, dialled the number and after a very brief conversation walked back over to Lucas.

"The fact that Dr Dunstable is caught up in a murder investigation gave Ms Hale no end of joy. She's very keen to tell us all about what happened; I said we'd meet her at her flat in half an hour."

Lucas looked at the address. The most expensive area in London; not somewhere he'd ever driven before. He took the car key out of his pocket and lobbed it to Nick.

"You're driving."

When Ms Hale opened the door, she rather took Lucas by surprise. He'd expected...well, he wasn't sure entirely what he'd expected, but not this young, slightly overweight, extremely bubbly girl who almost gave him a hug instead of a handshake.

"Come in, come in, lovely to meet you. Do you like the flat? It's amazing isn't it? I still haven't got it all re-decorated, but this is my favourite room."

She led them in to a spacious bright room, the large windows looking out over a very green and quiet part of London. Everything in the room was a complete miss-match of genuine antiques and modern kitsch, but the overall effect somehow worked and gave the same happy, bubbly, feel as it's owner.

"Have a seat, I've got tea and things ready."

The 'things' turned out to be a large selection of cakes and biscuits, on a Fortnum and Mason tray.

"The cakes are delish, you have to try them."

Lucas and Nick sat down on a deep black leather sofa, while Patricia Hale opted for a very cosy looking red armchair.

"Ms Hale," Lucas began.

"Oh, Pat, please."

He hesitated slightly and began again.

"Pat, I believe sergeant Fletcher explained over the phone…"

"That that awful bully could be a murderer!" She was even more excited now. "Yes, he did say that. And that you found my letter to Hugo Bonner and you want to know all about what a horrible person she is." Her eyes were positively gleaming with delight.

Lucas looked at the food. Pretty tempting after a not very special lunch. Best to just go with the flow. He put a few cakes on a plate – an example Nick immediately followed – poured himself a cup of tea, and sat back in the sofa.

"Why don't you just tell us the whole story, Pat."

"Nine years ago I left school with just a few GCSE's and no idea what to do next. I'm not from a rich family, you know. My mum's brother had gone to America the year before to do something with computers. We knew he was doing all right there, and he had always lots of money to spend when he came over, but we'd no idea just how rich he'd become until he died just over a year ago. He had one of these super-fast sports cars and lost control… it tore my mum up, that did, he was her only brother. Then it turned out he'd left me, his only niece, all his money. Millions." She stared past them into the distance and fell quiet. After a few minutes Lucas gently coughed, which brought her back to the present. "Anyway, when I left school I didn't have any money and needed a job; I temped a bit and then became receptionist at our local county archive. Ms Dunstable," she could clearly hardly bring herself to say the name, "was the senior archivist. Everyone else there was really nice, but she was horrible. Never a good thing to say about anyone, always criticising what everyone did. And in a really nasty way, to make you feel small. A proper bully. But a clever one; she could turn on the charm when she needed to and the county archivist thought she was wonderful." She pulled a face. "There were rumours that they were having an affair, but that just brings up all kinds of disgusting images. Whatever was or wasn't going on, she was untouchable."

"I see why…"

"Oh, that's not the half of it!"

Lucas took another piece of cake and settled back down in the sofa.

"One of her favourite taunts was my lack of education. She was doing a PhD at some university about archive management and would give me lectures about hard work and how lazy it was of me not to want to better myself." A sharp pain had crept into Pat's voice, suddenly making her seem even younger and very vulnerable. "Always going on about that, she was. She wouldn't tell anyone what her PhD was about or let anyone read it or anything – she made it clear to the archivists that their opinions would be worthless." She paused to take a big bite of a piece of triple chocolate cake. "Luckily she wasn't very good with technology; both her mentor and one of the archivists were called Ben and when she wanted to email the latest version of her thesis to her mentor, she emailed it to the archivist instead." A faint smile appeared on her lips. "He went through the roof. Her entire thesis was based on research she'd told him to do. She tried to wriggle out of it of course, but even the county archivist couldn't just ignore this. In the end they worked out a compromise: she dropped out of the course and left the archive and archivist Ben became the new Senior Archivist. No scandal, no blemish on her record – I bet she walked straight into a new job with a glowing reference." She sounded indignant now. "She wasn't really punished at all, for any of the things she'd done. And I bet she's been just as horrible to anyone else she's been in charge of. So when I saw her name on the Literally London website, I thought I could finally make her pay. Get her sacked. Show her it's not clever to be nasty to people who you think aren't important."

"Did you tell Mr Bonner?"

"Yes. He took me out to lunch last Wednesday and I told him the whole story. He said he was appalled, but that of course he would have to talk to Olivia first and hear her side." She looked straight into Lucas' grey eyes. "I offered him a quarter of a million to sack her. Believe me, he was going to."

Emma looked up from the report she was writing for a paying customer (they needed more of those!) and surreptitiously observed Tim as he walked back into the room, clutching the blue-grey folder he'd collected from the store. He looked a lot better now, his face relaxed, his cheeks no longer quite so pale. He was probably just worrying too much about his job and what Olivia might do next. Or at least try to do next. She quickly looked away as he turned round and walked over to her desk.

"Time for pudding, I think."

Emma obediently took the paper bag with mini custard tarts out of her handbag; going out for lunch was always dangerous of course, but at least this time they'd limited themselves to toasties and had brought treats back for everyone to share.

Tim joined Jennifer and Marie in the staff room, while Emma went through to the kitchen and put the tarts on a plate. Theresa burst in while she was making two cups of tea; she fished her bottle of coke out of the fridge and looked longingly at the plate.

"Yes, please, take it through, they're for everyone."

Theresa quickly popped a whole one in her mouth and took the plate with her; by the time Emma followed, more than half were gone already.

"So what did you make of Mrs Beecher, Marie?"

Emma handed Tim his cup of tea and sat down next to him on the sofa, cradling her yellow mug in her hands.

"A very nice lady," was Marie's assessment, "we'll be all right with her in charge."

"She came down to conservation," Jennifer added, "and was very interested in the work. Unlike Olivia."

"Olivia was toadying up to her no end, but she wasn't having any of it."

Theresa laughed.

"You just happened to overhear?"

"Damn right I made sure I overheard - this is about our jobs, Tessie."

"I know, I'm sorry. I'm glad you look after us Marie."

Emma looked at the clock.

"Shouldn't you be heading back?"

Theresa threw her bottle of coke back in the fridge and ran down the stairs.

"I'll wash up," Jennifer offered and she went into the kitchen, taking empty cups with her.

Thirty seconds later Olivia strode into the staff room and made her way straight to the kitchen. She switched the nearly full kettle on, spooned some instant in her mug, looked disgruntled at the nowhere near boiling kettle and strode out again. Once she'd safely gone, Tim brought his and Emma's cups through.

"I'll give you a hand," he offered.

Jennifer smiled, pushed Olivia's mug out of the way, and handed him the tea towel.

Nick parked the car as near to the archive as he could and switched off the engine.

"How do you want to play this?"

"Have you been watching American cop shows again?"

"She's not an easy person to talk to, boss."

Boss? That was a yes, then.

"We do what we always do: ask questions and see what kind of reaction we get."

They walked through the big sliding door; Lucas wasn't even surprised when Marie dashed out to greet them before they'd managed to get to the stairs.

"Anything I can help you with, inspector?"

"No, thank you, Mrs Thorpe." Seeing the disappointment on Marie's face he quickly added, "Perhaps later."

"Come."

"Really?" thought Lucas, "*come*? Who says *come*?"

Olivia looked momentarily surprised as they entered, but quickly recovered and indicated two empty chairs that stood against the wall. Nick grabbed both, plonked them in front of the desk and both he and Lucas sat down. She looked older than yesterday; maybe she wasn't as immune to her surroundings as she seemed.

"Yes, inspector?"

"As part of our investigation, Dr Dunstable, we look into the past of everyone involved..."

"*Everyone* involved? That would take up an awful lot of valuable police resources. If you mean all suspects, please be clear about that."

Lucas breathed out slowly; he'd meant to be diplomatic, but now she'd asked for the direct approach.

"We had a conversation with a Ms Patricia Hale earlier today. Does that name mean anything to you?"

"You know very well that it does."

"Ms Hale made some allegations about the time you worked together." He paused, but as there was no response he continued. "Bullying, was one, plagiarism another."

"Some people would describe Ms Hale as a sweet girl with a very active imagination... I on the other hand have always considered her to be quite an accomplished little liar. I'm sure a man of your intelligence would have seen straight through her."

The sarcasm in that last remark rang out loud and clear.

"Whether I believe her is irrelevant, Dr Dunstable. Hugo Bonner was certainly impressed by what she had to say and was planning to fire you."

She gave him a very disappointed look and took a sip from the almost empty cup of coffee on her desk.

"Oh dear inspector, it looks like you did take her seriously. Whatever *Ms* Hale may have believed, I assure you my position here was under no threat whatsoever."

"Did Bonner confront you?"

"We discussed the matter, yes."

Lucas was getting impatient.

"You don't seem to appreciate Dr Dunstable that this is a murder investigation and that Ms Hale's claims give you a very clear motive. I suggest you stop playing games and tell me what happened."

A smile flickered momentarily across Olivia's face; damn, he'd let her rattle him and she knew it.

"Hugo came to see me last Thursday morning... He told me about Ms Hale's allegations and her 'offer' to the archive if I were to leave. I'm sure that's illegal, wouldn't you say inspector? Would that constitute a bribe?" The same small smile re-appeared briefly. "Either way, I made it clear to Hugo that I had no intention of leaving and that if he dared fire me I would sue him personally for wrongful dismissal... He assured me there would be no need for that."

With a final gulp she finished her now cold coffee.

"Now if you'll excuse me, I have work to do."

She turned back to her computer screen and started typing.

"Maybe you were right," Lucas said fuming as they walked down the stairs, "maybe we should have had a play."

"She was lying through her teeth."

"No way to prove it now that Bonner's dead. If he'd mentioned the possibility of sacking her to anyone else here they would have told us by now."

"I bet that's what he came to do on Monday and she headed him off."

Lucas paused at the bottom of the stairs.

"Did you notice she was speaking more slowly than usual?"

"Yes, she seemed to be searching for her words. Maybe there was more than just coffee in that cup."

Helen stared at the phone, hoping the ringing would just stop. She'd had too many calls already today, too many people interfering. This caller was being very persistent though. She grabbed the phone and pressed the button.

"Helen, at last. I need to see you.'

"Why? We'd agreed it would be better not to be in touch for a while."

"I...I miss you."

Helen took a deep breath and tried to stay calm – was the sex really good enough to justify all this neediness? But then again, now was definitely not the time for further complications.

"Fine," she said, trying not to sound too impatient.

"When?" came the eager reply.

"Lunch tomorrow, while Matt's in school. I'll meet you at Ronaldo's at twelve."

"I'll be there."

"Good. I need to go."

The door to the dining room opened as Mathew walked in, still looking very pale.

"Who was that?"

"Just more condolences, darling. How did it go?"

Matthew shrugged his shoulders.

"No one really knew what to say. Mr Harris said I could postpone taking my A-levels if I wanted to, but I said I'd rather get them done. Dad helped me prepare, I don't want to waste..." His voice trailed off and he looked at his mother, hoping she'd understand.

"Of course, darling, you want to make dad proud."

Matthew's face flushed with relief.

"I'll go up and study for a bit."

"Mrs Flint has promised us her famous fish and chips tonight, followed by trifle."

Matthew smiled and started to leave the room.

"I think I can eat that."

Helen listened as the sound of his footsteps gradually diminished the higher up the stairs he got; she convinced herself she could hear him all the way to the second floor, could hear the click as he closed his bedroom door, could even hear the chair being pulled nearer the desk. He was being brave, holding himself together, doing what was expected of him. No doubt he would sail through his exams, probably getting even better results than had been predicted. But then what? Once that pressure was off, once he could relax, would that be when it really hit him? Had it really hit her yet? Yes, she thought, she could honestly say it had. It had been a shock, obviously, and she'd never wished Hugo dead, but any love there had been between them had vanished years ago. His multitude of affairs, her own current dalliance; if he hadn't been such a great father for Matt, she'd have divorced him by now. And if she wasn't so ridiculously wealthy, he would have certainly left her. She had no tears to waste on him, no great feelings of loss or loneliness; the realisation that her future was entirely her own again, was actually quite appealing. She looked up to the ceiling and could picture exactly how Matthew was sitting at his desk, studiously leafing through his maths or chemistry books. She'd keep him busy, get him through this – perhaps it would never need to hit him.

Amanda poured herself a second glass of wine, stared at it for a while, then took it over to the sink and poured it away. One of them really ought to stay sober, she decided. Alex had passed out after confessing the affair and its consequences in between gulping down several more whiskeys. How did she feel about it? Confused, certainly. Hurt by the betrayal, but then, that had happened a long time age. Or had there been others? If she was totally honest, what hurt most was Matthew. Alex hadn't wanted children, had persuaded her she didn't want them either. And now it turned out he had a son after all, while she never would. Seeing Elise had brought back the memories of their time criss-crossing the Midlands, in search of the big stories even Londoners would want to read about. She'd been ambitious, seeing her partnership with Elise as a step towards a London-based job and maybe even television. She'd been good too, if maybe a little too naive at times. But then she'd met Alexander. Suave, handsome, wealthy, powerful, slightly older Alexander. And she'd been completely swept off her feet...That bottle of wine was looking very tempting again. She shook her head – no, that wasn't the answer. She opened one of the kitchen cupboards and took out the packet of flour; she always thought more clearly while baking.

Five on the dot. Marie looked at the signing out sheet: no one had left early, but she could hear footsteps coming down the stairs behind her.
"Scuuuuse me, Marie."
Marie spun round.
"Theresa, where did you spring from? Sneaking up on me like that!"
Theresa laughed.
"I can be very quiet when I want be."
She reached past her and signed herself out. Emma and Tim had reached the door by now as well and were joined by Jennifer. Marie waved them goodnight and continued her closing checks. It was five fifteen when she returned to the door; Frederick and Richard had gone, but Olivia still hadn't signed out. No surprise there. She walked round the building again. Nearly half past five. Marie checked the signing out sheet again, but no, Olivia was still in the building. Best not to be seen hanging around the door waiting for her, not after the day this had been. She went back to her desk, picked up her book and continued reading a particularly disturbing torture scene.

A terrified scream echoed through the foyer, followed by a heavy thump. For a few seconds Marie sat rooted to her chair, not sure whether her imagination had gotten the better of her. Then she ran into the foyer and nearly tripped over the lifeless body of Olivia Dunstable.

Lucas sat on one of the comfortable searchroom chairs and looked through the glass door at the multitude of people gathered in the foyer. Nick was heading his way - poor Alfie would have fallen asleep listening to second class funny voices again.
"Flo confirmed that Dr Dunstable has a broken neck; she would have died on impact. They're taking her to the mortuary now."
"How's our Mrs Thorpe doing?"
"I don't think she's stopped talking yet."
"What do we think, Nick? Suicide?"
"The kick stool is still standing on the second floor landing. She must have climbed on it and jumped over the railing."
"Why would she kill herself though? Can you honestly see her as Bonner's killer and then feel so guilty about it that she jumps down two flights of stairs?"
"Can you honestly see anyone getting that very overweight, short woman over that metal railing and throw her down two flights of stairs? Dead she'd be a horrendous weight and alive – well, I imagine she'd struggle and shout for help, wouldn't you?"
"Right. Let's send Mrs Thorpe home and finish off here. I'll call Dr Owen and give him the news; he'll have to let his staff know they won't be able to come in till after lunchtime tomorrow. I'm not letting any of them in the building until we've had Flo's report."

FRIDAY 12 APRIL

Fourteen

At 6.30 am Emma had already been on the laptop for an hour. She'd started off in her bedroom, not wanting to wake anyone else, but was now installed in the kitchen so she could have a more regular supply of green tea. And dark chocolate digestives.

"Emma, what are you doing?"

Elise wandered into the kitchen in her dressing gown, still half asleep, and re-filled the kettle.

"I didn't sleep much, all I could think about was Olivia killing herself like that. She must have killed Mr Bonner, but why? I woke up at about half four and just kept thinking about that."

"Darling, no need for you to lose sleep over that strange woman. I'm sure your inspector..."

"He's not *my* inspector, mother. Anyway, he's bound to want to talk to us all again, isn't he, to see whether we can think of a reason?"

Elise nodded.

"Well then, I was thinking about your theory..."

"Which one sweetheart? I do tend to come up with quite a few."

"Someone stealing documents. Olivia was perfectly placed to do it – she does the official cataloguing, so all she'd have to do is not include something and no one would ever know it had been stolen."

"Yes, you explained all that yesterday."

"So how would you sell a literary manuscript or letters written by some famous author?"

Elise was beginning to feel a bit more awake, having drunk half her cup and tried to concentrate.

"Find private collectors?"

"And what's the easiest way to find them?"

"Darling it's not even seven o'clock yet, far too early for a quiz."

"The same way you find anything – on the internet!"

"Is that what you've been doing at this ridiculous hour then?"

"At first yes, but I didn't get anywhere. Private collectors clearly like to be just that – private. So I started looking for websites selling manuscripts."

Elise was definitely awake now.

"And?"

Emma sighed.

"The opposite problem – there are hundreds of them. I've spent ages looking through sale catalogues and browsing websites, but without knowing what I'm looking for it's pretty impossible. It's easy enough to find stuff from London born authors, but proving any of it came out of our collection – that's just not going to happen."

Disappointed she shut the lid of the laptop and grabbed another biscuit. Elise looked at the nearly empty packet.

"How about some real breakfast?"

"No, I think I'll just go back to bed." Emma was sounding very tired and disillusioned now. "I really thought I was on to something."

She got up and started to leave the kitchen.

"It's a pity you can't work it the other way round" Elise said.

"How do you mean?"

"If you knew something was missing, you could look for something specific. But of course that would have to be something you'd seen and knew wasn't there anymore, or an author you knew you had everything from. Ah well, get some sleep, darling."

Emma walked back to her bedroom, almost opened the door and then rushed back into the kitchen, all thought of sleep gone.

"Mum, you're a genius!"

"Obviously," Elise agreed, "but what about specifically this time?"

"Marcus Whitten." Emma sounded triumphant.

"Who?"

"Marcus Whitten is a Victorian writer. No one here much cares about him, but he visited America and wrote various novels set in New York and other cities, which makes him important for their literary and social history."

"I'm going to need another cup of tea."

"It's simple mum: a few years ago the Trustees bought Whitten's archive from his great-granddaughter. All of it. Every manuscript, every note, it's all in there. I know, I helped pack it all up into our boxes – at least thirty of them – and I regularly have to hunt through the collection to answer queries about him."

Elise sat back down with her new cup of tea.

"Ok, I think I've got it so far."

"A few months ago Olivia asked Tim to box list the collection. That's nearly three years after it came in."

Elise still looked puzzled.

"An important collection like that mother! It should have been given priority, but she didn't ask Tim to work on it for nearly three years. Why would she have done that if not to give herself time…"

"…to go through it and sell off some of the most interesting pieces. You could be on to something there."

"I know I am." Emma sat down again and opened up the laptop. "Right, let's find Marcus Whitten."

Elise saw the determined look in her daughter's eyes, picked up what remained of the biscuits, put them back in the cupboard and took out the porridge.

Lucas snatched his pieces of toast from the toaster, spread them with margarine and marmalade and sat down at his small kitchen table. Someone was getting very excited on Radio 4 about something or other and no doubt someone else would be getting very cross about it all in a minute. He usually enjoyed listening to the Today Programme as it cleared his head for the day ahead, but this morning the heated discussions just annoyed him and he switched the radio off. Why would she have killed herself? Granted, he hadn't known Olivia Dunstable well, but someone that arrogant shouldn't kill herself – she would always assume she'd get away with, be certain that whatever she'd done had been a justifiable thing to do. He took a sip of coffee and savoured the taste; only one cup a day now, just to wake up properly. He still missed it during the day, but he had to admit the dull headaches he used to get had disappeared. Ah well, he'd get used to tea eventually. The image of last night flitted in front of his eyes again – the pale, broken body lying in the middle of that grand foyer. The way she'd spoken to him and Nick, the way the other staff reacted to her presence, all indicated a bully and her type of bully didn't usually become violent; they didn't need to. It was difficult to picture her as the murderer of Bonner, which then made her suicide even more puzzling. But Nick was right of course, you wouldn't exactly be able to pick her up and throw her over the banister, either dead or alive. And if Mrs Thorpe heard the scream, she must have still been alive and would surely have struggled and called for help. But why would she have killed herself? This was getting him nowhere; he switched the radio back on and tried to concentrate on the news.

"Yes!"

Emma's shout resonated through the flat and brought Elise running out of the bathroom.

"Look mum, look" Emma said excitedly, "there on that page."

Elise moved a chair next to Emma's, sat down and looked.

"What is it I'm looking at, exactly?"

"It's the website of a dealer in old books and manuscripts. See, right here on his sale catalogue."

Elise read the entry Emma indicated.

"*An Evening Adventure in New York,* original hand written manuscript by Marcus Whitten, 1891. Price of..." She looked up at Emma. "Seriously? Thirty thousand pounds? For one manuscript?"

"They're very rare. I mean there shouldn't be any for sale anyway, we're supposed to have them all."

"So what's the plan?"

"Call inspector Bohr and show him the evidence."

Emma reached for her phone and dialled the number.

"Bohr."

"It's Emma Baines, inspector. I've just found proof that Olivia was stealing from the archive."

"That's very impressive Miss Baines; what exactly have you found?"

Emma hesitated.

"It's a bit difficult to explain over the phone."

"I could come over to see you in about half an hour?"

"Great, it'll be much easier to show you."

Elise was looking at her expectantly as she finished the call.

"He's coming here in half an hour." Emma said as she reached for her mug.

"You might want to be dressed before he gets here."

Emma looked puzzled for a moment, then, realising she was still in her dressing gown, blushed and ran into the bathroom, shutting the door quickly so as not to hear her mother's laughter.

Lucas arrived slightly later at the flat than he had expected – it had been impossible to find a parking space anywhere nearby. No wonder Emma Baines took the bus to work. A few minutes later he found himself in a large, cosy, dining-cum-living room. While Emma got her laptop out of the kitchen he looked at some of the hundreds of books that lined every available bit of wall space; some were modern, some antique, some fiction, some factual, poetry and plays, all jumbled together in an unapologetic celebration of words.

"Do you like books, inspector? They're not in any order whatsoever, I'm afraid."

Emma had come back in and put the laptop on the small dining table.

"We got fed up having to re-arrange everything every time we bought a new book."

"We?"

"My flat mate and best friend, Jessica Clarke. She's still asleep; as an actress she's used to late nights and lie-ins."

Lucas spotted a few popular science books crammed in between the complete works of Shakespeare and a P.D. James novel, and took one out.

"I do love books," he admitted, "which one of you is the scientist?"

"If I were a scientist I'd hardly need to read the simplified versions," Emma objected, "but I am fascinated by space and physics." She hesitated for a moment before adding "You're not related to Niels Bohr, are you?"

Lucas smiled.

"My grandfather is Danish, but I have been assured that Bohr is a reasonably common name there and that as far as he's aware we're not related."

She was standing next to him now, also looking at the books.

"I did study maths, but found I wasn't quite exceptional enough to be anything else than a maths teacher, a job I didn't enjoy. But my sister is a scientist, so who knows, maybe one day I *can* boast about being related to a famous physicist called Bohr."

He replaced the book exactly where he'd found it and followed Emma to the table; they had to sit quite close together to both see the screen. As Emma found the right website again she explained how documents could have been stolen and how this one manuscript was bound to be one of the ones that belonged in their Whitten collection. Lucas listened carefully; when she triumphantly showed him the description in the sale catalogue, he wasn't sure how to phrase what he had to say.

"So you say this manuscript came out of a collection of about thirty boxes that are in your archive?"

Emma nodded.

"And that Dr Dunstable stole it and sold it on to this seller?"

She nodded again.

"And that Hugo Bonner discovered this and she killed him for it, but then out of contrition killed herself?

Emma was looking very pleased now.

"Exactly."

"Can you prove any of that?"

Confused, Emma pointed to the laptop.

"The manuscript is right there."

"Yes, but if it was stolen before it had ever been officially recorded as belonging to the archive, how will you prove it belongs to the archive?"

"We bought the entire archive from the author's great granddaughter."

"And there is no chance that a different family member sold a manuscript to someone else at some point? Or that the author himself gave a manuscript to a friend? Or that it mistakenly got thrown away and rescued by an innocent member of the public?"

"I suppose…"

"I don't doubt that you believe it has been stolen, but you simply wouldn't be able to prove it."

Lucas gestured to the website.

"It is of course possible to find stolen goods on the internet, but not by doing a simple search. This would seem like a very solid, respectable business, which means if the manuscript was stolen it would have passed through other hands before getting to this shop. Again, very difficult to find a link to your archive."

Emma was starting to look a bit pale now.

"And even if you could prove somehow that the manuscript was taken from the archive, why would that have been done by Dr Dunstable? There is no evidence whatsoever to show that she was a thief, or that she was involved in Mr Bonner's death. Even her own manner of death is still in question, certainly until we have the report from the pathologist."

Emma was sitting very still, not looking at him. He wasn't sure what to say next, how he could soften the blow a little.

"It was good detective work to find that manuscript and I will of course send someone to talk to the owner. You may well be right about all of it, but we can't just jump to conclusions like that."

Lucas got up from the table and hoped that had sounded less patronising out loud than it had inside his head. Emma got up as well and walked with him to the door. She was desperately trying to regain control, so as not to sound too pathetic when she finally spoke. She almost succeeded.

"Thank you for coming inspector. I'm sorry it was a waste of your time."

"Not at all Miss Baines, it was a pleasure to see you again." He did mean that, but he could see it wasn't helping. "I'm sure we'll meet again soon."

They shook hands and Emma gently closed the door behind him.

"So that went well," Elise commented from the kitchen door.

But Emma had already stormed into her room and slammed the door behind her.

Fifteen

Lucas was still thinking about his morning's meeting with Emma, wondering whether anything she'd told him had actually been useful and trying to forget the look on her face as he explained the problems with her theory. As he reached his desk he heard Nick on the phone.

"He's here now, hang on." Nick indicated the phone on Lucas' desk. "Flo."

Lucas picked it up.

"Good morning Flo, what have you got for us?"

"Because you weren't sure about that suicide yesterday I sent some blood for analysis and asked for it to be prioritised."

"And?"

"And you were right to be suspicious. The lab found a very high level of an anti-depressant in her blood."

"Would it have made her drowsy?"

"At the concentration they found it would have been possible to wake her and make her move around, but she'd have been completely spaced out."

"How quick for it to take effect?"

"If it was one dose, about an hour before she'd have been totally out. In several doses she'd just get gradually drowsier over the course of several hours."

"Thanks Flo."

"No problem."

Lucas looked extremely annoyed with himself.

"We should have seen that, Nick, the sleepy look, the searching for words."

"It looked exactly as if she'd been drinking, why would we have thought anything else?"

"I knew there was something odd about it at the time, but it didn't fully register – there was no smell of alcohol on her breath or in the room."

"A few hours at most; that means she was drugged at the archive."

"Get forensics back down there. I want every foodstuff, every cup, every plate bagged and checked."

Nick grabbed his phone to relay the instructions, while Lucas switched on his pc. Amongst the emails that had appeared since last night was one containing some very interesting information about Tim Edwards.

"Our Mr Edwards has been hiding a very big secret, Nick. Look at this."

Nick walked round and looked at the screen. The headline from a local newspaper screamed out at him: PAEDO WORKING IN LOCAL SCHOOL.

"Wow. Worth killing someone who found out?"

"We'll see. I'll call the police in Eastbourne first and see if I can talk to whoever was in charge of the case."

Emma could hear the tell-tale sounds of Jessica waking up; soon she'd be pouring herself a cup of coffee in the kitchen while Elise filled her in on the morning's developments. Early morning's that is, it was still only nine o'clock. Damn, she'd been so sure she was right. And that he'd be impressed. He must come across amateurs like her all the time, with ludicrous theories he'd have to try not to laugh at. Fine, she'd learnt her lesson. Leave it to the professional. With the amazing grey eyes. She daydreamed a few minutes about losing herself in those eyes, but then shook herself back to the present. Wait a minute – ludicrous theories? There was nothing ludicrous about anything she'd said, there just wasn't any proof. That Marcus Whitten manuscript, that was just too much of a coincidence – surely it was stolen from the archive? And ok, that would be difficult to prove, but she'd helped box it all up, wouldn't she recognise it if she saw it? There was no image of it on the website, but the shop itself had a London address. She grabbed her bag and coat from the dressing table and strode into the kitchen.

"Come on mother, you're driving."

The startled look on Elise's face made her feel even better.

"I'll explain on the way."

With that she headed out of the flat, head held high, wishing she felt as confident as she'd sounded.

"What did Eastbourne say?"

Lucas sighed.

"A much more complicated story than those newspaper headlines suggested. And I very much doubt worth killing for. But we might as well go and talk to him now."

"Hang on, I've found something else interesting."

Lucas looked at him expectantly.

"I went through Bonner's credit card statements. He had four by the way, all used for very specific kinds of expenses. One was mainly for hotels and restaurants and I noticed one particular hotel in London came up very regularly – the Willow Tree. Apparently quite an exclusive place."

"And why would Bonner need a hotel in London, if not to take his girlfriends to?"

"Exactly. I phoned them and they had a reservation for Mr and Mrs Bonner on Monday night."

"You drive – I've already been in unfamiliar parts of London today."

Nick was surprised, but far too happy to be given the keys to question the reason why.

The car pulled up in front of a row of large Victorian detached houses, the kind that had once housed families and their servants but had long since been turned into flats. No big sign making it obvious that there stood a hotel here, just a discreet plaque next to one front door proclaiming this building to be The Willow Tree. The small lobby gleamed of polished brass and old leather; the elderly man standing behind the reception desk looked every inch the reliable, discreet, courteous kind of person you would expect to work here.

"Yes gentlemen?" he enquired. "We have one double room available at the moment."

Ah, thought Lucas, at least that was one way in which the hotel *had* embraced the modern world. He showed his police ID and said:

"I'm Inspector Bohr, this is Sergeant Fletcher. And you are?"

"Potter, Sir, Edmund Potter."

Lucas waited a moment to see if there would be an 'at your service', but was left disappointed.

"We're investigating the murder of Mr Hugo Bonner – I believe he was a regular visitor to this hotel?"

"Oh dear, Sir, I'm very sorry to hear that. Yes, Mr Bonner visited us often; he was a very generous man."

"Did he usually come alone?" Nick asked, trying to sound as if he didn't already know the answer.

"No, Sir, he was always accompanied by Mrs Bonner."

"Always the same Mrs Bonner?" Lucas asked.

Potter hesitated slightly before answering.

"Mr Bonner did seem to re-marry rather regularly, Sir."

Lucas smiled encouragingly.

"We would very much like to find the current Mrs Bonner; perhaps you could describe her?"

"Let me see now, the current Mrs Bonner has been coming for about five months now. Nice looking lady, mid-thirties, beautiful shoulder length auburn hair."

Lucas tried to think who the description reminded him off, but frustratingly he couldn't quite add a face to the picture.

"Would a photograph of the lady help, Sir?"

"You have a photograph of her?" Lucas exclaimed.

"We have very sophisticated CCTV in the lobby and all corridors, Sir. We may appear old fashioned, but this is the twenty-first century after all."

Potter scrolled through the booking diary on his screen.

"The last time Mr and Mrs Bonner were here, was last Monday. I'll just call up footage of that day."

A few mouse clicks on he'd found what he was looking for.

"They usually came in around six o'clock and dined in our restaurant, where we also have CCTV. Ah yes, this is a nice view of the lady."

A near-soundless printer gently whirred into action and a moment later Potter handed Lucas a full colour photograph of the current Mrs Bonner. Also known as Ms Jennifer Marr.

Sixteen

Not much had been said in the car so far. Elise wasn't very familiar with this area of London and was trying to listen to the satnav while not causing an accident when suddenly being told to turn right. But now that they'd managed to find a parking space she felt she had to say something.

"Let me get this straight: you're going to pretend you want to buy this manuscript, so you can see it up close and then hope you recognise it from when you boxed up the collection at the archive."

"Yep."

"And what if you do?"

"If I don't we can still ask him where it came from and..."

"I said, what if you *do*? How will you prove it? Are you just going to accuse the shop owner of theft?"

Emma was getting annoyed now.

"I'm not going to accuse anyone of anything; I'm not a total idiot you know."

"So what...."

"I would just like to see it," Emma said slowly, almost spelling out the words. "I'll figure out the rest after that."

Elise looked surprised and then smiled.

"I never knew you could be as stubborn as your father."

The small shop was remarkably modern and neat looking – not at all the jumble of antiques Emma had imagined. Old looking books were arranged smartly on gleaming white shelves and several museum style display cases housed a variety of letters, pamphlets and photographs. No price tags were on show anywhere, but there was a very noticeable, sleek, CCTV camera following their every move. Elise dutifully started examining the spines of the books, while Emma feigned interest in the letters in one of the display cases. Not that that was difficult to do, as they were signed by Jane Austen, one of her favourite authors. Maybe one day the little note she'd received from another favourite, Terry Pratchett, would lie in a display case like this, to be admired and possibly bought provided you could afford to buy things in a shop without price tags. It would be after her death though; she couldn't imagine any circumstances in which she'd part with it.

"Good morning ladies, may I help you?"

The sudden smooth voice startled Emma and she felt quite disorientated, having been deep in thought, about fame and mortality. Luckily Elise always managed to stay down to earth.

"What a fabulous shop you have!" she exclaimed enthusiastically. "Is this a first edition Dickens?"

The shop owner turned his attention to her, giving Emma the opportunity to collect herself; still pretending to be interested in the contents of the display case, she was able to observe the man who's voice had surprised her so. He was much younger than she'd expected – mid-thirties or so – with sleek short black hair and large black-rimmed glasses. His public school voice sounded rather obsequious as he was trying to convince Elise of the merits of a special edition David Copperfield; an apt novel to discuss with someone with such Uriah Heep-like qualities. But how to broach the subject of the Whitten manuscript?

"Lovely as this book is, we're here to get my daughter her birthday present," Elise said while gesturing at Emma, "and as you can see, she's more interested in manuscripts than published works."

Uriah (what had it said on the website? Owner James Brooker; a pity, that wasn't creepy enough at all) turned round and gave her the least sincere smile she'd ever seen. She briefly considered pretending to be a very haughty snob, but this whole situation was complicated enough already without testing her rather dubious acting skills, so she gave him a big smile instead.

"It's just so amazing, because you're handing a piece of paper they actually handled themselves and it's their own handwriting."

"I totally agree," Brooker purred, "it's the best way to get very close to one's favourites. Such as Jane Austen, perhaps?"

Emma looked at the display cabinet; it was very tempting to agree and have him open it so she could touch the letters, but no, she needed to stay focussed.

"Ah dear Jane – mum bought me a letter of hers last year." It wasn't easy to say that and keep a straight face; her admiration for Jessica soared. "This year I'm looking for someone else." She certainly had Brooker's full attention now, his eyes gleaming at the prospect of a big sale. "I studied literature at Harvard for a year, where we read some of the works of Marcus Whitten – you know, contextualising late nineteenth century New York society." Did that actually mean anything? Brooker was nodding his head in agreement, but then he'd probably have done that whatever gobbledegook she'd come out with. She briefly glanced over his shoulder and could see Elise trying very hard not to burst out laughing. Stay focussed Emma! "I absolutely loved his descriptions of New York and have been trying to find something original by him ever since, but without any luck. " She looked straight at Brooker and gave him her most glorious smile. "Until we came across your website this morning."

"Absolutely dear lady, I do happen to have an extremely rare manuscript by Marcus Whitten in my possession at the moment." He hesitated for a moment. "I must warn you though that it is *rather* expensive, as of course it is a whole manuscript and, as you yourself noticed, extremely rare."

"My dear man," Elise said angrily from behind him, making him turn round to face her, "do you really think we would be here if money was an issue?"

"I do apologise madam, I will of course get the manuscript for you."

With that he slid through the door to the back of building. Emma took a deep breath and was about to remark that he should have 'humbly' apologised, but she saw Elise was firmly staying in character, so she turned her attention back to the display case instead.

They only had to wait a few minutes before he returned, carrying a beautifully constructed cloth-covered box. Emma's heart skipped a beat when she saw it and she only just managed to stop herself shouting "yes" – the box looked exactly like the ones Jennifer made to house manuscripts in the archive. Even the blue-grey colour of the cloth was identical. He placed the box on a small table next to the counter, opened it up and took out a thick wad of leaves. Emma didn't have to pretend to be excited as he handed them over; her hands trembled as she gently turned the pages. Some of the manuscripts she'd boxed up had been in terrible condition, the edges eaten away by mould, the paper disintegrating if you dared touch it. And here was one of them, gorgeously, delicately, lovingly repaired in exactly the way Jennifer would have done. Had done, surely? Emma started to get furious now. All of Olivia's disparaging remarks about conservation and the whole time she'd been profiting from Jennifer's work. It was clever though, she had to admit that. Take a document in such a terrible state that no one had been able to read or even describe it in years, get Jennifer to repair it as part of her normal schedule and then sell it on before it is catalogued. It would be almost impossible to ever trace it back to the archive; even if Jennifer testified to having carried out the repairs, it would be her word against the others, no way of proving any of it. Emma suddenly became aware of Brooker's expectant gaze upon her. She didn't know what to say, didn't dare open her mouth.

"My dear girl," Elise came to the rescue, "you seem to have become quite speechless." She leaned over to have a closer look at the manuscript herself. "It's been rather heavily restored," she said in a dismissive tone, looking straight at Brooker, "which does affect the value quite a bit."

"Ah no madam, ordinarily you'd be right of course, but hardly any of Whitten's manuscripts survived and those that did were very badly damaged. I only know of two others and they needed even more repairs than this one."

Emma couldn't contain herself any longer; the anger that had been rising within her since this morning burst out.

"Three very badly damaged manuscripts," she hissed, almost in tears, "I unpacked three very badly damaged manuscripts. I carefully put them in folders and put a 'do not handle' tag on them. And here is one, beautifully repaired by my friend Jennifer, and you say you have the other two as well?"

Charles Brooker was looking utterly astonished now, clearly not understanding what was going on.

"These belong in the Marcus Whitten collection in Literally London." Emma enunciated every word precisely and carefully so there could be no misunderstanding. "They were bought by the Trustees from his great-granddaughter so the whole world would have access to them, not so that some miserable second class salesman could make a profit."

Brooker tried to snatch the manuscript back, but she cradled it close against her chest.

"I have no idea what you're talking about!" he shouted, all humility vanished. "How dare you come here and accuse me of dealing in stolen goods."

Elise gently pulled Emma back and positioned herself between the two.

"We're not accusing you of anything." She sounded very calm. "I'm sure you had no idea these manuscripts were stolen."

"This is ridiculous, I bought this item from a respectable dealer."

Emma moved next to her mother; she'd calmed down now and followed Elise's conciliatory lead.

"Then I'm sure you won't object to passing on this dealer's contact details so we can get to the bottom of this."

Brooker looked doubtful. Emma took her phone from her pocket.

"Of course I could just call my friend Inspector Bohr and he can ask you instead. But then, as he's investigating two deaths, he might want to talk to you for much longer."

"What deaths?" Brooker looked utterly confused again.

"Two people have died at the archive – one murder, one suicide. All because of these thefts. I can give Lucas your name or the name of the person you bought them from; it's your choice."

Brooker was looking scared now.

"I only bought the one, I wasn't sure there'd be any interest. He still has the other two."

"Who?" Elise asked gently.

"Craig Morris. He's a dealer in all kinds of antiques. I honestly thought he was above board, I've bought quite a few things from him the past couple of years."

Emma sighed. Maybe Brooker wasn't the bad guy she'd imagined after all.

"How do we contact him?"

Broker rifled through a drawer behind the counter and handed them a business card.

"That's his number. He has a warehouse in East London."

Elise took the card.

"Thank you. Now Emma, please take a photograph of the manuscript, here in Mr Brooker's shop, with Mr Brooker in the shot."

Emma put the manuscript down on the counter, positioned Brooker next to it and took several shots with her phone.

"I'm sure Mr Brooker will take extremely good care of the manuscript now he knows it is vital evidence in a police enquiry."

Emma looked surprised.

"Aren't we taking it with us?"

"No dear, it is currently legally Mr Brooker's property."

Emma placed the manuscript back in its box; definitely Jennifer's work. Elise looked straight at Brooker.

"Should anything happen to this manuscript you will be arrested for falsifying evidence and be implicated in a murder investigation."

Brooker took the box from the counter and looked straight back at her.

"I have nothing to hide."

Seventeen

As they pulled up outside the small Victorian terrace where Jennifer Marr lived, Lucas wondered whether she'd moved house after her husband's death. A quick flick through the file told him she'd lived here for the past seven years, so no, she hadn't. She still lived in the house they'd shared, the house she'd found him in. In the same circumstance he felt he would definitely have moved. Then again, this was one of those situations where you couldn't know what you'd do until it happened. Escape your ghosts or cling on to them? He hoped it would be a long time yet before he found out what his reaction was. It took a while for the door to be opened; when it was, Jennifer looked quite pale and shocked to see them. She led them into her small, sparsely furnished front room and went to the kitchen to make some tea.

Calm down, calm down, calm down, Jennifer told herself as her trembling hands took three mugs out of the cupboard. She put a tea bag in each, poured some sugar in a bowl – one of them had asked for sugar hadn't he? – and some milk in the jug. She took a deep breath, grabbed hold of some kitchen towel and mopped up the spilt sugar and milk. Why were they here? What could they want? What had they found out? Surely not... The noise of the kettle starting to boil got her to focus on the present again. She managed not to spill as she poured the steaming water in the cups and even fished the tea bags out without any nefarious results. She carefully placed everything on a tray; just listen to them and don't say anything rash and everything will be all right she told herself, as she walked steadily back to her front room.

Lucas sipped his tea – no, he still preferred coffee – and looked at the pale, tired woman sitting opposite him. He had assumed that Bonner's violent death had brought back terrible memories for her and that that was why she'd been so shocked; only now did he realise she was in mourning for a man she'd loved and lost. Again.
"I'd like to offer you my condolences, Miss Marr."
Jennifer looked confused.
"I'm not sure I..."
"The Willow Tree has an excellent security system and was able to supply us with a photograph of Mr *and* Mrs Bonner."

He lay the picture on the little black Ikea table that stood between them, turning it round so it was the right way up for her. Jennifer glanced at it and then looked up at him; she tried to speak, but her voice was barely audible, her eyes welling up with tears.

"How long had you been together?" Lucas tried to sound his most re-assuring and comforting.

Jennifer stared into space for a few minutes, but managed to gather herself together and eventually answered.

"We'd met quite a few times over the past six years, but only briefly, whenever Hugo came round to visit the archive. Of course I was married for most of that time and after Simon's death..."

She took a few more sips from her tea, desperately trying to regain her composure.

"About five months ago we all got dragged to this major fundraiser for the archive. Lots of wealthy people, or people from wealthy institutions, we had to smile at and convince to give us money. A very unpleasant experience. Rather demeaning actually, having to beg to be given enough money to be allowed to do your job." She sounded quite bitter now. "Olivia was disgustingly obsequious; at least Richard managed to keep some dignity. The rest of us just smiled as best as we could and wished we could go home." Her face softened as she went on. "Hugo was marvellous. He had this knack of making everyone he spoke to feel as if they were the most important person in the room; I'm sure he raised a lot of money for us that night." She hesitated again and took another sip of tea. "Every time he walked past me he gave me such a warm smile." She started to put the cup down, changed her mind and took another sip. "It was an early evening event – you know, snacks, no actual meal – so by seven thirty most people had left and we could escape. I was putting my coat on when Hugo appeared and held it for me. He offered to take me out to dinner to celebrate the success of the evening." The memory made her smile. "I have to admit, I had felt attracted to him all evening and I suddenly thought – why not? Why not have some fun for a change? Finally move on..."

Lucas waited a few minutes, but Jennifer seemed totally lost in her thoughts.

"So you started a relationship?"

She seemed surprised to hear his voice and answered dreamily.

"It was just meant to be fun. He said his marriage had ended ages ago and he was just waiting for his son to leave home before doing the same. I didn't expect to fall in love. I'm sure he didn't expect to fall in love with me either."

A deep sigh seemed to bring her back to the present and she looked at Lucas much more steadily now.

"You want to know about Monday. Yes, he came to see me. It wasn't planned, so I don't think he just came for me; he'd never turned up like that before. He came into conservation around half past one, just after Olivia left. I assumed he'd been to see Richard, I had no idea no one else knew he was there. I mean, Olivia must have met him on the stairs, she can't not have seen him. He stayed about five minutes; we kissed and talked about meeting up that evening." She looked at the photograph. "It really is a lovely hotel." She realised she was still holding her now empty tea cup and set it down on the little table. "When he left I thought he'd just go out of the building and I'd see him that evening. When he didn't turn up I assumed something had happened at home; his son always came first. As he should. I wasn't even worried when Emma made her discovery, it just didn't occur to me…Not until you told me."

"But you didn't say anything."

"What was I supposed to do? No one else was admitting to having seen him; that was very confusing, I couldn't understand why no one was saying anything. And I couldn't exactly say 'Yes, I saw him, because I was having an affair with our married boss."

She was getting agitated again now, picking up her empty tea cup and putting it down again.

"Over the past few months, did Mr Bonner ever say anything about the archive he was worried about? Any disputes he was having with anyone?"

Jennifer shook her head.

"We never talked about the archive. He did tell me a lot about his bookshops; I don't think his wife was particularly interested in those. He was having problems convincing his business partner to agree the way forward. Hugo was all about taking risks, expanding, borrowing to grow whereas his partner was running scared and wanted to reduce the number of shops. He was getting very frustrated about that."

"But you can't think of any reason why he would have been in the archive in secret?"

"No idea. I'm sure he must have been there to meet someone though. It's a scary thought that one of my colleagues is a killer."

"What do you think?" Lucas asked when they were back in the car.

"She obviously had the opportunity to kill him, but it's difficult to see a motive."

"I wonder why she was so certain Dr Dunstable had seen Bonner."

"She must have done if he came in straight after her, they would have met each other in the corridor or on the stairs."

"Not necessarily. Remember we thought that store room would have been a good place for a clandestine meeting; if he'd come out of there, she wouldn't have seen him."

"She could have seen someone else though."

"Someone coming out of that room?"

"Well it wouldn't have seemed odd to her at the time if it was one of the staff, but what if she realised afterwards it must have been the murderer?"

"And they killed her for it? Very possible."

Jennifer turned on the tap to do the dishes and so remove any residue of her unwelcome visitors. She went over and over the conversation in her head, wondering whether she should have phrased things differently. She was so lost in thought she only noticed how hot the water had become when it started to scold her fingers and she hurriedly had to switch to the cold tap so she could run the cool soothing water over her hand.

Jess had listened open-mouthed to Emma's account of what had happened in the antiques shop.

"Wow Em, you were right all along." She slapped her friend on the back. "Well done!"

Elise returned from the kitchen with a tray of tea and coffee and a pack of dark chocolate digestives and set them on the dining table.

"What are you going to do now?" Jess asked as she grabbed a biscuit.

"Not sure" Emma mumbled with her mouth full.

Elise put her coffee down.

"Simple. We call our friend 'Lucas'...", she winked at Emma who immediately blushed, "...and give him the business card."

Emma didn't look convinced.

"What have we got that we didn't have this morning?" she asked. "I can't prove that manuscript came from us or that Olivia stole it. He'll just be as dismissive as he was earlier."

"He can talk to this Craig Morris though."

"Or we can talk to him first," Emma said with a sparkle in her eyes.

"What do you mean?"

"We call this Morris and tell him we're interested in the other Whitten manuscripts. We do exactly like we did this morning and if we think he's involved in the thefts, we call inspector Bohr."

Jess looked worried.

"I'm not sure about this Emma. If this is the guy who bought them from Olivia, he's a crook and could be dangerous."

"We're just going to talk to him."

"And tell him the manuscripts are stolen, like you did in the shop?"

"I won't get angry this time, I know what to expect now. Come on mum, we make a great team."

Elise hesitated.

"I suppose it couldn't do any harm. We'd just look at the manuscripts, tell him we'll think about it and call the inspector."

"Don't you let her convince you like that." Jess still sounded worried. "Have you two forgotten that two people have died? What if this Morris is involved in the murder?"

"Really Jess, not you too." Emma was getting quite exasperated. "Olivia was stealing manuscripts, Hugo caught her, she killed him and then killed herself. Morris may well be a fence, but he's not involved in murder."

"It's just a bit of investigative journalism, isn't it?" Elise was definitely warming to the idea.

"Exactly." Emma picked up her phone, took a deep breath and punched in the number.

"Yes?"

"Mr Morris? My name is Emma...Clarke," she hoped he hadn't noticed the slight hesitation there. "I got your number from James Brooker, from Ancient Scrolls."

"And?"

This wasn't going to be as easy as she'd hoped.

"I was tempted to buy the Marcus Whitten manuscript he has, but then he said you have two more and I'd be more interested if I could buy all three. I'm not in London for long, so I was hoping I could see the other two this morning?"

Silence on the phone.

"Mr Morris?"

"Fine. Did Brooker give you the address of my warehouse?"

"Yes, I have your business card here."

"I'll meet you there in an hour."

He hung up.

"His warehouse in one hour." Emma felt a shiver of excitement as she relayed the message to Elise.

"It'll take us at least forty minutes to get there, so let's leave in ten."

Jessica was still worried.

"Text me when you get there and when you leave again."

"All right, if it'll stop you worrying."

Emma and Elise took their cups in to the kitchen, while planning how to approach their next adventure. Jessica looked at the business card on the table and couldn't shake the feeling that this was a big mistake.

The door to the flat was opened by a slim, short woman in her thirties. She looked very annoyed when Lucas introduced himself.

"He hasn't done anything wrong. He didn't then and he hasn't now."

Her voice had a soft Scottish lilt to it – east rather than west coast, Lucas thought.

"I've spoken to the police in Eastbourne, Ms?"

"Gill. Isobel Gill."

"We know the accusations were false, but we do still need to talk to Mr Edwards."

Reluctantly Isobel stepped back and let them follow her into the main room, which combined a comfortable seating area with a small dining table and computer area. No books to be seen here; rather there were stacks of CDs surrounding an impressive looking sound system. As they sat down on a black sofa, Tim Edwards appeared. He obviously hadn't had much sleep the night before and stifled a yawn as he perched on the settee opposite; Isobel sat down next to him and put her hand in his.

"Tell us about Eastbourne," Lucas said gently.

"I was a teaching assistant at a primary school, getting experience before getting a degree. Isobel was already a teacher, at a different school." At the mention of her name Isobel squeezed his hand and looked even more defiantly at Lucas. "It was the height of those celebrity child abuse cases; every day the papers were full of new allegations, new investigations. Every man wanting to be around children was suddenly viewed with suspicion. The head teacher warned us to be extra careful, not to put ourselves in situations that could be misinterpreted..." he looked straight at

Lucas now "...but what are you supposed to do when a child is upset and needs your help? Ignore them until you can find a second adult? Tell them to find a female teacher instead and teach them no man can ever be trusted?" He was sounding quite bitter now and stopped for a moment to compose himself. "To be honest, it never occurred to me there might even be a problem." His voice took on a dreamy quality as he stared into space, re-living that moment. "Some of the infants were playing hide and seek during lunchtime play. I was setting out chalks round the back of the school – we were going to use them in an outdoor maths lesson. Suddenly a year one girl came running round the school, obviously looking for somewhere to hide. They weren't supposed to come that far during play time and I was just about to tell her to go back to the playground, when she fell over. I ran over to her; she'd started crying and had grazed her knee. I helped her back up and gave her a hug. One hug. She was crying and had hurt herself and needed a hug. Just one hug." He stopped again and took a deep breath. "She stopped crying, gave me a smile and ran back to the playground."

"What happened next?"

"I forgot all about it. The bell went, maths started; it didn't seem important to tell the teacher what had happened – after all, nothing *had* happened. The next morning the head called me into her office and asked about it. Apparently one of the reception girls had followed the other girl and told her parents that she'd seen Mr Edwards hugging Sally behind the school building and that Sally had been crying at the time. They told Sally's parents who exploded; I was suspended pending an investigation and the police were called in. Someone went to the press; I'm sure you saw the headlines? They didn't wait to see what the investigation found, they named me, put a picture of me on the front page, called me a monster. Poor Sally had to sit through questioning by specialists – I can just see them giving her a doll, saying show us where Mr Edwards touched you." He'd gone very pale now and Isobel had tears in her eyes. She squeezed his hand, went into the kitchen and returned almost immediately with two mugs of coffee. She gave one to Tim and glared at Lucas, daring him to ask for refreshments for him and Nick.

"I was never charged. The police said they were satisfied nothing had happened and that my account of the events was true. The 'experts' agreed that Sally hadn't been molested and that the whole investigation had been far more traumatic for her than any hug she'd received. I was re-instated, but that caused a revolt by some parents." He looked straight at Lucas again. "No smoke without fire, you know." Another squeeze from Isobel. "The head was prepared to stand by me, but it was pointless. And very stressful and confusing for the children. So I left. And then I realised no other school in Eastbourne would touch me." He drank some coffee, stealing himself for the next part. "One evening Izzy and I were walking home from this little Italian restaurant. We'd been trying to figure out what to do next and I still wasn't quite prepared to give up on the possibility of becoming a teacher. This group of people – just ordinary people – walked past us and one of them recognised my photo from the newspaper. They started shouting abuse at me. And at Izzy. It was..." he took a deep breath "...very frightening. There was no way we could talk to them; they started to follow us and looked like they could get violent, so we ran for it. The following day Izzy started applying for jobs – anywhere far enough away. And I realised I would never be a teacher. Someone at some point would come across that newspaper story and it would all happen all over again."

"So you came to London?"

"It was the first job Izzy found. I was quite depressed for a while; not all that surprising, is it?"

"But then you got the job at Literally London."

"Richard and Hugo Bonner interviewed me. At the end they asked whether there was anything they ought to know about before they carried out some background checks. Well, you can imagine, I thought that was the job gone. So I told them." He looked quite surprised as he went on. "You know what they said? With my permission they'd check with Eastbourne police and if they confirmed my story I could have the job. I couldn't believe it! You've no idea what that felt like, being believed like that. I'd sort of given up on people, but they gave me hope."

"And on Monday?"

Tim shook his head.

"I've no idea. I didn't know Hugo Bonner was there and regardless of why he was there or what was going on, I would have stood by him. And Richard. I'd do anything for either of them."

"How about Dr Dunstable?"

Isobel jumped up from the sofa, absolutely furious.

"How dare you! How bloody dare you! After everything Tim's just told you you're still trying to frame him for something. You should be ashamed of yourselves."

Tim took hold of her hand and gently pulled her back down.

"It's all right Iz, they have to do their job." Still looking at Isobel, he went on. "Thing is, I was very worried after Olivia made it clear she wanted to be in charge, and soon. If she'd found out, she wouldn't have reacted like Richard or even have fired me; she'd have held it over me the whole time, threatening to tell everyone if I didn't agree with everything she said." He turned back towards Lucas. "That's the kind of person she was – a nasty bully. I thought for ages what I should do, but I have to say killing her wasn't one of the options I considered." He remembered his coffee and drank another sip. "In the end I made up my mind – I'm fed up constantly worrying that someone will find out, how they'll react, whether they'll believe me, whether I'll need to start all over again. All that fear when I never actually did anything wrong, never did anything to be ashamed off." He put his cup down and faced Isobel. "No more running. I'm writing a letter explaining everything that happened and I'm going to ask Richard to hand it to the Trustees; hopefully he can persuade them to keep me on. I'm also going to tell everyone at work – I don't know how they'll react, but at least the sword of Damocles will be gone."

Isobel smiled proudly and she and Tim embraced, seemingly forgetting all about Lucas and Nick, who were still quietly sitting opposite. Lucas got up and motioned to Nick that they were leaving.

"Thank you for your candour Mr Edwards. We can show ourselves out."

"What do you think?" Nick asked as he was starting up the car. Lucas shrugged his shoulders.

"He could still have a different motive for killing Bonner. And if he was prescribed anti-depressants during his depressed period, he could have had some left over and drugged Dr Dunstable."

"It seems surprising she lasted this long without someone killing her."

"It does seem like everyone who works there has a motive for *her* death at least."

"Even Miss Baines?" Nick asked innocently.

Lucas refused to take the bait.

"All of them," he said sternly.

Eighteen

The warehouse was an anonymous looking one story building, sitting amongst a host of similar buildings on a quiet industrial estate. A large four by four was parked right outside the door; the only vehicle visible anywhere. Emma felt nervous getting out of the car – this wasn't quite like popping into a shop. She looked at her mother, who also seemed to be hesitating slightly. This was silly though – they weren't going after some kind of master criminal, just an antiques dealer who might not be totally legit. She sent Jess a quick text ' We're here' and had to admit she felt better for having done so. Elise had wandered over towards the other car now.

"There's no one in here, he must already be inside."

Emma linked her arm through her mother's as they walked to the door. Their knocks produced no results, but when they tried the handle the door opened, so they decided to go in.

"Hello?" Elise called "Mr Morris? Anyone here?"

There were a few lights on inside, but most of the building was in darkness. They moved towards the brightest area, where a table and several chairs were clearly lit. Out of the darkness appeared a rather unassuming, short, slightly overweight and balding man. Emma realised just how tense she'd been, as she felt herself relax. She managed a big smile, held out her hand and walked towards him.

"Mr Morris? I'm Emma Clarke; this is my mother, Elise."

Morris gave her a rather limp hand and grunted an acknowledgement.

"So you're interested in Whitten?"

"Absolutely! I studied in Harvard for a year where we examined some of his work in great detail and I've been hoping to find some original material by him ever since."

"When Mr Brooker said you had two more manuscripts," Elise added, "we decided we simply had to see them."

"To buy all three?"

"Well, they don't exactly come up for sale often," Emma exclaimed, "how did you ever manage to get hold of these ones?"

"I have my sources."

Morris took a cardboard box from a nearby pile, set it on the table and took out two more handcrafted blue-grey boxes, identical to the one they'd seen in the shop. Emma's heart started racing again, but this time she tried very hard to stay in control.

"Oh look, mum, the same cute boxes."

She opened one up – yes, this one had needed a lot of repairs as well.

"They do all seem to have been very heavily repaired," Elise remarked, looking over Emma's shoulder. "What sort of provenance do you have for them?"

Morris glared at her.

"I bought them off an old lady who'd found them in her attic. Are you interested or not?"

"What kind of price are you looking for?"

"Twenty thousand each."

"Any deal you could do for the two together?"

"This isn't some bloody TV-show! Twenty thousand each or forget it."

He snatched the manuscript out of Emma's hands and placed both back in their boxes.

"Do you accept cheques?"

The look on Morris face was a sufficient answer to that question.

"Well, we obviously didn't bring that kind of cash with us. We'll need to go to the bank and meet you back here...what? Tomorrow?"

Morris gave Elise a faint smile and walked up to her with his hand outstretched. As she shook his he suddenly pulled her towards him, held her in a tight grip against his body and with his other hand pointed a gun at Emma.

"Now," he said very calmly and deliberately, "I suggest *you* young lady sit down on this chair here." The gun briefly indicated an ordinary kitchen chair, which stood next to the table. Emma couldn't move; her legs were shaking and she felt decidedly light-headed. "Maybe you'll do it if I point the gun this way?" he asked, pressing the gun against Elise's head. Emma swallowed hard so as not to be sick and managed to walk the couple of metres she needed to before sliding onto the chair.

"Good girl. Hands on the table, please."

Emma carefully placed her hands palm down on the table in front of her; she was desperately trying to work out what was happening and what she could say to get them out of this. The voice in her head shouting 'THIS IS ALL YOUR FAULT!' wasn't helping. Morris walked over to Emma, still holding on tight to Elise.

"See that rope there?" he asked Emma. She spotted a length of twine lying on the table and nodded. "Take it and tie this lady's wrists together."

Elise held out her hands and Emma looped the twine round her wrists.

"Much tighter than that. If it's not tight enough I'll shoot her in her arms instead."

Morris' voice had turned decidedly nasty, so Emma tightened the rope as much as she dared. She'd been desperately trying to stay calm, but she couldn't stop the tears trickling out of her eyes as Elise winced in pain.

"I'm so sorry mum," she said almost inaudibly. "This is all my fault."

"You're not the one with the gun, sweetheart." Elise was trying to sound calm, but Emma could see her legs were shaking as well.

"So we do have a mother – daughter combination then? Good." Morris shoved Elise down in the other chair and thrust his face – and the gun – so close to Emma's she could smell the faint linger of a bacon cob breakfast on his breath. "Because that means you're not going to try and do anything silly that will result in your mummy getting killed, will you?"

Emma shook her head slowly, taking care not to get any closer to Morris' cheek than she already was. He'd only have to tilt his head slightly and his mouth would be there and there would be nothing she could do to stop him. To her surprise he pulled back, took a second length of twine from the table, grabbed her wrists in one hand, placed the gun next to him on the table and tied her wrists together. She felt so relieved it didn't even occur to her to struggle or reach for the gun until it was too late and she was tied up; probably a good thing she decided, who knows what could have happened if that gun had gone off in a struggle.

Elise's voice suddenly rang out from the other side of the table.

"I told you, we don't have any money with us."

Emma looked at her mother. Robbery? That hadn't even occurred to her. Of course, if you say you can go to the bank and withdraw forty thousand pounds, you must be worth quite a lot. Kidnap maybe? Trying to get money out of a wealthy husband or father? In both cases he would need to keep them alive, at least for now, which was something.

"Do you think I'm stupid, lady? I do business with people who have money. They don't wear Marks and Spencer clothes, or cheap watches, or drive fucking Polo's!"

He perched on the edge of the table and stared hard at them both.

"And dear old Jimmy Brooker would never, ever do himself out of a commission by giving his clients my name. You're no cops, that's obvious. So who are you?"

Emma suddenly saw a way out.

"I work at Literally London" she said, sounding nowhere near as confident as she was trying to be.

"What the hell's Literally London?"

Emma felt confused, but then, why would he need to know the name of the place the manuscripts came from?

"The Whitten manuscripts. They were stolen from there. The woman who stole them is dead. She sold them to you." She took a deep breath and tried to stop rambling quite so much. "That means you no longer have a source for some very lucrative merchandise. Unless I steal them instead. I know how she did it, how she got away with it without being detected. I sell them to you - for less than she wanted -" she added hastily "you sell them on for a big profit and everyone's happy again."

Morris still looked puzzled.

"What woman?"

"Olivia." Emma said in disbelief. "Short, overweight, long brown hair? She sold you those manuscripts."

"Nice try, but I didn't buy these off a woman."

"Then who..."

"Some tall rich looking bloke. Always wears nice suits, talks posh."

Emma felt as if the ground had just been pulled away from under her: Hugo was the thief?

"He's dead too," said Elise, "murdered. But perhaps you already knew that?"

Morris turned to her.

"What the hell're you getting at?"

"An argument between thieves? Squashing his head won't have destroyed all evidence of bullet holes. I bet the police are looking for that gun right now."

"Why would I kill some bloke who keeps bringing me..." he looked at Emma "...lucrative merchandise?" Morris paused, reflecting on everything he'd just been told. "If that bloke's been murdered, that does change things."

Several minutes went by in silence, each of them trying to work out what to say or do next. Emma had just decided to try her offer again – after all, Hugo was dead too – when Morris spoke.

"If the police are involved I can't allow you two ladies to go tell them all about me, now can I?"

"We won't," said Emma quickly, "We'll never say anything."

"No you won't," Morris agreed, "you're not going to be saying anything at all anymore." He looked round his warehouse. "If you found me, then the cops will too, so I can't have any trace of either of you in here." He grinned at them. "Two ladies officer? A mother and daughter? They sound utterly delightful – no they were never here."

Emma and Elise looked at each other, both desperately trying to think of something to say.

"Right" Morris said in a very final sort of way. "We'll go for a little ride." He grabbed hold of Emma, hauled her up her feet and held her tight against him, sticking the gun in her side. "All right mummy," he was looking straight at Elise now, "up you get, slowly, and walk to the door."

Elise had to push the big door open with her shoulder; the big four by four still stood there, with the little Polo looking forlorn at its side. Morris opened the back door and told Elise to get in; he then shoved Emma in after her and slammed the door shut behind her. With a big grin on his face he started to turn round to get into the driver's seat, when he suddenly felt the cold metal tip of a gun pressing against the back of his head.

"They don't often let me play with guns," Lucas hissed. "I would love an excuse to pull this trigger."

It wasn't a particularly stimulating environment, the relatives' waiting room at the police station. Emma surveyed the rather old-fashioned chintzy comfy seats, interspersed by small wooden coffee tables. The kind of environment some man would have assumed women found comforting, without thinking that first of all not all women were stuck in a time warp and secondly surely men counted as relatives too? A water cooler stood in one corner, dispensing free drinks. No hot drinks were available though; perhaps they were considered too dangerous in the hands of hysterical women. She looked at Elise, sitting deep in thought besides her. She'd nearly got her mother killed. Not a very constructive thought to have just right now, she realised, as she felt the contents of her stomach starting to travel back up her oesophagus. Surely there was nothing left in there? After the inspector's miraculous appearance – how would they ever be able to thank Jess for alerting him? – the stocky sergeant had helped them out of the car. She'd been shaking so badly while Bohr cut through the twine around her wrists it must have been very difficult for him not to scratch her. Then, as soon as he'd finished, she'd been sick all over his shoes; what a way to show your gratitude Emma! He'd wanted to take them to hospital, but they'd both insisted they were fine so he'd driven them to the station instead, with sergeant Fletcher following in Elise's Polo. He hadn't said anything in the car; a very young constable had shown them through to this 'cosy' room, saying Inspector Bohr would be along shortly. She'd even promised them some tea, which hadn't appeared yet.

"I'm sorry, Emma."

Elise's quiet voice shook Emma out of her thoughts.

"What for?"

"For putting us in danger. In the whole of my career I was never stupid enough to take a risk like that." She took hold of Emma's hand. "It was just so much fun, gallivanting around London with you, I stopped thinking."

"Oh mum, don't be silly, it was all my fault."

Emma put her arms round Elise; they both held each other tightly, neither wanting to break the hug or wanting the warmth to stop.

"I believe the order was for two teas?"

Lucas was standing in the doorway, holding a large tray in both hands. Emma and Elise let go of each other and sat back in their chairs, while he put the tray on the little table in front of them: two large white mugs full of steaming tea, a little milk jug, a sugar bowl, two teaspoons and a large plate of biscuits.

"This one's green tea," Lucas explained while turning the mug towards Emma, "this one's just tea. You both still look very pale." He sounded worried.

"This is just what we needed," Elise said gratefully, "thank you."

Emma added her thanks; she noticed he'd changed his shoes but decided it was probably better not to mention that. Lucas moved one of the flowery seats opposite theirs and sat down.

"Now," he said, suddenly looking very serious, "would you mind explaining what on earth you were doing, going to that warehouse?"

They hesitatingly told the story of their morning's adventures, in between sips of tea and nibbles of biscuits. Emma could barely look at Lucas as the disbelief on his face grew clearer and clearer.

"Did it ever, at any point, occur to you to call me? Going off like that to meet a possible murderer..."

"But he isn't, surely? Olivia killed Hugo." Emma realised this wasn't much of a justification for what they'd done, but still. Lucas however shook his head.

"Olivia's death wasn't suicide. So even if she did kill Hugo, that still leaves a murderer on the loose." He looked straight at Emma now. "Quite possibly Hugo's accomplice, don't you think?"

"I thought..." Emma didn't even try to finish that sentence, her mind was spinning round too much.

"Look, I do appreciate that you were trying to help, but please leave the investigating to us. I'd rather not have two more murders to solve." He got up from his seat. "PC Flinders will collect your written statements and then show you to your car; go home and if you have any more bright ideas, call me."

"We could take Jess to dinner somewhere special," Elise suddenly suggested in the car, breaking the silence that had reigned since they'd spoken to Bohr. "You know, to thank her."

"Yeah, good idea." Emma wasn't really listening as she'd been busy checking her texts. "Actually mum, could you drop me off at work? Richard sent a text about half an hour ago to say we were allowed to go back into the building. "

Elise stared at her in utter disbelief.

"You were nearly killed this morning Emma, I'm sure Richard will give you the day off."

"I have to tell them. They deserve to know what happened. What Hugo was doing." She looked at her watch – almost one o'clock. It seemed totally incredible that it could still only be lunchtime. "Please mum."

Elise sighed and started looking for somewhere where she could do a U-turn without killing any cyclists.

Nineteen

Ronaldo's prided itself on both the quality of its food and the discretion of its staff; the perfect place for expensive secret rendezvous. Not that there was anything dark about the place: the décor was very now, light and airy and of course there was free Wi-Fi, but if you asked for the right kind of table when you booked you ended up in one of the little alcoves, invisible to everyone but the waiters. Helen stood outside the door for a moment, wondering how often Hugo would have dined in here with someone very much not herself. Or perhaps he'd found a different meeting place – London wasn't exactly lacking in discreet restaurants.

He was already there, of course, studying the menu, pint of Guinness in his hand. He looked up as she slipped into her seat and gave her a warm smile.

"G&T, extra ice," Helen ordered before sending a quick smile back. "Well, here I am Sam."

"Yes you are. How's Matthew coping?"

"Concentrating on his studies."

The waiter returned with Helen's drink; she ordered a Niçoise salad, Sam steak and chips.

Sam made some attempts at small talk, but Helen wasn't in the mood.

"Why did you want to see me?"

"Like I said, I miss you...and I'm worried about the police. What if they find out about us?"

"That's not very likely is it? And even if they did, it doesn't matter. Hugo was killed in that archive, so it must have had something to do with that place."

"The police won't see it that way. They'll see a jealous lover and a wife who's having an affair; that's an easy solution for them."

"So what if they think we're guilty? They can't do anything without proof and as we didn't kill him there isn't any proof to find."

The waiter returned with their orders and they ate in silence for a while, each following their own train of thought. Eventually Sam smiled.

"How long do you want to wait? Six months? Or would that be too soon?"

Helen looked confused.

"What *are* you talking about?"

"Well, we don't need to be a secret anymore now, do we? But we do need to let a decent amount of time pass before we go public." He paused to swallow down the piece of steak he'd been chewing. "I suppose it will take a while for Matthew to get used to it all." He gave Helen another bright smile. "Don't worry, I'll wait in the shadows until he's ready."

Helen was staring at her salad, not the least bit hungry anymore. He meant it. He actually, really meant it. The last thing she needed was another love-struck man to deal with. She slowly put down her cutlery, raised her head and looked him straight in the eyes.

"Don't get me wrong, Sam, it was a lot of fun. But that is all it ever was." She got up from her seat, gathered her coat and handbag and turned back to him as he sat there looking totally nonplussed. "And now it's over. Goodbye Sam." She started to move away when she remembered why she'd agreed to this meeting in the first place.

"My solicitor will be in touch regarding the bookshops. You can buy me out or we can liquidate the business and split the profits – your choice."

With that she strode out of the restaurant, smiling at the maitre'd as he held the door open for her.

Before entering the archive Emma popped into a sandwich shop; apart from the tea and biscuits at the police station she hadn't had anything to eat since breakfast and she suddenly realised just how hungry she was. The big outer door was shut, a hastily printed sign stuck to it with blue tack: *Closed due to unforeseen circumstances.* It wasn't locked though, so some of her colleagues must be there at least. She glanced into the eerily quiet searchroom and tried not to stare too hard at the cordoned off area on the floor to the side of the stairs. As horrible as Olivia had been, no one deserved to be thrown to their death like that. She could all too easily imagine the terror Olivia must have felt in those last few seconds when she would have realised she was about to die. Painfully. The inspector hadn't given any details about the murder and as Emma climbed the stairs she began to wonder how on earth anyone had managed to push Olivia over the railing. Her stature, her weight – you'd need two people, surely? Would Morris have brought an accomplice? Or maybe he'd killed her before throwing her over? She was still considering these possibilities when she reached the second floor and heard voices coming from the staff room.

They were all there: Richard and Frederick sitting at the table, Jennifer, Theresa and Tim together on the sofa, Marie in the kitchen boiling the kettle. There was something odd about the picture though; Emma couldn't quite work out what it was, but something was definitely different. Theresa jumped up when she saw Emma standing at the doorway and rushed up to her.

"There you are Em, we wondered what had happened with you. Did you hear? It wasn't suicide, she was murdered!"

"Yes, I know."

Theresa carried on excitedly.

"She must have been poisoned and then thrown over the railing – the police have taken all the food and drink and plates and mugs and cutlery and everything away."

That's it, thought Emma, that's what looked odd: no colourful mismatch of mugs of tea and coffee anywhere.

"Marie's just been down to the shops and got some mugs and tea and things."

Emma let Theresa drag her onto the sofa and plopped down next to Jennifer. Both Jennifer and Tim were looking rather pale and seemed not to be in very talkative moods. Marie came in from the kitchen handing round mugs.

"Emma, good to see you. I'll make you a cup as well. Emma gave her a watery smile and took her sandwich out of her bag.

"Tell Emma about last night Marie, about what you heard." Theresa was still excited as she perched on the edge of the sofa holding a bottle of lemonade. Marie sat down on the chair opposite and told the whole story yet again.

"Hang on," Emma said, trying to swallow a mouthful of chicken and salad. "How can you have heard Olivia's scream if she'd been poisoned?"

"Who says she'd been poisoned?"

Emma stared at Theresa, who looked defiant.

"Well why else would the police have taken away all the food and stuff?"

Emma chewed slowly, trying to make sense of it all.

"Maybe it wasn't poison, maybe she'd been drugged with something to make her sleepy?" As she phrased her thoughts out loud, it suddenly all made sense. "Of course, that's it! If Olivia was drowsy Morris could have easily coaxed her out of her office and maybe even got her to stand on something next to the railing – she'd have been too dazed to realise what was going on until it was too late."

All eyes were firmly fixed on her now.

"Who's Morris?" asked Theresa.

Twenty minutes later the staff room was completely silent. Emma had finished recounting her morning's adventures and was now surrounded by open-mouthed colleagues, trying to digest what they had just heard.

"The bastard." Jennifer's eyes were welling up from anger as she considered what had been happening. "Using my work to profit from. Selling my work…" Her words choked in her throat; Emma put her arm round her, but she shook it off and sank into the sofa in a haze of fury.

"So the police are questioning this Morris character?" Richard asked quietly.

"I assume so. Hopefully he can tell them what other works they've stolen and who he sold them to."

"I still don't understand why Olivia ended up dead." Tim looked at Emma expectantly.

"Maybe she saw Morris on Monday and he wanted to silence her?"

"But then why didn't she tell the police straight away?"

"I don't know, I don't have all the answers. We'll just have to see what Morris tells Inspector Bohr."

Theresa suddenly burst out laughing.

"I'm sorry Jennifer but it really is funny. All those hours you spent doing those little repairs and then Hugo Bonner comes along and sells the manuscript. No wonder he liked conservation – I'm sure Olivia wouldn't have tried to get rid of you if she'd realised how profitable your work could be."

Jennifer gave Theresa a venomous look and stormed out of the room.

"Honestly Theresa," Frederick said, "that was extremely tactless."

"And a very hurtful thing to say," Tim added.

"All right, all right, I'll apologise to her later." Theresa still couldn't stop smiling. "It *is* funny though."

Richard got up from his seat and took his mug to the kitchen.

"I suggest we try to get some work done. I should be able to access Olivia's email account."

Everyone got up and started to leave the room; Emma thought Richard was looking rather pale, so she lightly put her hand on his arm.

"Don't worry Richard, everything will be back to normal soon."

He gave her a not very convincing smile.

"I'm sure it will, Emma."

There was nothing flowery or cosy about the interrogation room: it just contained a sturdy table with two wooden chairs either side. Craig Morris was sitting sullenly, staring straight ahead of him; he hadn't said a single word since his arrest. Lucas busily leafed through the file that was lying on the table in front of him; Nick sat next to him, scrolling through emails on his phone.

"Right, Mr Morris..." Lucas began.

"I'm not saying anything without a solicitor." Morris sounded more bored than anything else. Time to shake things up a bit, Lucas decided.

"That's fine Mr Morris." Lucas got up from his seat. "When you call your solicitor, do tell them that you are under arrest for the attempted murder of Ms Elise Horton and Ms Emma Baines and the actual murders of Mr Hugo Bonner and Dr Olivia Dunstable." Was that surprise on Morris' face? "And of course the smaller matter of theft of literary manuscripts and the illegal selling of those. But then, when you're doing life in prison a few extra years for fencing isn't going to make that much of a difference, is it?"

"Hang on, hang on!" Morris was sounding worried now.

Lucas had already reached the door; he turned round slowly, trying to indicate he didn't want to waste any more time in this room.

"Yes, Mr Morris?"

"Look, I bought those manuscripts from a posh bloke who said they were his, but he needed money quickly and didn't want the hassle of going through more conventional channels. I've bought his stuff before, always found a buyer really easily, so I gave him twenty grand for the three. I'd no reason to think they were stolen – the most you can do me for is not keeping proper books."

"And I just imagined watching you force two women into your car at gun point? Two women whose hands were tied and who you'd told were going to kill?"

Morris was speaking hurriedly now. "I wasn't going to hurt those two ladies, just scare them, you know, stop them being such busybodies."

Lucas sat back down and stared at Morris.

"Is that how you treat all your clients?"

"I'm not an idiot, inspector. James Brooker would have never sent anyone on to me if he thought he could make a profit out of them. I agreed to meet them because I was curious. I even wondered whether they were police – you know, the art squad. But then they started talking about theft and murder; I thought they were going to try and blackmail me. That's why I wanted to scare them."

Lucas got back up.

"Good luck convincing a jury. And without proof that you bought those manuscripts you're still my best candidate for a double murder."

Morris was beginning to panic now.

"Wait! The guy I bought them from, the posh tall one – is he really dead?"

"Hugo Bonner? Yes."

"What about the other guy?"

"What other guy?"

"About five years ago, the first time I met this Bonner to buy some stuff, another guy came with him. Short, balding...a bit overweight. He was very nervous about it all. He can confirm what I've told you."

Lucas searched through the file he was holding and took out the photographs of all the men at Literary London. The first one, Hugo Bonner, Morris recognised straight away as the 'tall, posh one'. One by one Lucas placed the other photographs on the table.

"That's him." Morris snatched the photograph off the table. "If those manuscripts were stolen, he knows all about it. And he knows I bought them for a fair price."

Lucas looked at Nick.

"We'd better have another conversation with Dr Owen."

Twenty

Emma sat in front of her computer, trying to concentrate on the incoming emails, but it was pretty pointless. On top of everything that had happened that morning, those blond curls and grey eyes kept staring out at her from the computer screen. She glanced over at Tim who had also given up any pretence of working; he seemed to be writing a very long letter by hand, a rather unusual thing to do when there's a perfectly good pc right in front you.

"What'cha doing?" Emma asked, deliberately trying to sound jolly.

Tim looked startled.

"What?"

"Must be very special if you're writing it out by hand."

Tim went bright red and looked close to tears; not exactly the reaction Emma had expected.

"I'm sorry Tim, it is of course none of my business." She got up from behind her desk and headed towards the door. "I need a cup of tea – shall I bring you one?"

He didn't reply, just looked at her utterly miserably and dejected before hunching back over his desk and continuing writing. Five minutes later Emma put a mug on his desk, followed by a packet of hobnobs.

"Marie got some biscuits; you look like you could use them."

She took her mug to her seat and continued to stare at her emails.

"Em?"

"Yep?"

"It *is* important. It's a letter to the trustees." He looked at the pages lying on his desk as if he was afraid they would come to life and attack him. "I don't know how they'll react. They might sack me." He looked straight at Emma now, his eyes pleading for understanding. "I'm so tired of being scared."

Emma rushed over and gave Tim a big hug.

"Whatever are you on about? Why are you scared? Why would they sack you?" She let go of the embrace and looked at him. "Whatever it is Tim, I'm sure it'll be all right."

With trembling hands Tim picked up the scrawled-on pages and handed them to her. "Read this, then tell me whether it'll be all right."

135

Theresa looked around the empty searchroom; she'd plumped up all the book cushions, straightened out the reference books and tidied away all the little book weights. The room had never looked tidier. There weren't any emails to respond to – Olivia had always sent on the ones she felt Theresa was capable of answering – and of course no customers to steer in the right direction. Maybe she could give someone else a hand; she was willing to have a go at pretty much anything to stop being so bored. Perhaps Jennifer had some more documents to repair before they got sold? Theresa burst out laughing thinking about that whole situation; all right, it wasn't fair on Jennifer, but it *was* very funny. Maybe she could help Jennifer see the funny side?

"Daydreaming, are we?"

"Marie! Where did you spring from?"

"Saw you through the door, staring into thin air."

"I'm so bored, I've got nothing to do."

Marie's eyes lit up.

"A volunteer's as good as twenty men. Here..." she handed her a dust cloth "I'll get another one and you can help me dust book shelves."

Theresa took the cloth and wandered into the foyer. What would be more boring, she wondered: doing nothing or dusting off books? Surely Marie could do without her for a little longer; she dashed through the staff only door, descended into the basement and knocked loudly on the door to conservation.

"Yes?"

"Hi Jennifer," Theresa began as she entered the room. She saw Jennifer's face darken and added "I'm sorry about earlier. I didn't mean to upset you."

Jennifer visibly relaxed and Theresa walked over to the large bench in the centre of the room, which was covered in letters with small weights on top of them.

"What are you working in now?"

"Eighteenth century correspondence. They're still in their envelopes, see..." Jennifer gestured towards a pile of waiting documents "...so all the letters are folded several times over. Eventually those folds become tears, which I'm now repairing."

She handed Theresa a neatly repaired letter, the old tear barely visible.

"Wow, that must take ages to do." Theresa gave the letter back. "I don't think I know anyone who's more patient than you." A mischievous glint appeared in her eyes. "So how much do you think these are worth?"

Jennifer's face went as white as the tissue she'd used to carry out the repairs.

"Get out."

"Jennifer, it's just a joke."

"GET OUT!"

Seeing the fury in Jennifer's eyes, Theresa rushed out of the room, ran up the stairs and kept going up until she saw Marie merrily cleaning shelves. Some people just couldn't take a joke.

Emma glanced over at Tim, who was studiously avoiding looking in her direction. What on earth could he have written to have gotten so upset about? At least his handwriting was easy to read. She settled down in her seat, took a sip of tea, and started reading. Within moments the hot tea was forgotten – she barely even remembered to breathe. Halfway through her hands started trembling, mimicking the writer's. She could barely read the last page, her eyes wet with tears. She wasn't sure what she felt most of at the end – anger, frustration, pity? But she did know there was only one possible way to respond; she put the pages on her desk, walked over to Tim and put her arms around him. It was the longest hug they'd ever shared; no words were needed or said.

Frederick stared at his computer screen, trying to make sense of the emails Richard was sending him. He'd tried talking to him, but Richard wasn't answering his calls and had locked the door to his office. There were all kinds of attachments: minutes of trustee meetings, the latest budget figures, correspondence with researchers from all over the world, personnel files for all the staff – what was Richard up to? Now he'd even sent the password to his email account! Frederick jumped up from his chair, suddenly feeling alarmed, and knocked loudly on Richard's door.
"Richard! Open this door so we can talk." He waited for a moment to see whether Richard would react and then started knocking again. "Richard! For god's sake don't do something stupid – let me in!"
To his relief he heard trudging footsteps nearing the door, before it was unlocked and slowly opened. Richard was looking very pale.
"You'd better come in."

Lucas and Nick climbed the steps to the closed door of Literally London; they were about to open it when Lucas' phone went. A quick conversation later he turned to Nick.

"The lab boys haven't found any trace of that anti-depressant anywhere. None of the food they took from here is contaminated and all plates, mugs and cutlery had been washed."

"They do seem to have a very regular dishwashing thing going."

"I guess not everywhere is as tolerant of dirty sinks as the police station is." Lucas looked thoughtful. "She must have ingested it somehow though. How would anyone have been able to add something to her food without her noticing? She didn't even eat in the staff room."

"According to Flo the pills would dissolve easily in hot drinks."

"She was drinking coffee when we saw her, wasn't she? Of course that still doesn't answer how he could have put them in there."

Lucas opened the door and walked into the foyer.

"Let's go and ask him."

"Inspector! Sergeant!"

Lucas sighed. To be honest he'd been surprised not to have been immediately confronted by Marie Thorpe the moment he entered the building – three quarters of the way up to the first floor was definitely a record.

"I knew I heard someone come in." Marie stood on the first floor landing, duster in hand. As they got nearer Theresa joined him.

"Emma's told us about everything that happened this morning." She smiled at Nick as she went on. "How she was rescued by you and how you caught the murderer."

"Not quite yet," Nick answered and he followed Lucas further up the stairs.

"What's that supposed to mean?" Marie called after them. She and Theresa followed them upstairs; all the noise had alerted Emma and Tim, who came out of their office. Emma smiled at Lucas; he looked at her rather ruefully – she wasn't going to be happy about this. Lucas knocked on Richard's door.

"Dr Owen? It's Inspector Bohr; I think you know why I'm here."

The door was opened by the looming figure of Frederick Samuels, who stepped out of the office, followed by a very pale looking Richard.

"Dr Richard Owen I am arresting you for the theft of literary manuscripts and…"

The corridor broke out in a cacophony of questions; the silence that followed was broken by only one.

"What are you doing?"

Emma sounded shocked.

"I'm sorry Miss Baines, Mr Morris has identified Dr Owen as Mr Bonner's accomplice."

Everyone looked at Richard, who was staring at the floor, studiously avoiding eye contact. Nick took Richard by the arm as Lucas continued "...and on suspicion of the murders of Mr Hugo Bonner and Dr Olivia Dunstable."

That made Richard look up. "No, no, I had nothing to do with their deaths," he said, sounding horrified. Nick led him down the stairs; Lucas was still surrounded by incredulous faces.

"If you'll excuse me, I..."

"Lucas," Emma whispered, her eyes pleading with him to stop, to say it was a mistake. "It can't be true, it can't be Richard."

Seeing the pain in her face Lucas wished there was something he could to help, but he just said 'I'm sorry' and walked away.

The corridor was deadly quiet; even Marie was lost for words.

"I thought I heard shouting." Jennifer had just arrived at the top of the stairs. "What's going on?"

Everyone started talking at once, until Frederick's voice rang out over all the noise.

"Everyone in to the staff room, please."

Frederick surveyed the room full of anguished faces; he knew how they felt, he'd felt exactly the same – what, only fifteen minutes ago? Now they were looking at him to tell them it was all some horrible mistake, that Richard would be right back, that he hadn't betrayed them. They were about to be sorely disappointed.

"As you know I was with Richard in his office when the police came," he began. "He had just confessed to me that he and Hugo Bonner had indeed been stealing manuscripts from the collection and selling them on to various dealers. He has kept a list of everything that was taken, a copy of which he will hand over to the police; we may be able to recover some items this way." He looked apologetically at Jennifer before continuing. "I'm afraid they did mainly select badly damaged uncatalogued items which Richard added to Jennifer's workload; hopefully Jennifer's conservation notes will also help the police track down the documents."

"So it was a good thing you did all that work Jennifer," Theresa offered, but Jennifer didn't even look at her.

"Yes, well," Fredrick continued, "Richard has left me temporarily in charge and has given me access to all his files and emails, etcetera. I will notify the Board, of course; it will be up to the Trustees to decide what happens next."

"Did Richard say anything about the deaths of Hugo and Olivia?"

Emma sounded as pale as she looked.

"No, and I find it hard to believe Richard could be a murderer. " He hesitated for a moment, but decided total honesty was probably best. "I have to admit though that after today's events I don't know what to believe anymore."

Everyone nodded in agreement, except for Emma.

"I know Richard betrayed our trust," she said quietly "but I'm not willing to simply abandon him. There's still a big difference between murder and theft."

As no one else seemed to have anything to say, Frederick got up.

"I think we've all had enough drama for today. I suggest you finish whatever you were doing and then go home. We'll remain closed to the public tomorrow; hopefully I'll have some news from the Trustees by then." With that he left the room, going straight back into Richard's office.

Twenty-one

"No one will ever know, Richard."

"I can't believe you just said all that Hugo...I mean, it's theft."

"Theft? It's my collection. My family paid for all of it, they put it all together. I'm only selling what's rightfully mine."

"That's poppycock. The collection is now a trust – you may be the chairman, but it's not your property."

"And how unfair is that? My father basically disinheriting me like that. Do you think he would have wanted me to suffer rather than be able to sell off a few pieces?"

Yes, Richard thought, that's probably exactly why he'd set up the Trust.

"Books matter Richard. The old ones, yes, but also the new ones. Which means bookshops matter. Independent ones, where you can still find surprises lurking in unexpected corners. Where the staff care as much about the stories as they do about the paper, the leather, the illustrations."

Richard had had to agree, he loved those old fashioned shops.

"The internet is killing us, Richard. How can you compare browsing on a website to actually browsing in a shop, with the smell of newly printed books around you? We can't just let cheap and easy win, Richard, we must fight back."

"But like this?"

"If these authors were here now, if we could ask them what was more important, would they want their manuscripts to be lying in a box somewhere gathering dust or would they be auctioning them off to save independent book sellers?"

Richard still hadn't caved.

"They're not ours to sell, Hugo."

"Only because of a mistake my father made. Please Richard, if we can't pay off this loan, the bookshop will have to fold. Helen won't help, she doesn't value books, all she cares about is money. She doesn't get it the way we do, Richard. I have to squeeze all my books into one room so they don't create a 'mess' everywhere. Don't let this bookshop go under, Richard. Just this one manuscript will save it; will save all those books."

The silence lasted several minutes.

"Just this once."

The room was surprisingly pleasant. Richard had expected some dingy, dark attic, hidden away in a back alley – he wasn't prepared for the bright modern loft they'd been sent to. Hugo of course looked as self-confident as ever, striding in to the room as if he'd been there dozens of times already.

"Gentlemen."

The woman was seated behind a large buttercup yellow table which dominated the room. She was a surprise too – all smiley, blond and glamorous looking. Nearer fifty than forty at second glance and perhaps slightly too fond of chocolates judging by the near empty box standing lonely on the corner of the table and by the plumpness of the hand that indicated the chairs for them to sit on, but nothing like the villain he'd imagined. He took the seat next to Hugo, who was already in full flirting mode.

"Miss Saunders, I presume? Delighted to meet you."

As they shook hands and he was completely ignored, Richard accepted his role and sat back to let Hugo do the negotiating..

"You have something to show me?"

Hugo took the blue-grey box out of his briefcase and placed it delicately on the table in front of him. With a big smile he pushed it towards Miss Saunders.

"Only twenty-thousand pounds. A bargain for such a one-off."

Even Richard noted the slight hesitation as she opened the box and took out the manuscript; Hugo had done his research and chosen his buyer well. Miss Saunders was a pro as well though and didn't give away any more signs of being excited.

"This has been quite extensively repaired. That affects its value."

"It is because of the state it was in that no one has seen it for about two hundred years. That's what makes it so totally unique."

She gently placed the manuscript back in its box.

"I could manage fifteen."

Hugo slid the box back towards himself and put it back in the briefcase.

"Nice to have met you Miss Saunders."

Richard followed his lead and started to get up.

"Eighteen. My final offer."

There was Hugo's most charming smile again. He held out his hand and she shook it; the deal was done.

"You see what a wonderful place this is, Richard."

He had to agree. It was the kind of bookshop you wanted to spend hours in, getting lost in the aisles, forgetting all about the outside world. Being here made him feel very guilty about the books he'd bought online recently. Hugo ushered him in to the empty manager's office.

"Sit down Richard. I'll make you a coffee."

Richard made himself as comfortable as possible in the wooden visitor chair and accepted the mug of sweet, milky coffee. Hugo sat down on the other side of the desk, reached into his pocket and took out a thick envelope.

"Here," he said as he handed it to Richard, "for you."

Astonishment at the contents immediately turned to concern.

"What's this?"

"Three thousand pounds."

"I don't understand..."

"The bill I needed to pay turned out to only be for fifteen. I wouldn't want to personally profit from the sale of the manuscript, but I do want to thank you for your help."

Richard dropped the envelope on the table and turned bright red.

"I didn't help you for money, I helped you to save the bookstore. I don't want this money."

"Richard, Richard, I'm not suggesting for one moment you were expecting a pay off." Hugo's voice remained very calm, soothing even. "I just want you to understand that I didn't do it for profit either. Give it to charity if you like."

Richard relaxed. He hesitated for a moment, then picked up the envelope and put it in his pocket. Charity. That's what he'd do. Of course.

"NO. Absolutely not Hugo. No."

"Richard..."

"One time. I agreed to one manuscript, one time. An emergency to save the bookshop. We are not doing it again."

"I can't turn my back on the store now."

"You have a second shop now, you actually expanded. You can't possibly expect me to agree that this another emergency."

"But we're winning, Richard. We're fighting back against the soulless grasp of the internet. People are visiting the stores, are buying books. Just not quite enough of them yet. Another manuscript will buy us enough time..."

"No Hugo, I'm not falling for it all this time. Once I could live with, but this? You're just going to come here, selling off manuscripts every time you need money for the store. I can't possibly allow that."

Hugo remained very calm, as always.

"I'm afraid you don't have a choice."

"What do you mean?"

"You didn't give that money to charity, Richard. I saw it in your eyes when you took the envelope. What was it? A holiday? Presents for the grandchildren? It doesn't matter – your hands are as dirty as mine."

"Are you threatening me? You can't go to the police, it was all your idea."

"My dear Richard, who do you think they'll believe? Who has the best lawyer? Who will end up in jail and who won't?" Hugo's tone turned slightly menacing. "You'll find another manuscript for me. Today. Getting one that Jennifer had repaired was a stroke of genius. Better get her to repair a few more, in case of future need."

Hugo got up and walked to the door. "I've found a new buyer, somebody Morris. We're meeting him tomorrow night. So you'd better find something good."

Richard stared at the door for what seemed like hours; then he got up and went down to the stores.

"And what happened on Monday? Did you refuse to co-operate anymore? Perhaps there was a struggle? Self-defence?"

"I didn't kill Hugo." For the first time Richard lifted his head and looked straight into Lucas' eyes. "I never found the courage to stand up to him."

"Then what happened?"

"Hugo needed another manuscript. I'd agreed to meet him at twenty to one and let him in through the basement fire door. Jennifer always goes up for lunch at twelve thirty and no one ever goes down to the stores at that time. I put my coat on pretending to go out for lunch, but went down to the basement instead; Hugo was waiting outside."

"Where did you go?"

"The storage room. Only Marie ever goes in there and she also has her lunch at that time."

"Where was the manuscript?"

"Still in the store. Hugo waited while I got it out. A lovely little notebook, repaired by Jennifer. She'd made a box for it as well."

"You gave it to Hugo?"

"Yes."

"And then?"

"I went back upstairs – it must have been around one o'clock. Frederick was waiting for me outside my office."

"And Hugo?"

"He should have let himself out through the fire exit. I have no idea how he ended up dead."

"Do you seriously expect us to believe that?"

Richard remained silent.

Emma closed down her computer and glanced over at Tim, who was also getting ready to leave.

"Are you ok Tim?"

He walked over and perched on the edge of her desk.

"I just don't know what to do now."

The fear in his voice cut straight through Emma.

"Look, the police know all about what happened and they're not going to tell anyone, are they? Richard..." She paused, finding his betrayal too painful to talk about. "Frederick will have an awful lot to do in the next few days or even weeks. Maybe you could wait until all of this settled and then have a word with him if you still want to? Besides, they still need to catch the killer."

"What do you mean?"

"Richard may be a thief, but I don't believe for one second that he's the killer."

Tim shrugged his shoulders.

"I don't know what to believe anymore."

He walked over to the coat rack, picked up his coat and waited for Emma to join him out of the door.

"I think you're right though. The last thing Frederick will want at the moment are more problems. I'll wait till all this has blown over." He gave Emma's arm a squeeze. "Thanks."

Emma tried to smile.

"You're welcome."

Marie was in the foyer, talking to Jennifer, as Emma and Tim came down the stairs.

"Ah good, that's most of us then. I was just saying to Jennifer I still can't believe what's happened today. Although I have to say, I always thought there was something a bit dodgy about Richard."

"No you didn't Marie, don't be ridiculous."

Everyone stared at Emma; she could feel herself turning red, but she just didn't care – she wasn't going to abandon Richard that easily.

"We all liked and trusted Richard and the fact that he stole manuscripts is very difficult to comprehend, but he's no murderer."

"Who is then?"

Before Emma had a chance to reply to Jennifer's calm, quiet question Theresa ran up to them.

"God, I thought you'd all gone and I'd be locked in! What are we talking about?"

"Emma doesn't believe Richard is the murderer," Marie answered.

"And I was just wondering who it is then."

"Easy! It's obviously this guy who tried to kill Emma earlier today. Right Em?" She didn't wait for a reply before continuing. "I am going to forget all about this this weekend, especially at what will be the party of all parties in the Black Circle on Sunday. Are you still coming Tim?"

Tim looked quite stunned and had obviously forgotten all about their discussion on Monday.

"You know what, I just might."

Theresa looked delighted.

"How about you two? Jennifer, it'll help you get over how Richard abused all your hard work – poor Jennifer – and Emma, you can find some bloke to forget all about that inspector."

Both Marie and Tim started talking at the same time.

"We really should be..."

"I think we'd better..."

Theresa burst out laughing.

"Oh relax, it's only a joke. See yous tomorrow!"

With that Theresa almost skipped out of the door. Emma gently took Jennifer's arm.

"Are you ok? It is pretty horrible what they did to you."

Jennifer shook her arm free.

"I'm angry, yes. What do you expect? As far as I'm concerned Richard can rot in prison."

"I think we all need to go home and calm down." Frederick had appeared unnoticed behind them. "You can lock up now Marie."

Nick stood in front of the flip chart Lucas had positioned behind his desk, checking Hugo Bonner's Monday afternoon's timeline.

"We know Bonner was still alive when Richard Owen left him at one o'clock, as he went to see Jennifer Marr afterwards and he stayed with her till two o'clock."

"Could he have gone back downstairs then? Perhaps he caught Bonner stealing something else and snapped?"

Nick searched through the statements.

"Tim Edwards spoke to Owen in his office at about ten past two, but that was very brief. No one seems to have seen him after that."

"So he had opportunity and motive. Ms Marr had opportunity as well of course, but I can't see a motive."

"Lover's tiff?"

"So bad that she kills him? If she'd wanted him dead she could have met him anywhere outside the archive and avoided all suspicion."

"If Bonner was still hanging around after two, maybe trying to find more stuff to steal, any one of them could have caught him at it."

"And fought with him? It's possible."

"It's still most likely to have been Owen though. He has a clear motive for killing Olivia Dunstable if she'd found out about the stolen manuscripts. And if she knew he'd killed Bonner she'd be more likely to have tried to blackmail him rather than talk to us."

"We'll let him stew overnight and have another go at him tomorrow." A glance at the office clock revealed it to be just after six. "Go home, Nick, you might just catch Alfie awake."

Lucas perched on his desk, staring at the flipchart, not really seeing what was written on it anymore. Something felt wrong. Owen had certainly had the opportunity to commit both crimes, but the motive for killing Bonner was weak. And killing him in the archive downright stupid, as it would inevitably have led to the discovery of the thefts. Even without Miss Baines' assistance. And where had he got the pills from to drug Olivia Dunstable? How had he managed to slip them in her coffee? He'd have to go over everything again in detail. Talk to Owen again. Maybe after a night in the cell Owen would be ready to confess. Maybe.

Amanda sighed as she put down the phone; the last thing she needed was more problems at Literally London. Not when she had her own crisis to deal with. She still hadn't been able to talk to Alex – he'd just grunted at her when he'd finally woken up. He'd had a shower, gone out and still hadn't come back. How had it suddenly got to this. Suddenly? Was it really that suddenly? They'd only known each other eight months when they'd got married. A true fairytale wedding with hundreds of guests, a beautifully handmade white dress with endless trail, bridesmaids and pages, a four-tier wedding cake and a fantastic jazz band to dance the night away. The honeymoon had been pure bliss and she'd been absolutely certain the rest of her life was going to be perfect. How had she pictured it back then? A successful career, children, perfect husband - yes well, maybe she had been just a little bit naïve. Being the wife of a big time banker had made her journalistic credibility nosedive; possibly she could have still had both, but it had been easier to give in and become the dutiful housewife who sits on the boards of charities and networks like crazy to help her husband's career. It had felt like her decision at the time, but had it really been? And when they'd finally discussed children...

Amanda looked round the kitchen – there were only so many loaves you could justifiably bake. But she certainly didn't feel like cake.

Emma was sulking on the sofa, having hardly eaten any of the dinner Elise had prepared.

"Richard is no killer."

"Yes darling, you've said that already."

"Well I'm sorry if I'm getting boring."

"Em, we know you're upset." Jess sat down beside her on the pale blue sofa. "There's no need to take it out on us, we're on your side."

Emma blushed.

"Sorry. I just can't believe he thinks Richard is the murderer."

"The inspector didn't exactly have much choice sweetheart. Richard did steal those documents..."

Emma jumped up from the sofa.

"THAT DOESN'T MAKE HIM A MURDERER!"

"We know it doesn't Em. Come on, sit down."

"I'm sure the investigation is far from over, sweetheart. Have some faith in your inspector."

"He's not *my* inspector."

With that Emma strode to her room and slammed the door behind her.

SATURDAY 13 APRIL

Twenty-two

Emma groaned as she hit the snooze button on her clock radio; the archive had been open on Saturday mornings for over a year now, but she still very much resented this intrusion in her weekends. Even with the extra pay. To her surprise Elise was already having breakfast in the kitchen.

"Morning mum. You're up early."

"Morning sweetheart. Sleep well?"

"Fine."

Emma could feel her mother's constant gaze on her as she prepared and ate her breakfast.

"Was there anything, mum?"

Elise hesitated, then carefully put her cup of tea down on the table.

"I was just a bit worried about you, Emma."

"I'm fine...Sorry about last night."

"I don't mean last night. Yesterday was quite an extraordinary day, what with getting held at gunpoint and then Richard admitting to stealing and getting arrested."

"I guess it was all a bit much. But I'm fine, really."

Elise wasn't convinced.

"You've always gotten on so well with Richard, what he did must feel like a personal betrayal. And for Inspector Bohr to be the one to arrest him..."

Emma got up so quickly, her chair clattered onto the tiled floor. She took a deep breath so as not to shout, but the words still insisted on coming out quite loud.

"Mum, stop fussing, for heaven's sake. I've told you I'm fine."

Elise watched her daughter grab her coat and bag and rush out of the front door.

Nothing about this whole situation seemed *fine* to her.

Amanda jumped up from the sofa as she heard the front door open.
"Alex?"

She rushed out of the room and followed her husband into the kitchen.

"Alex, where have you been? You've been gone since yesterday morning, I've been worried sick."

Alex sat down on one of the wooden chairs and glared at her with bloodshot eyes.

"I went to talk to the mother of my son. At least, I tried to. She refuses to see me, says I have to stay out of their lives. How's that fair?"

Amanda clenched her left hand and dug her fingernails into her palm; stay calm, she told herself.

"You reek of alcohol."

"Well excuse me if I needed a drink."

"Have you had anything to eat recently? I'll make you some breakfast, then we can talk..."

Alex slammed his fist so hard on the kitchen table, the biscuit tin fell on the floor.

"Talk? Really? We're going to have a nice chat about it all and put it behind us, are we?"

He walked up close to Amanda and grabbed her arm.

"As if nothing ever happened?"

"Alex, you're hurting me, what are you doing? Why are you angry with me, I'm trying to help."

Alex pulled Amanda closer, gripping her arm even tighter and hissed "Why can't you be more like Helen?". He abruptly let her go and stormed back out of the flat. Amanda fell down in the chair and tried hard not to cry. He'd only ever hurt her once before, years ago, when she'd brought up the subject of children yet again. They'd visited Helen in the exclusive maternity hospital where she'd given birth to Matthew and on the way home Amanda had suggested perhaps it would be nice if they did...Alexander hadn't even let her finish and for one moment she'd been afraid of him. Afraid he was going to hit her, really seriously hurt her. He'd explained it all to her before, his own neglectful, abusive childhood, his unwillingness to be a parent himself, but he'd always stayed calm before. That time, in the back of the car on the way home he'd looked at her just as he'd done this morning. She'd never mentioned children again.

The steps to the front door seemed steeper than usual, this Saturday morning. To be honest, Emma thought, they always seemed steeper on Saturdays, but still, today was pretty exceptional. Olivia dead, Richard arrested. Her mother being annoying – God, she could be seriously annoying. She marched into the office and glared at Tim, who was sitting behind his computer not really noticing whatever it was that was on the screen and looking as glum as she felt.

"Hey" was the best she could muster as greeting today.

"Hey" came the feeble reply.

"Right you two…" trust Marie to sound as energetic as always "…Frederick wants us all in the staff room, so chop, chop."

She vanished before either one of them had time to react.

"Come on," Emma said as she led the way, "a cup of tea is just what we need."

They entered at the same time as Theresa, who very pointedly sat down as far away from Jennifer as she could. Oh dear, Emma wondered, had there been words again? She didn't have time to contemplate this any further, as Marie entered, followed by Frederick who looked very serious and remained standing.

"I just wanted to let you all know that I spoke to Mrs Beecher last night. Needless to say she's as shocked as we are about yesterday's developments. Richard gave me a list of the manuscripts he and Hugo sold; I will start going through the list and work out how we can attempt to recover the documents. Mrs Beecher will come over on Monday to discuss the matter in detail and she will liaise with the police and our insurers. Jennifer has already confirmed that she repaired most of the stolen documents and has copious notes and photographs to prove this; Mrs Beecher may want to speak to you as well on Monday, Jennifer."

Jennifer nodded.

"I'll get all my notes together."

"Thank you. Mrs Beecher has asked me to be Acting Director until the Trustees can meet and decide how to proceed; she also asked me to assure all of you that as far as she is concerned there is no danger of the archive closing or anyone losing their job." A communal sigh of relief filled the room. "We now have a backlog of enquiries to answer; please check your emails as I've forwarded on quite a few. I'm sure getting some work done is the best way for all of us to get through this difficult time."

Lucas stared at the piles of paperwork on his desk – weren't offices supposed to be paperless now? Or to at least try to reduce the amount of paper they used? He tried to sort them in new piles, ranking from very important and urgent down to not important and not urgent, as he'd been taught on the time management course he'd been sent to a few months ago, but ended up spending so much time trying to decide in which pile each folder should go, he gave up. If he was going to waste time, at least he'd do it in a way that made sense to him.

"Anything useful in amongst all that?"

Nick had appeared in the office and wheeled his chair round to Lucas' desk.

"Not for this case, no. But you look like you've got something?"

"The CD with the accounts for Books Galore arrived yesterday, but of course we didn't get a chance to look at it then. I was just going to send it straight on to Fraud to check, but then I thought I 'd just have a quick look in case anything stood out straight away."

"Which was?"

"Regular business expenses for meals at a restaurant called Ronaldo's."

"Doesn't seem that odd."

"Not unless you happen to know that it's a place known for intimate, clandestine encounters."

Lucas looked surprised.

"And you know this because?"

"A case I was on a couple of years ago. Husband had followed his wife there and then shot her and her lover as they came out."

"There are a lot of married women in London Ripley could be having an affair with."

"True. But the manager of Ronaldo's, who very much doesn't want the restaurant to be involved in another murder case, identified Ripley's girlfriend from her photograph. It's Helen Bonner."

Lucas looked surprised.

"I suppose killing Hugo Bonner in the archive would be a clever way to distract us from the family angle. Bring him in, Nick; let's see what he has to say for himself."

Sam ended the call, stood still for a moment, and then hurled the phone against the far wall of the office. Not even the concerned looks from Melissa and Martin calmed him down. How dare Hugo do this to him? Make him grovel to the electricity company so they wouldn't disconnect the newly opened Leeds shop. He'd actually had to use payroll money to pay the bill. The very same bill Hugo had assured him he'd pay. Had absolutely guaranteed he'd pay. Now how were they going to pay the salaries? Sam paced up and down the office, swearing at Hugo, getting angrier and angrier as the minutes went by. Then he made his decision – he wasn't going to be the only one to lose sleep this time. He rushed out of the office, ignoring the staff, jumped in his car and drove to Hugo's house.

How the other half live, Sam thought as he stood outside the front door. He'd only been there once before a few years earlier and had felt extremely unwelcome. A surge of anger as he remembered the phone conversation made him press the bell – no, Hugo was going to have to deal with this right now regardless of how badly he wanted to keep family and business separate. The door was opened by an older lady, presumably the housekeeper, who ushered him into a room full of antique looking figurines. No books though. A few minutes later Helen Bonner entered.

"My husband is on a business trip to Leeds, Mr Ripley. I'm surprised you would have forgotten that."

"He never mentioned any business trip to me. He never goes to Leeds, I'm the one who does that. I bet..." He managed to stop just in time. "I mean...eh...Leeds...of course...eh..." He could feel himself turn red under the stare of those bright blue eyes and stuttered to a halt.

"Don't worry Mr Ripley, I know what my husband means when he mentions a 'business trip'. Why do you need him so urgently?"

Sam wasn't going to say anything at first, but Helen Bonner was not a woman to accept no for an answer; soon he'd explained exactly what had happened.

"I think you'd better follow me next door and have a drink."

"I don't normally this early in the day, but I suppose I could make an exception."

Helen held the door open for him and as he left the room her arm brushed against his ever so lightly, but ever so deliberately. Oh yes, Sam thought, a drink is exactly what I need.

"So that's how it started?"

Sam gradually adjusted to the present: the bare, small interrogation room, the wood veneer table, the sergeant and inspector sitting opposite.

"Yes, inspector, that's how it started. About eighteen months ago." He took a sip from the glass of water that stood in front of him. "And Helen ended it yesterday."

"She ended the relationship?"

"You almost sound as surprised as I was, inspector. It started as a way for both of us to take revenge on Hugo, of course it did, but I totally fell in love with her." He took another sip. "Helen comes across as a bit of an ice queen, but once she drops the mask she's a funny, wonderful person to be with. She'd talked often about leaving Hugo once Matthew went to university and didn't need his father home any more. I thought she meant she'd leave him for me..." He looked straight at Bohr now. "I was happy to wait, by the way. No need to kill Hugo, I'd already won as far as I was concerned. Except of course that I haven't..."

Lucas and Nick exchanged a quick glance.

"That's all for now Mr Ripley. Sergeant Fletcher will see you out."

Twenty-three

Emma looked at the clock. Again. Nearly twelve now, another hour before they could go home. She'd never known the atmosphere in the place to be this awful; not even on days when Olivia had been at her worst. Everyone was angry with Richard and any time she suggested he might not be a murderer, they refused to listen. Of course he was the killer, they said, it made perfect sense. She couldn't even blame them. He'd betrayed everything they stood for, everything they worked for; had even used Jennifer's skills behind her back. And yet she was convinced he wasn't a murderer. His motive for killing Hugo was presumably some kind of argument amongst thieves – no, she didn't buy that at all. Richard simply wasn't that stupid. He must have known any investigation into Hugo's death was likely to lead to the discovery of the thefts. And how was he supposed to have killed Olivia? None of it made any sense. She tried to distract herself with the email she was supposed to be answering, but it was no use –the grey eyes of Lucas Bohr kept floating in front of the screen. He ought to be more intelligent than this, ought to know it wasn't Richard.

"Emma? You all right?"

Emma gradually remembered where she was and realised she had angry tears streaming down her face. She took a tissue from her bag and blew her nose.

"I'm fine."

Tim didn't look convinced.

"It's just this business with Richard and everything."

"I know, it's awful." He gave her a wry smile. "I don't suppose you've got any emergency chocolate left?"

"I never run out of emergency chocolate."

She delved into her drawer and they shared a bar of 70% pure heaven.

"Munching away on chocolate again? You two are terrible!"

"What is it Marie?" Emma mumbled.

"Frederick says we can go home."

Tim almost ran back to his desk to shut down his computer and had his coat on before Emma had finished the last piece of chocolate. He waved a quick 'see you Monday' and rushed out of the door. Maybe he and Izzy had plans this afternoon, Emma pondered while she put on her coat. As she came down the stairs she heard angry voices by the front door.

"It was only a joke!"

"A very nasty, horrible joke."

"Oh lighten up Jennifer."

Emma quickened her steps and saw how very pale Jennifer was looking.

"Honestly Theresa," Emma interrupted, "you do go too far."

"She should learn how to take a joke."

Emma put her hand lightly on Jennifer's arm and felt how badly she was shaking.

"It's not very funny for Jennifer, Tess. They exploited her terribly; can you imagine what it would be like to be so horribly betrayed like that?"

"Well I don't care. I'm not going to think about any of this or any of you for the rest of the weekend; at least I've got a party to go to on Sunday to have some fun."

Emma turned to Jennifer as Theresa stormed out of the door.

"It's just her way of trying to cope with it all, Jennifer, she doesn't mean it."

Jennifer glared at her.

"At least *she's* not patronising."

With that she shook her arm out of Emma's hand and left the building.

Oh great, Emma sighed; and I thought this day couldn't possibly get any worse.

"You look a mess." Helen sat down at the little café table. "And you've been drinking."

"I wonder why that might be."

Alex finished his coffee and indicated to the waitress to bring another one.

"God, you're beautiful."

Helen groaned.

"I'm only here because you threatened to tell Matthew. If you're going to start behaving like a pathetic teenager, I'm leaving."

She started to get up again.

"No you're not." Alex looked her straight in the eyes. "Or I *will* tell him."

The waitress brought over the coffee; Helen asked for a latte and sat back down.

"What do you want, Alex? And don't say Matthew."

"We were great together, Helen, you and me. I've never stopped loving you and I know you still want me. You were never truly happy with Hugo and Amanda...well, let's just say she's not you."

"Alex, I don't..."

"Let me finish. It's simple: I'll divorce Amanda and you and I get married."

He held up his hand to stop her interrupting.

"I know, I know, Hugo's not even buried yet, Matthew needs time to grieve. The divorce'll take some time to come through anyway, so it won't happen for another year or so. But then we'll be together and I'll be a part of my son's life without ever telling him our little secret."

He looked expectantly at Helen, who slowly drank a few sips of her latte.

"You pathetic little shit. We had adequate sex a few times, that was it. I don't love you or want you and if you ever come near me or my son again I will make your life a living hell."

Without once looking back Helen walked out of the café, leaving a speechless Alexander behind.

"Well that got us nowhere."

Nick wheeled his chair round to his boss's desk and sat down.

"He's not going to crack, is he?"

Lucas sat down in silence, thinking through the conversation they'd just had with Richard Owen. Yes, he'd stolen the documents, yes he'd met Hugo on Monday, no he hadn't killed him and no, he hadn't killed Olivia. That's what two hours of interrogation boiled down to. Exactly what he'd said yesterday.

"It must have been him though, surely? He must have fallen out with Bonner and Dr Dunstable must have seen or heard something."

Lucas could hear Emma's voice, asking whether *that* counted as jumping to conclusions.

"We don't have any proof, Nick. No forensics, no witnesses, no murder weapon... Have we found a link between those anti-depressants that drugged Dr Dunstable and Owen?"

Nick shook his head.

"They're prescription only; as far as I've been able to track no one involved has ever had them prescribed."

"So they got them illegally – another dead end."

"They? You seriously think the killer could be someone else?"

Lucas slowly shook his head.

"It's just too unlikely. If Ms Marr had wanted to kill her lover she'd have been mad to do it there, with her colleagues all around her. The same goes for Ripley – killing his rival, maybe, but in a place he doesn't know well, where he could have so easily been seen? Not very likely."

"You could make the same argument for Owen."

"You're not helping, Nick."

They both sat silently for a while, trying to come up with a new angle, a sudden insight that would re-arrange all the facts into a neat solution.

"Weren't you supposed to have the weekend off?" Lucas suddenly asked.

Not quite the insight Nick had expected to hear, but it was certainly true.

"No time off when there's a murder to solve."

"Damn it Nick, it has to be Owen. Go home – if anything dramatic turns up, I'll call you."

"You sure?"

"Go."

Lucas watched a relieved Nick almost run out of the room – at least someone was going to enjoy themselves this weekend. He stared at the ever increasing pile of files on his desk, took the top one and started to read.

"What a disaster today has been."

Emma sighed as she scooped a spoonful of cream from her extra luxurious hot chocolate. She'd needed the one with the marshmallows, cream, chocolate sprinkles – all of it double helpings.

"Cheer up, Em."

Jessica had her hands wrapped round her skinny latte, trying to recover from an afternoon window shopping in the unseasonably cold wind.

"You've had a bit of a tough week, that's bound to catch up with you after a while."

"A *bit* of a tough week? Finding a dead body with its head squashed to a mush, have a colleague murdered, get threatened with a gun and then find out someone you like and look up to has been lying to you all along." She shuddered at the memories. "I think that counts as the absolutely worst week *ever*, actually."

"You've left out the bit where you fall for a not particularly handsome but certainly quite interesting stranger, who then turns out not to be able to live up to your ideal image of him."

Emma glared at Jess from behind a mountain of cream.

"I haven't fallen for him."

"Oh please Em, you do this every time. It takes you about two minutes to fall head over heels in love and then as soon as he does or says something that doesn't fit with how you imagined he was, you run away."

"Great way to cheer me up Jess, thanks a lot."

"I'm only saying it because you deserve a lovely guy who falls madly in love with you and makes you deliriously happy. But that's never going to happen if you don't accept no one is perfect and you don't take the time to actually get to know them properly."

"I just want to find my soul mate."

"I know, you're a horrible romantic. But your soul mate is going to have to accept your imperfections, so perhaps you should be willing to accept his?"

Emma had finished the cream and chucked all of the marshmallows into the still very hot chocolate. Definitely time to change the subject.

"I can't believe how annoying mum was this morning. She just can't accept I'm a grown woman."

Jessica hesitated – ah well, maybe it was about time some things got said.

"Are you?"

Emma nearly choked on her marshmallow.

"What?" she managed to mumble.

Jess tried very hard not to burst out laughing at the sight of Emma with her cheeks rounded from marshmallows and with a trickle of hot chocolate curling its way down her chin.

"Obviously Aunt Elise is the best mum in the world ever, but she can be a little...over protective of you. Still. And you do rather give in to that..."

"Jesus Jess, since when do you have a degree in psychology? You're supposed to be cheering me up with a hot chocolate and telling me none of it's my fault, not analysing my 'imperfections' and showing me what a pathetic kind of individual I am."

"Em...I just mean that most mothers and daughters argue sometimes. It's a way of showing that there are limits to the relationship, just as there are limits to all relationships. Boundaries that shouldn't get crossed. Interference that doesn't get tolerated. Little girls that grow up."

Emma didn't look up from her drink.

"Every time anything happens you call your mum. And every time she drops everything and rushes down to sort it all out and make you feel better." Jess gave Emma's shin a gentle nudge with her foot under the table. "Actually, when I say it like that, it sounds nice. Maybe I'm just jealous."

Emma kicked back – only slightly harder.

"No, you're right. Come on, let's go home. I may run away from soul mates, but not from my mother."

Amanda threw the dough down hard on the flour-strewn kitchen table. She was probably overworking it, but the rhythmic kneading, the touch of the smooth mixture against her fingers, the wisps of flour caressing her face and the anticipation of the feel of the heavy wooden rolling pin in her hands were having the desired effect: she'd calmed down. She had no idea where Alex had been all day or even whether he'd be home that night and she was gradually coming to the realisation that maybe, just possibly, she didn't care. If anyone had asked her yesterday she'd have said yes, of course she loved her husband and together they would be able to overcome anything. After the scene this morning, she wasn't that sure anymore. The possibility of her marriage ending should have made her feel sad, confused, anxious, frightened, angry – any of those surely, in any combination. But the overwhelming feeling was one of relief, tinged with excitement at the prospect of being entirely her own person again. She could honestly say she'd been madly in love with Alex when she'd married him, but now? She didn't know. She'd just decided the dough couldn't take any more, when she heard the front door open. Alex staggered in to the kitchen and plonked down on one of the chairs.

"I'll make you a coffee."

"Don't want coffee."

"You're drunk Alex, it'll help you sober up."

"Why the hell would I want to be sober?"

"Look, I know it's difficult..."

"Oh you do, do you? Know what I'm going through, do you?" He picked up the rolling pin and slowly turned it round in his hands. When he spoke again there was a menacing tone in his voice that went straight to Amanda's heart and made her shiver.

"Know what I'd like to do, do you?"

"Alex just..."

He banged the rolling pin on the table so hard, Amanda jumped back against the cooker.

"Alex what..."

Whirling the rolling pin around, he jumped up from his seat and walked towards her, shouting.

"LEAVE ME ALONE!"

Amanda ran out of the kitchen, slamming the door behind her. She was shaking in anger and disbelief and not at all sure what on earth to do next. She stood still in the front room for a few minutes, then quietly tiptoed back to the kitchen door, through which she could hear Alex sobbing; she could just about make out Helen's name. Deep in thought she went into the bedroom and locked the door firmly behind her.

"Mum?"

Elise was in the kitchen, preparing dinner.

"Hello sweetheart. The chicken's nearly ready to come out of the oven and..."

"I'm sorry about this morning."

Elise walked over to the cooker and pricked a potato with a fork – not quite ready yet.

"That was nothing, darling."

Emma moved a little closer.

"I'm nearly thirty, mum. Maybe it's time I learnt to stand a bit more on my own two feet?"

Elise checked the potato again – no, still not done.

"I know I can be there a bit too much for you, Emma." She kept her eyes firmly on the water, watching it bubble away in a frenzied dance. "After your father died, I just didn't want anything to happen to you."

Emma stood next to her mother now, almost touching.

"And it's been wonderful to have you so close to me, mum. But I think it's time I tried to sort out my problems on my own."

Elise blinked away her tears and pricked a different potato.

"I'll try not to interfere so much."

Taking the fork out of her hand, Emma gave her mother's shoulder a nudge.

"But still a little bit?"

Elise laughed, turned round and brushed a stray hair off her daughter's forehead.

"Always a little bit."

SUNDAY 14 APRIL

Twenty-four

Elise was running through the dark street, hot in pursuit of the prime minister. "Why won't you answer the question?" she screamed at him, but he ignored her and kept running. At the end of the street he turned into the sunny Derbyshire countryside and began to climb a green hill – 'Now I've got him', Elise thought, and she turned into the woods for the secret shortcut to the top of the hill. Music was swirling through the trees, getting louder and louder, encouraging her to run faster, and...she woke up to the insistent tune of Für Elise emanating from her phone.

"What? I mean, hello?"

"Elise, it's Amanda."

The panic in Amanda's voice burnt away the lingering dream and made Elise sit up.

"What's wrong Mandy?"

"It's Alexander. I don't know what to do, he just came for me. I don't know what to do."

Amanda was sounding hysterical now.

"Mandy, listen to me. Take a deep breath and tell me what's happened."

There was a worrying silence on the other end of the phone.

"Mandy? Are you still there?"

"The door's not locked," came the sobbing reply, "you can see for yourself."

"Mandy what do you mean? Mandy?"

"Why are you shouting, mum? It's eight o'clock in the morning. On a Sunday."

"She's hung up. Quickly, we have to get over there."

Elise grabbed her bag and started to head for the door, but Emma took her arm and gently held her back.

"In our pyjamas?"

Elise tried to think clearly, but Amanda's panic had engulfed her too.

"Something terrible's happened to Amanda, we have to get to her flat straight away."

"Of course we'll help Amanda, but don't you think we can do that much better if we stay calm and put on some clothes first?"

Elise finally became fully aware of her surroundings, of Emma in her pale blue shorts and T-shirt, with her tousled hair and bare feet and of her own stripy nightgown and red slippers.

"She sounded so scared."

"Five minutes to get dressed, then we go."

Elise reluctantly nodded and headed back to her suitcase, while Emma dashed into her bedroom.

"How do we get in?"

Emma and Elise were standing in front of the ornate building that housed the Beechers' flat. The front door was locked and pressing the bell of number 12 had yielded no results. Elise pressed another random bell and waited for the owner to answer.

"Flower delivery." she said clearly into the telecom. A buzzing sound followed and they quickly went through the door.

"Learnt that a long time ago," she smiled nervously at Emma, "no one can resist getting flowers."

The front door to number 3 stood ajar; Elise knocked as she pushed it open.

"Mandy? Alexander?"

No sound came from anywhere. They gingerly walked through the hallway, Emma following Elise who at least had been there once before and had some idea of the lay-out. The kitchen door stood wide open, plate and cup on the table with remnants of tea and a half eaten slice of toast. Opposite the kitchen was the door to the large open plan dining room and lounge Elise had been in a few days ago, with its luxurious sofas, marble fire place and lush pristine cream-coloured carpet. Elise hesitated at the door; she wasn't sure why at first, but then realised there were signs that it had been forced open. Careful not to touch the handle and destroy evidence, she used her foot to open the door further. At first sight there was nothing unusual in the room, so she ventured further in. Then she saw him, on the not quite so pristine carpet, just in front of the sofa she'd sat on the day before. The last time Elise had seen Alexander Beecher had been at the wedding, a grand affair with several hundred guests in a massive marquee in the grounds of what had once been a stately home, but was now a very exclusive hotel. She'd never warmed to Alexander, but then she'd only met him a few times and he clearly hadn't felt she was the right kind of friend for the future Mrs Beecher either. On his wedding day he'd been resplendent in his handmade tuxedo; now however he was lying there in his dark green silk dressing gown, his greying black hair matted together by the blood that had oozed out of the gash on his forehead. The wrought-iron fireplace poker lay beside him, presumably where Amanda had dropped it. Elise became aware of Emma's hand in hers and turned round.

"My second body in a week," Emma whispered, "this seems to be becoming a habit."

Elise gingerly crouched down and reached out to feel his pulse.

"Nothing. Nothing at all," Elise concluded. "Let's get out of this room."

They quickly checked the other rooms, looking for Amanda, but she was nowhere to be found. Back in the hallway Elise took her phone from her bag.

"Have you found him?"

"Mandy, where are you?"

"I'm not sure. I had to get out of there, I've just been walking around."

"Focus on your surroundings and get to somewhere easily recognisable. A public building, like a library or a museum. Then call me back and wait there for me."

"Yes, ok, Elise."

Elise turned to her daughter.

"I'm going to find Amanda, sweetheart. Can you call your inspector and stay here till he gets here?"

"He's not my inspector," Emma rather feebly replied. "But, yes I'll call him. What do I tell him about Amanda?"

Elise hesitated slightly.

"I'll bring her to the police station."

"He's just supposed to accept that?"

"I'm sure he will if you ask him."

Lucas looked down on the body of Alexander Beecher and felt a pang of guilt. Nonsense, of course. The chain of events that had let to this were not his fault; even so, he was the one who had insisted Alexander be told he was Matthew's father. That he'd been investigating a murder, that any of his colleagues would have done the same, that he wasn't responsible for the actions of either Alexander or Amanda Beecher – none of it silenced the little voice in his head that was blaming him. He walked back into the hallway, where Emma was still standing. Just.

"Have you had anything to eat today?"

She shook her head.

"Amanda's call woke us up and we just rushed straight here."

He took a chair out of the dining room and made her sit down.

"Once the forensic team arrives I'll drive you down to the police station to give a statement. And have a cup of tea."

"No sergeant Fletcher today?"

"He was looking forward to having a whole day with his family; I'm not going to deny him that unless I absolutely have to."

"I'm sorry. You must have had plans today as well."
Lucas looked quite surprised at the thought that he might actually have anything to do that wasn't work related.
"Nothing that couldn't be changed – one of the advantages of being on your own."

"Mandy?" Elise's voice was full of relief; she'd started to think the call would never come. "Where are you now?"
"The V&A."
"Where?"
"Outside the V&A."
"Great. Wait by the entrance, I'm on my way."
Elise re-started the car; she'd guessed wrong and had driven in the opposite direction of where she needed to be. All she could do now was hope that Amanda would wait for her.

Lucas walked round the flat again, puzzling together what had happened that morning. The breakfast leftovers were most likely Amanda's; it would be difficult to imagine the pink small suitcase standing next to the kitchen door belonging to Alexander. But which one of them had locked the door to the front room and which one of them had broken it down? He'd been involved in enough domestic abuse cases not to make gender assumptions about anything anymore – he'd just have to wait for forensics to tell him. And Amanda Beecher of course, although she had now had plenty of time to work out exactly what to say. How had he allowed himself to be persuaded not to go after her? Why on earth had he agreed to wait for Elise to bring her to the police station? She was a journalist for goodness' sake, she could be helping Amanda to get her story straight. He went back into the hallway.
"I can't wait any longer, I have to start the search for Amanda Beecher."
"Of course, I understand. Do you mind if I call mum and ask her what's happening?"
Lucas looked at her pale face and worried expression and relented.

After driving round the same streets four times, getting more and more anxious at the time wasted, Elise parked her car next to a permit holders' only sign. She hastily tore a piece of paper out of her notebook, scribbled an apology and her phone number, stuck it behind the windscreen wiper and rushed to the V&A's entrance. She started to panic as she neared the door and couldn't see Amanda, but then she spotted her, sitting on a bench a little bit further along the street.
"Hey Mandy."
Elise sat down next to Amanda, who looked like she'd been crying for hours. She put her arm reassuringly round her and Amanda let herself be pulled close. After quite a while, when she'd finally stopped shaking, Elise pulled back slightly and asked what had happened. Before Amanda could answer, Elise's phone went.
"Oh hello sweetheart. I'm with Amanda now."
"Inspector Bohr is getting quite anxious to talk to her."
Elise looked straight into Amanda's eyes as she continued talking.
"I think we're about ready to come to the police station."
Amanda looked startled at first, but then nodded her head.
"We should be there in about forty minutes, depending on traffic. Bye darling."
Elise helped Amanda up from the seat and together they slowly made their way back to the car.

The forensic experts had taken over the flat, searching for all the little material clues that would help the investigation along. They'd fingerprinted Emma and would need to do the same to Elise...and Amanda of course. Assuming they would actually turn up at the police station. Emma could feel the panic rise up from her stomach at the thought that her mother might be helping Amanda escape. Or maybe it was just hunger taking over completely. Lucas had been talking to various of his colleagues, but he seemed to be satisfied now and walked over to her.
"Nothing more I can do here – shall we go?"
Emma felt a little dizzy as she got up; she never had been able to cope without breakfast and it was now pretty nearly lunchtime. She tried not to show it though and walked steadily down to the car. To her surprise Lucas didn't open the door, but

walked on, heading straight for a coffee shop. He looked back to check she was coming and even held the door for her; she didn't understand, but the glorious smell of food and hot drinks overwhelmed her and she decided to concentrate solely on getting a soy latte and a ham and cheese toastie. And a blueberry muffin. Lucas sat opposite her with the biggest cup of coffee she'd ever seen and a BLT sandwich.

"I've had confirmation that your mother and Mrs Beecher have arrived at the police station, so as I don't need to worry about them anymore and as you look as if you're about to faint from malnourishment..."

Emma gave him her warmest smile.

"Thanks. I did desperately need something to eat."

They ate in silence for a few minutes, Emma resisting the temptation to gulp everything down, instead fully savouring every mouthful as the tastes and smells prickled her senses and her complaining stomach gradually settled down.

"So did you grow up in the Derbyshire countryside?" Lucas broke the silence.

"Yes, all very rural, very pretty. A bit boring I suppose, but I never minded. We visited cities often enough for me to appreciate the benefits of a small town." She glanced up from her muffin. "How about you?"

Lucas held his enormous cup in mid-air, staring at it wistfully.

"We never settled down anywhere. My mother's a GP and my father's a maths teacher, so they never had any problems finding work. They both enjoy regularly seeing new places, not being stuck anywhere."

"But you don't?"

Lucas had never heard a simple question asked so tenderly before and he found it difficult to answer.

"I've lived in the same flat for nearly twenty years now." He glanced at her as she looked at him intently. "I suppose that answers your question."

He looked back at his nearly empty cup of coffee, drained the last remains out of it and got up.

"We'd better go."

He held the door open for her again and she walked slightly closer past him than was necessary. Maybe he was her inspector after all.

What to do, what to do? Amanda still couldn't quite believe the decision she was nearing. She spread her slice of toast with some thick-cut marmalade and poured another cup of tea. Leave him? Could she really leave him? Should she have left a long time ago? Yesterday, for

the second time in her married life, she'd felt frightened of her husband, frightened of the way he'd looked at her, frightened when he'd banged his fist on the table so hard when he mentioned her name. Why was she even questioning staying with a man who'd frightened her? Why was it still so hard to go? Silently, almost tip-toeing, she went back into the bedroom, took her small overnight bag and packed a few clothes. She could hear Alexander snoring loudly in the spare bedroom; hardly surprising after the amount of alcohol he'd consumed the night before. She put the bag ready in the kitchen and sat back down at the table. Was she actually going to do this?

"What do you think you're doing?"

Amanda jumped up at the sudden appearance of her husband. The harshness in his voice frightened her even more than the shouting had done the day before.

"Creeping around the house like some kind of intruder, packing a bag...you weren't thinking of walking out on me, were you my dear?"

Amanda tried to think clearly but a blind panic was starting to overtake her. At least he was standing in front of her, at the other end of the table, which meant the way to the door was clear.

"I couldn't allow that, you know. Being humiliated again, first by Helen..." his voice almost broke as he whispered her name "...and then by you? I don't think so, my dear."

She could run to the front door, but it was still double locked – she'd never have enough time to get it open. The front room. That door locked and the key was on the inside of the door. It was meant to give added security in case of intruders, although she'd often wondered whether the door would withstand any kind of effort to break it down.

"You're going to be a good little wife..." he was starting to walk towards her now "...I'll make sure of that."

Amanda screamed as loud as she could, which surprised him and stopped him in his tracks. She then hurled the chair towards him and ran out of the kitchen, into the front room, frantically locking the door behind her. Only then did she realise she was trapped, with no way to call for help. Her mobile was in her purse in the kitchen, the landline phone not in its charger. She desperately searched for it as Alexander started banging on the door, shouting at her to open it, threatening she'd regret her actions. She finally saw the phone lying next to the television remote, on top of the mantelpiece, but it was too late – Alexander burst through the door and rushed towards her, waving that same big heavy rolling pin he'd slammed so close to her face the day before. She walked backwards and stumbled against the elegant bucket containing the ornamental iron pokers for the fake gas fire. She reached behind, grabbed one, closed her eyes and started slashing it about; when she realised she'd hit something she opened her eyes to find Alexander lying on the floor, eyes wide open, blood gushing out of his forehead.

Amanda took a sip of the glass of water Lucas had placed in front of her.

"I panicked. I didn't mean to kill him, I just didn't want him to hurt me. He was so very clearly dead." She shuddered at the vivid image. "I can't remember what I did next, but I must have taken my purse and left the building. I vaguely remember calling Elise...the next thing I remember is getting Elise's call, her wonderful calming voice telling me to go somewhere safe, promising she'd find me. And she did."

Emma and Elise got up as Lucas entered the waiting room.

"What happens now?" Emma asked.

"Assuming the forensic evidence bears out Mrs Beecher's story, she killed her husband in self-defence and won't be charged."

"What do you mean assuming? You can't possibly think..."

Emma gently took hold of her mother's arm and pulled her back slightly.

"Mum, calm down, let the inspector do his job."

"Can I at least see Amanda?"

Lucas opened the door and beckoned a constable.

"Show these ladies where Mrs Beecher is waiting for her solicitor."

Elise followed the constable, but Emma hesitated.

"Is this a normal week for you? Murder, domestic violence..."

"...rescuing damsels in distress? The last one not so much, the rest rather comes with the job."

Emma blushed.

"I suppose that was a silly question."

"Not at all; I have no idea what counts as a normal week in your job either."

"NOT this one."

A slightly awkward silence followed, neither quite sure what to say next.

"I'd better get on with the paperwork."

"And I'd better find my mother."

Emma gave him a parting smile and went through the door. Lucas took a deep breath. *I'd better get on with the paperwork.* Of all the things he could have said, he'd unfailingly chosen the most boring one.

Twenty-five

"So how's Amanda?"

Elise didn't answer straight away, as a parked car decided to shoot out onto the road in front of them and she needed to do an emergency stop to avoid a collision.

"Bloody idiot. Honestly, some people have no patience and even less sense." She took a deep breath and drove on. "Better than you'd think. Her solicitor seems very sensible; he's convinced he can get her out on bail."

"I don't know how I'd feel if I'd killed someone, even if it was in self-defence."

"Well, let's hope you never need to find out. I'd be more worried about your job and the archive, if I were you."

Emma looked confused.

"Why?"

"How much time do you think your chair of Trustees will have to devote to the place? I would guess she'll have other things on her mind."

Emma stayed silent for a while, as the implications of what had happened slowly sank in.

"I'd better call Frederick."

Frederick stared at the phone, debating whether to call Melanie. She'd given him her number – in case of a cooking emergency – and in normal circumstances he wouldn't have hesitated to use it. But the past few days hadn't exactly been normal. It took him a moment to register that the phone had started ringing; maybe she'd decided to call him instead.

"Frederick, it's Emma."

When Emma had finished he thanked her for letting him know, put the phone down and glared at the empty room.

"Shit."

He paced round the room for a while, trying to come up with some kind of plan for what to do next. In the end he grabbed the phone from the table and phoned Marie. It went straight to voicemail. He left a quick message and wondered who else he could call. No, things were definitely not going as planned.

Twenty. That was enough laps in front crawl; Marie moved on to the more relaxing backstroke. She started thinking about her daughter's wedding plans; the big day was less than a year away now and there was still so much to do. Molly was the last one to leave home; Jerry had a decent enough job working as a paramedic, he'd look after her all right. The third wedding in five years. Another dress to find, venue to sort out, bridesmaids' dresses, food, decorations. More money to find. Where was it going to come from this time? Marie got out of the pool, showered, got dressed and checked her phone. Strange to have a message from Frederick; she quickly listened. Damn. Did this mean everything had been for nothing?

"Tim, can you get the phone?"

"Can't we just leave it?"

"Just answer it, will you – you're making me nervous standing right outside the door like that."

Tim walked through to the front room, picked up the phone and walked back into the bedroom.

"Hello?"

"Tim? It's Frederick. Sorry to disturb you on a Sunday, but there have been some developments you need to know about."

"Now's not the best time..."

"Amanda Beecher has killed her husband."

"You what?"

"Apparently he attacked her and she killed him in self-defence. You can imagine the problems this is going to cause..."

The door to the bathroom opened and Tim stopped listening when he saw Izzy's wide smile. Time seemed to stand still as she walked towards him. He suddenly realised Frederick was still talking.

"Sorry Frederick, I'll have to talk to you about this tomorrow."

He ignored Fredericks protestations, flung the phone on the bed and carefully put his hand on Izzy's belly; their future was in there. There was no choice now – he'd have to do anything necessary to keep his job.

"Yes Frederick...absolutely...thanks for letting me know...yes, I'll see you tomorrow...bye."

Jennifer slowly walked over to the mantelpiece and placed the phone back in the charger. What an odd development. She pressed the play button of the digital radio and sat back down on the sofa accompanied by the mellow sounds of Radio 2. Her embroidery was sitting invitingly on the little black coffee table. No, a cup of tea first. She got back up and went to the kitchen.

Life was full of difficult decisions, Theresa contemplated. Her favourite little blue dress was of course totally a party knock-out, but her new sparkly black mini skirt was crying out to be worn. Which to choose? Absent-mindedly she answered her mobile.

"Hi."

"Theresa? It's Marie. Have you heard what's happened?"

Theresa's annoyance at being reminded about work on a Sunday soon evaporated and she burst out laughing as she listened to Marie.

"That's hilarious! Do you think she'll go to jail?"

"Let's hope not – she protects our jobs, remember?"

"I can't worry about that now, I've got a party to go to. Bye Marie."

Mmm...might be worth starting to look for another job though. But first things first; she examined both options closely once again and slid into her little blue dress.

"So Em, do you think you'll manage not to find a body tomorrow?"

"Very funny, Jess."

"You have to admit though, you're getting rather good at it."

"I wish I was any good at finding murderers."

Elise came back from the kitchen with the apple pie they'd bought for pudding.

"You still think it wasn't Richard?"

Emma took a generous portion and poured on some custard.

"I *know* it wasn't Richard."

"It must have been someone at your work though." Jess said as she demolished her pie.

"I'm not even sure about that. Mum, you've done lots of investigating, what would you do?"

Elise thought for a moment.

"I always just went to the people who knew and asked them lots of questions. That's the difference between being a journalist and a detective, I suppose."

Emma suddenly pushed her half-eaten plate away.

"Oh, come on! We've all read plenty of detective novels and watched murder mysteries on TV – we must be able to work out what to do. Jess, you were even in one!"

"Only for about two minutes, until I got pushed in front of a train," Jess protested.

"They look for clues. Surely?"

"Yes sweetheart, I'm pretty sure the police have done that. That's what's led them to Richard, remember?"

"Then they've missed something...they haven't found the murder weapon yet, have they?"

Elise and Jessica shrugged their shoulders.

"No of course they haven't, Lucas would have told me."

Jess looked at Elise; *Lucas?*, she mouthed. *Apparently*, Elise mouthed back.

"It's just not possible none of us saw anything," Emma continued, oblivious to the silent hilarity around her. "Whoever saw something can't have realised the importance of it."

"It could even have been you, Em."

"You're right," Emma conceded slowly. "Right," she added, with a very determined look on her face. "I'm going to find out what it is that's been missed. There has to be something and I will find it and I will prove Richard's innocence."

Elise gently put the half eaten apple pie back in front of Emma.

"Of course you will darling. How about some more custard?"

"Tim! You did come. Not too old after all?"

"No one's ever too old to party, surely."

They joined the throng of scantily clad partygoers and made their way through the double doors, down the stairs and into the club. Tim headed straight for the bar to get them both a drink, while Theresa ran towards a group of her friends who were already on the dance floor. After a couple of dances she saw Tim sitting on a bar stool and went over to get her drink.

"Come on, then, show us what you've got."

To her surprise Tim turned out to be a great mover, who manoeuvred her effortlessly in between the other dancers, not once losing his rhythm or poise.

"Wow, you should definitely come out more often!"

"That was great fun, I have to admit." He slowly got his breath back and sat down at the bar. "Listen, Theresa..."

"What?"

The music seemed to have turned up a notch and had gone from very loud to can't-hear-what-anyone's-saying.

Tim took Theresa's hand and led her back towards the entrance, where at least there was some chance of being heard.

"Listen, I had a great time, but I should be going now."

"Already? We've only just got here." She looked very disappointed.

"I just don't want to leave Izzy alone like this. Parties aren't her thing."

"She's got you on a tight leash, hasn't she?"

Tim hesitated.

"Promise you won't tell anyone?"

"That you're on a tight leash?"

"No, you idiot...Izzy's pregnant."

"Tim, wow, that's pretty exciting."

"We only found out today, no one is supposed to know yet. But you can see why I don't want to go out partying and leave her alone at home right now."

"Yeah, I get it. Go on then, go home. Don't worry, I know how to keep a secret."

"Thanks." He gave her a quick hug. "Don't stay out too late."

"Gee Dad, I'll try not to."

Tim waved goodbye, but she'd already disappeared in to the crowd, undoubtedly heading straight back to the dance floor. He quickly ran up the stairs; almost nine o'clock, Izzy should still be up when he got home.

Lucas switched off the television; watching a movie hadn't relaxed him either. He'd talked to Richard Owen again that afternoon and the more he talked to him, the less certain he became that he had his murderer. Maybe he shouldn't have dismissed Sam Ripley so easily – a jealous lover had a better motive than a thieving accomplice. But no, there was no way Ripley could have walked round that building without any of the staff noticing him; it simply had to be one of them. But was it Owen? He poured himself a vodka; tomorrow they'd go over everything again. Every statement, every fact, every piece of evidence. Just in case they – he – had missed something.

The music was attempting to bounce off the walls, but kept finding party-goers in its way. The dance floor was so full there was very little dancing being done and everywhere around people were sitting and standing, drink in hand, having conversations by shouting into each other's ears. Theresa was in the centre of it all, swaying her body to the music, while deftly avoiding collisions with other enthusiasts. A shame Tim had left early, although it had been brave of him to come – he must have been the oldest one here. Damn, that meant that some day she would be too old for these parties as well. Ah well, all the more reason to enjoy every moment now. She stopped for a moment to re-hydrate – not 'drink', that implied alcohol and she never drank when she was out on her own. Having gulped down the remains of her coke, she glanced at her watch: almost eleven. She threw herself back on the dance floor for one last frenetic dance, then weaved her way through the crowd and pushed through the door. Theresa stood still for a minute or so, deeply inhaling the cool night air and re-adjusting her hearing to the relative quiet of the street. Being a party girl didn't mean you had to be an idiot: no drinking or drugs when out on your own, no staying out too late on a work night and no accepting lifts from strangers. She huddled tighter into her jacket; the April air had turned quite cold again. She started walking towards the bus stop when she spotted a familiar face coming out of a 24 hour shop. Getting offered a lift home by a friend was of course a different matter; Theresa slid into the passenger seat, enjoying the warmth of the car and immediately started talking about the fabulous party she'd just been to. She only stopped when the hard, cold metal hit her head and she slumped unconscious against the door.

Lucas slowly opened his eyes and looked at his alarm clock: 2.07am. Who the hell was calling him at this time?

"Bohr"

"Sorry to wake you inspector. This is sergeant Madden."

Lucas sat up; Madden was on the homicide night shift this week.

"What's happened?"

"The body of a young woman was found about an hour ago; she's had her head bashed in."

Fear woke him up properly.

"We've just realised she's involved in your case so thought you'd want to know straight away."

Lucas could barely move now. She'd been so adamant Owen was innocent, had she confronted someone else, had she not trusted him again? He managed to force his voice out.

"Who is it?"

"A Theresa Woodward."

A wave of relief washed over him, immediately replaced by the bitter feeling of guilt. Emma had been right – the killer was still out there.

On any other night this would be a very ordinary street, all its inhabitants soundly asleep in their neat Victorian terraces; no bright police lights, multitude of police cars or coroner's van to arouse curiosity. A few had braved the rain and were standing behind the police tape, straining their heads, desperate to get a glimpse of the unfolding drama. Most had stayed dry indoors though and were observing procedures from behind partially drawn curtains. Lucas showed his badge and was ushered through the barrier, where Madden was waiting for him.

"This streetlight was reported last night by one of the residents as being broken. That turns this whole area pretty dark."

"The street has no connection to Miss Woodward?"

"Not as far as we can tell, sir. Doesn't look like she was killed here, more likely a body drop."

Lucas couldn't quite bring himself to look.

"Who found her?"

"Patrol car. They were doing their regular rounds and noticed her lying there. They thought she was drunk, so went over to help her get home and then they saw..."

"Any evidence of theft or molestation?"

"All her clothes are intact and undamaged and we found her purse in the inside pocket of her jacket."

"Looks like it is to do with my case then. Thanks for alerting me so quickly Madden; I'll take over now. Do you want to stay involved?"

"I've got plenty to keep me busy, sir. You'll have my report before I finish my shift."

Madden walked over to one of the police cars and drove off; two minutes later Nick Fletcher was rudely awakened by the sound of his phone.

MONDAY 15 APRIL

Twenty-six

As Emma climbed the steps the front door swung open and Marie appeared.

"Morning Emma."

"Morning Marie."

She quickly dashed up the stairs, threw her coat over on the peg and sat down behind her desk. Right, she thought, now how am I going to prove that Richard is no murderer? The determination she'd found the previous evening was still there, but she had to admit she had no idea how to begin.

"You're deep in thought, Em."

"Hey Tim, I didn't see you come in. Did you go to that party last night?"

He hesitated. "Briefly. But I couldn't stay, Izzy needed me at home."

"Is she all right?"

Tim's face lit up. "She's absolutely fine. Everything's going to be fine."

Marie appeared at the doorway.

"Frederick's waiting for the weekly staff meeting, come on."

She vanished again immediately to round up the others. Jennifer was already sitting on the sofa, mug of tea in her hands; Emma sat next to her while Tim made two more teas. Frederick came in looking serious and remained standing. A couple of minutes went by before Marie burst through the door.

"Sorry Frederick, I can't find her anywhere, she's definitely not arrived yet."

"Is that Theresa?" Jennifer asked.

Frederick nodded.

"She's not usually late for work."

"She probably overdid it last night at the party." Tim ventured "She'll turn up soon enough."

"Well I won't wait any longer then; Marie, can fill her in when she arrives. I'm sure you're all aware of the developments regarding Mrs Beecher."

Everyone nodded their heads.

"I haven't been in touch with the board yet, I'm sure they will want some time to consider what happens next. I do think it best we get ready for whoever is going to deal with the theft issue, so Jennifer, if you could go through your notes with me this afternoon, please?"

"Of course."

"I will let you all know as soon as I know any more about the future of the archive. For now, let's just get to work."

"Odd that Theresa still hasn't turned up," Jennifer said as she took her mug through to the kitchen and ran the water. Emma followed her and grabbed the tea towel.

"Tim must be right – she just stayed too late at the party."

Lucas made his way to his desk, carrying the two large cups of black coffee he'd been to get at the café down the street; they'd needed a serious drink after the night's events. Nick looked relieved at his approach.

"The inspector's just arrived, Mrs Bonner," he said in the phone, "I'm sure he'll want to speak to you."

Nick covered the ear piece.

"She's in a foul mood – something to do with Ripley."

"Mrs Bonner? This is inspector Bohr...Mr Ripley is missing? I don't quite understand..." The torrent at the other end slowed down slightly as Helen repeated everything she'd just said.

"Right. I can understand why you're upset Mrs Bonner. Don't worry I'll notify the fraud squad immediately."

"The fraud squad? Why do we need them for a missing person?" Nick asked as soon as Lucas was of the phone.

"It seems our Mr Ripley has not been entirely honest. He sent Mrs Bonner a document giving her his 49% of the business and telling her he has dismissed all of the staff."

"And?"

"She's just seen the accounts – all there is, is a mass of debts."

Nick let out a slow whistle.

"So he's scarpered with all the money?"

"Looks like it." Lucas dialled the fraud squad's extension. "Of course that doesn't automatically make him our murderer."

"Moves him nearer the top of the list, though."

While Lucas was talking to his colleague, Nick leafed through the mail that had arrived that morning. Internal mail was a daily occurrence, but getting an actual letter through the post was getting very rare. He picked up the envelope addressed to Detective Inspector Bohr, marked 'strictly private and confidential'. He heard Lucas finish his call and handed him the letter.

"This one's very definitely for you. Hand delivered."

Lucas tossed it on his desk; no time for silly letters, not when there was a dead girl waiting to see him.

Back at her desk Emma tried to concentrate on her work and even managed to send a few email replies, before giving in to the nagging voice in her head – how are you going to prove Richard is innocent. She ignored the second voice – if he really is – because of course he was, but what could she do about it? She tried to imagine what could have happened that Monday afternoon – presumably Richard had let Hugo in through the fire door in the basement, but then what? It was no use trying to do this at her desk; she got up and descended the stairs all the way to the basement area. She pretended to open the fire door and let Hugo in – now what? They'd need somewhere private to talk. The storage room, of course! Only Marie ever went in there so if Richard had timed it right – lunchtime say – he would have been certain not to be disturbed. She went in to the storage room and switched on the light. All the things you'd expect to be here seemed to be there: stationery, boxes of archival folders and polyester sleeves, cotton tape, large packs of the very thick blue-grey card Jennifer made folders out of, boxes and boxes of disaster supplies so they could salvage the collections in case of flooding and general cleaning supplies. Nothing unexpected there. She suddenly felt rather foolish: the police would have been in here already of course and would have taken anything out of the ordinary away with them. From the storage room she went in to the locked archive strongroom; she'd been in here herself on Monday and hadn't seen anything suspect. Not until she'd gone in Tuesday morning, that is. The stacks were still open where Hugo's body had lain; she avoided looking in there and quickly left the room. Well, this hadn't helped at all. On her way back to the stairs she passed conservation and wondered how Jennifer was coping looking through the notes of all that work she'd done and that had been so badly abused. There was no answer to her knock , but she went in anyway.

"Jennifer?"

That horribly noisy contraption was on again and there was the usual faint smell of nail varnish remover. Printed out photographs and notes lay strewn all over the large centre table, the letters moved in to the fume cupboard next to the old iron Jennifer used as a weight and the folders lying ready to receive the repaired documents. No Jennifer though, so Emma trudged back to her office. She hadn't learnt a single thing from that little expedition – absolutely nothing that would help Richard.

Lying naked on the cold mortuary table, Theresa looked extremely young. As she had been. What had this girl done or seen to deserve this? Lucas had grown used to seeing dead bodies, many of them more badly mutilated than this one, but on this occasion he felt sick. Was this his fault? He'd had his doubts about Richard's guilt, but it had been so much easier not to listen to them, to simply assume he'd be able to work it all out given a bit more time. With his boss clearly upset, Nick took control of the conversation.

"Time of death?"

"Between eleven pm and one am. She was found by a patrol car just after one."

"Cause?"

"Several blows against the side of her head. The first one probably didn't kill her, the second one certainly did. There were at least five more blows after that."

"A frenzied attack."

"Certainly looks like someone was angry." Flo sighed. "Or they wanted to be very certain. The indentations in the skin indicate an object with sharply defined edges, possibly curved. I'm working together with the forensic team to get you more details on that.."

"Would it have required a lot of strength?"

"No, I'd say pretty much anyone could kill like that."

"Thanks Flo."

Nick grabbed Lucas' arm and they walked out of the mortuary, back into the bright light of day.

"Boss?"

"This is my fault Nick. Owens' motive was too flimsy, I should have looked deeper."

"Lucas, there's no way any of us could have known she was in danger. If she knew something, if that's why she was killed, there is nothing we could have done to prevent it."

"She must have seen or heard something – why the hell didn't she tell us?"

"Perhaps she didn't realise what it meant and confided in the wrong person?"

Lucas took a deep breath – self-pity wasn't going to get him anywhere.

"Right, let's go and tell them the news and see how they react." He stopped for a moment. "The murders are getting more vicious, Nick. One of those nice people in that quiet archive is getting desperate – who knows what they'll do next."

The closed sign was still hanging there; Lucas ignored it, opened the heavy wooden door and pressed the bell on the sliding door. He watched Marie hurry over ready to explain they were closed, until she recognised the visitors and quickly opened up.

"We'd like to talk to everyone together Mrs Thorpe – in the staff room perhaps?"

"Of course inspector, I'll round up the troops. Mind, it will be without Theresa, she still hasn't turned up for work."

Lucas and Nick began to ascend the stairs.

"Well, they obviously don't know yet."

Lucas shook his head.

"It's going to be a nasty shock for them."

Emma felt the blood drain from her face. Sweet, joyous, vibrant, silly, infuriating, smiling Theresa. Anger started to mix in with grief – how dare someone take away the life of this young girl? She couldn't have had anything to do with the thefts, how could she possibly fit in?

"Perhaps we should go home."

The words floated towards her. She looked at Frederick and shook her head. Others must have done the same.

"Staying together makes more sense."

Tim this time. His voice sounded strange, as if his throat was being strangled.

"I agree."

Jennifer sounded pale again.

"We will need to ask you all more questions, I'm sure you understand." Lucas sounded strained as well. "Do any of you know what Miss Woodward did last night after she left here?"

"She went to a party," Tim said slowly, "I met her there."

"In that case I'd like to talk to you first Mr Edwards."

"We all knew." Emma's voice rang out clearly and deliberately. "Theresa had been talking about this party all week. We all knew she'd be there."

She looked at Lucas, who acknowledged with a slight nod that he understood what she was trying to say.

"There's nothing to hide." Tim sounded quite defiant now. "She'd asked me – well challenged me – to come along and I did. I met her outside the club just after eight; we had a drink, danced for a while and then I left."

"What time was that?"

"Nine o'clock. I looked at my watch when I came out and remember thinking Izzy would still be awake when I got home."

"Was she?"

"Yes, inspector, she'll be able to confirm that I got home at twenty to ten."

"You didn't stay very long, sir."

Tim looked at sergeant Fletcher.

"I know, I shouldn't have left her alone like that, I should have stayed, given her a lift home. I'll never forgive myself for that."

Emma shuffled closer to him and put her hand on his arm.

"This isn't your fault Tim, you couldn't possibly have known."

Tim gave her a wry smile.

"I just didn't want to leave Izzy alone." He took a deep breath before continuing. "We've just found out that she's pregnant."

A slightly muted chorus of congratulations greeted Tim's announcement.

"I wasn't supposed to say anything yet, but...well..."

"Did Miss Woodward say how she was planning to get home?"

Tim shook his head.

"She seemed to always take the bus everywhere," Jennifer offered.

"Thank you, we're looking into that possibility." Lucas slowly looked round the room. "Did she say anything about the other deaths last week, hinted perhaps that she knew something?"

"She regarded it all as a big joke," Marie chipped in. "I called her yesterday around seven to tell her what had happened with Mrs Beecher and she just burst out laughing. Poor Tessie."

Lucas stood thinking for a moment.

"The only two people left who have admitted going down to the basement on Monday afternoon are Miss Marr and Miss Baines."

Both looked startled as Lucas mentioned their names.

"We've already talked extensively to Miss Marr..." everyone stared at Jennifer "...but I think it might be useful to have another word with you, Miss Baines."

Emma was about to get up, when Jennifer rose instead.

"There's no point trying to keep it a secret – I was in a relationship with Hugo."
When the gasps had died down she continued. "He came into conservation briefly
Monday afternoon; that's why the police have already had an extra 'chat' with me."
She sat back down, arms crossed, staring straight ahead of her.

Lucas turned to Frederick.

"May I use your office for a moment Mr Samuels?"

"Of course, be my guest."

"I don't know what else I can tell you."

"Just tell us again about Monday afternoon, Miss Baines. You went downstairs to
get something out of the store?"

"Yes. But I popped into conservation first. I guess it was about twenty past two."

"Miss Marr was there?"

"She was at the central table, looking at some documents. She'd been busy with
solvents, removing self-adhesive tape."

"How did you know that?"

"She'd been doing the same in the morning – the awful smell of that solvent is
pretty strong."

"She didn't seem upset in any way?"

Emma paused, trying to recall her exact impression at the time.

"More excited, I'd say. I suppose that would be right if she'd just had a visit from
Hugo Bonner." She looked straight at Lucas. "They were really having an affair?"

He nodded.

"How long were you in the room for?"

"Not more than a few minutes. Then I went to the strongroom."

"Was the door locked?"

"Definitely. Strongroom doors are always locked – I would have noticed if it
wasn't."

"Anything unusual in the that room? Any odd smells or sounds?"

"No. If Hugo had been in there he certainly wasn't when I went in."

"Did you notice the door to the store opposite?"

"I didn't really look at it; if it was open I didn't notice." Emma sighed. "Sorry, I'm
not being much help."

"Never mind. Sometimes small things get remembered a few days after the event; it
was worth a try."

Nick entered the conversation.

"What was Miss Woodward like on Saturday?"

Emma could feel herself turn pale again.

"Theresa was as joyful and fun as always. She was convinced Olivia had been
poisoned, but didn't give any hints or anything – you know, to say she knew who it

was? And she thought it was funny how they'd chosen manuscripts repaired by Jennifer to steal." She paused again. "Poor Jennifer, no wonder she was so upset when I told them. She wasn't just betrayed by her employer, but by her lover."

Lucas turned towards his sergeant.

"Nick, could you tell the others they don't need to wait in the staff room for us? We'll go back to the station as soon as I've finished talking to Miss Baines."

Nick nodded and left the room, after which the atmosphere changed slightly.

"Thank you for not having said it," Lucas said quietly, "but you were right. Richard Owen couldn't possibly have killed Miss Woodward."

"This isn't your fault," Emma replied gently. "I just wish I could be of more help. There has to be something here, something that will show who the real murderer is."

Lucas looked worried.

"Leave that to me. Please. Someone you think of as a friend is a killer and I don't think they'll hesitate to kill again if they think you know too much."

Emma smiled.

"A good thing you're used to rescuing damsels in distress."

Lucas didn't find it funny.

"Promise you won't start asking awkward questions?"

"Fine, I promise."

Lucas only looked half convinced.

Twenty-seven

Back at the station, Lucas went down to the cells to talk to Richard Owen once again.
"Poor little Theresa. I *told* you it wasn't me."
"Who is it, Dr Owen? You know these people well, who do you suspect?"
Richard shook his head.
"I have absolutely no idea, inspector. I wouldn't have thought any of them capable of murder."
"And none of them thought you capable of stealing. What about Marie Thorpe?"
"Marie's a good worker, an honest woman. A bit garrulous, yes, and rather attention seeking, but she wouldn't hurt a fly."
"Mr Samuels?"
"A thoroughly decent man – seriously inspector, it's pointless going through them all like that. Tim has had his problems, but is the sweetest man you could imagine. Poor Jennifer has been through so much...and I don't need to tell you what a lovely girl Emma is."
Lucas got up from his seat.
"You're still under arrest for the thefts, but your solicitor should be able to arrange for you to be released on bail."
"Would you tell Emma I'm sorry I let her down?"
"I think you owe it to her to tell her that yourself. To all of them, frankly."

Outside the interrogation room Lucas stood still for a few minutes, working out a plan of action. All the information about last night, the interviews with other clubbers, with bus drivers and shop keepers, any CCTV footage from anywhere near the club – all of that should be arriving soon. The more he thought about his various suspects, the more convinced he became that only one fulfilled the motive, means and opportunity triangle, at least for the first murder. But how on earth were they going to prove it? Back at his desk he noticed the mysterious letter that had arrived that morning. He still didn't have time to look at it, but then, when would he? He tore open the envelope and began to read.

Dear Inspector Bohr

Knowing Helen she will have checked the accounts of the business pretty immediately, and will no doubt have phoned you as soon as she realised the state the it is in and that she's unable to reach me. You may even have already guessed that I am no longer in the country; by now I will have arrived somewhere safe, where I will not face extradition. I sincerely hope that when you've read my account (forgive the pun) of what has happened, you will conclude that spending a lot of resources on tracking me down would not be a very sensible use of tax payers' money.

I was a fool to let Hugo persuade me to go into business with him. Then again, whatever anyone might say about Hugo, he was certainly extremely persuasive and he even probably was genuinely interested in the book shops. The problem was that he didn't need the business to succeed; he still had enough family money – not to mention his wife's money – to be able to treat it all as a nice little hobby. In retrospect it is difficult to understand why I ever signed a deal giving him 51% of the business, but as I said, he could be very convincing. It actually took me several months to realise that owning 49% of a business is useless if the other 51% are in the hands of one other person. Every time we disagreed, every time there was a problem, a decision that needed making, there was only ever one outcome – we did what Hugo wanted. I can't tell you the number of nights I lay awake thinking what would happen if he got bored and decided to sell his half to someone else; or he might even consider the business not worth saving and declare it bankrupt. Whatever he might end up doing, I would have no way to stop him and I would be the one who would have lost everything. I must say though, even in the darkest of sleepless nights, killing him never occurred to me. I embarked on a much simpler solution instead.

Hugo loved being the man in charge, making the big decisions, but he was very happy to leave the actual day to day running of everything to me. From the start that meant I was in charge of the accounts. Of course Hugo did look at them, so I couldn't see a way of putting a little emergency money aside for myself; until, that is, we employed our very own accountant. My idea and Hugo immediately agreed – every proper business had its own accountant. I told Hugo that obviously we couldn't just give all the accounts to Martin; I would continue to check the totals as they came in from the shops (we had two at this stage) and then hand over to Martin to check the details and especially to make sure we would never get in trouble with the tax office.

It was so easy. I'm not a greedy man, I only ever took small amounts out before handing the week's takings over to Martin. The shop managers were happy not to have to do all the adding themselves and I knew as long as the figures Martin came up with were close enough to sound true, they would never suspect. Over the past eight years I have amassed a very modest thirty thousand pounds; I'm sure you'll agree that's a sum hardly worth being pursued for.

After Hugo's death I'd assumed Helen and I would eventually get married and continue the business together. I had every intention of ploughing my savings back in and had already started to work out a five year plan; on my far more cautious terms this time. But when Helen dumped me she also made it clear she wanted no part of the business and expected to get money instead – either from me, or from liquidating the shops. That's when I decided it was time to bail out. I pooled together all the money the business still had and divided this sum equally between our 14 members of staff, as a dismissal payment. I have sent them their notice and included excellent references with each one. That leaves Helen with quite a few debts, but believe me, the total is not an amount she will lose any sleep over.

Thirty thousand pounds doesn't get you much these days, but where I'm going it's enough to start a little bookshop. And this time I will stick with the one.

Kind regards,

Sam Ripley

PS In case I haven't made myself clear, I did not kill Hugo and was not in any way involved in his death. As far as I know and believe, neither was Helen.

Lucas wandered over to Nick's desk, wordlessly handed him the letter and walked out of the office – he urgently needed more coffee.

Emma had hoped the fresh air of a lunchtime walk would have made her feel better, but it hadn't worked. She still didn't feel the least bit hungry and no sudden revelation had shown itself. Back inside she slowly climbed the stairs to the second floor, where she saw Jennifer enter Frederick's office – of course, going over all those treatment notes she had. Incredible to think Jennifer had been having an affair with Hugo, the very man who'd used her so abominably. It must have felt like a terrible betrayal when she found out. Emma could easily imagine how furious she'd have been, how she would have wanted to lash out. She froze. No, Lucas said they'd spoken to Jennifer at length; they must have eliminated her as a suspect. She sat down behind her desk – no point to even pretend to do any work, she had to find what it was that was niggling away at the edge of her mind, telling her she'd missed something important. Was it when she'd found Hugo? Had she glimpsed him or someone else down there on Monday afternoon? She realised she was fiddling with her nails, as she always did when trying to concentrate. She never bit them now, but still pulled at bits of skin. Nails. No nail polish, she only did that on special occasions – the smell of nail polish remover alone was enough to put her of. The smell. Something was wrong with the smell of nail polish remover. She jumped up, ran down the stairs and didn't stop until she was standing outside the door to conservation.

Emma waited a minute to catch her breath. She still wasn't sure why she'd come back down – no point bursting into the room panting, frantically searching for something if she didn't know what it was. Do this methodically, she told herself, pretend it's Monday afternoon. She slowly opened the door and went in; this is when the strong solvent smell had hit her at the same time as the awful whirring of the fume cupboard, which was still on this afternoon. She stood still – why would the smell have been that strong with the fume cupboard on? A vague sensation of nail polish remover, yes, but why had it been so strong? More importantly, why as soon as she came in? It hadn't been anywhere near so strong when she'd gone over to talk to Jennifer and that was closer to the big table and the fume cupboard itself. She closed her eyes, trying to remember. Her left, that's where it had come from. She turned round: the big old iron press and empty space where all those cardboard boxes with disaster supplies had been on Monday. Gingerly she put her hand on the press, letting her fingers glide over the very sharp, unforgiving corners. She pressed her nose against the very cold, strong metal, certain now that this is where the smell had come from. Squashing the head between the mobile racks would have destroyed evidence of what the original wound had looked like – otherwise the connection to the press would have been very obvious. She could picture it clearly: an argument, a struggle, a fall. An accident then. Maybe even self-defence. So much easier to believe than cold blooded murder. She straightened up – of course Olivia's death hadn't been an accident. And poor little Theresa getting her head bashed in with – how had Lucas put it? - a heavy object with well-defined edges. Emma looked back at the fume cupboard – why was it on today? Slowly she walked across the room; the iron in the fume cupboard. How had she missed that this morning? Why would any weights have solvent on them, there should be no reason for it to be in there. She didn't dare touch it, this heavy lump of curved metal with its convenient handle. It was always lying about somewhere in the room, it was Jennifer's favourite. *You need a lot of pressure to make the repairs stick, Emma. These old irons are perfect, they're so heavy.* But why would she...Emma became aware of movement behind her, of a rush of air. She tried to spin round, but then her head exploded in pain and she fell into a dark sea of nothing.

Lucas and Nick were sitting in front of a large monitor, looking through CCTV footage from the previous night.

"This tape is from a 24-hour convenient store a bit up the road from the club. If Theresa was going to take the bus, she'd have had to walk past here."

"According to the other party-goers she left sometime between ten thirty and eleven thirty, so let's look from ten thirty onwards."

After a few minutes of screen staring, Nick started to get restless.

"I'm sure you're right, boss, it must have been her. It just must have been."

"Ah well, if you say that in court we're bound to get a conviction."

"She had motive and opportunity." He paused. "And that room is full of heavy objects you could kill someone with."

"Jennifer Marr certainly had the best opportunity to kill her lover. And if she'd found out what he was doing, that would have given her a strong motive. Killing him in the archive wasn't very clever, though. "

"So it wasn't pre-meditated."

"The murder of Olivia Dunstable was. How did she get that drug in her coffee? Even more to the point, where did she get it from? We know her doctor didn't prescribe it."

A few more minutes of screen staring passed in silence.

"The husband!"

Nick's sudden exclamation almost made Lucas fall out of his seat.

"He killed himself because he suffered from depression right? Didn't he take an overdose of a prescription drug? What if she'd kept some?"

Lucas looked impressed.

"You could well be right, Nick. You'd better go and check."

Lucas kept staring at the screen; the time stamp was getting near eleven now and still no sign of Theresa. And then there it was. It all happened so quickly, such a fleeting moment, he wasn't at all sure he'd actually seen it. He rewound the tape slowly, frame by frame until he found it again: Theresa talking to Jennifer Marr.

Why couldn't she have left her alone? She was just like all of them, always watching, always listening, always snooping around. Causing problems. How was she supposed to get rid of this body? Jennifer checked Emma's pulse – still alive. That gave her an idea. A quick look out of the door showed an empty corridor, so she put on some thin rubber gloves and dragged Emma's body into the storage room next door. *Silly girl*, they'd say, *she must have wanted to destroy the evidence of where she'd killed Hugo by starting a fire. A pity she underestimated the danger of what she was doing*, they'd say, *she was clearly overcome by the smoke and couldn't get out.* It seemed a shame to use the beautiful hand crafted pure linen repair paper as kindling, but it should burn pretty well. There was only one spare box of matches in the room; Marie had never liked them being in there, but as Jennifer had so often explained, she needed some way to light the Bunsen burner when she wanted to melt wax to carry out seal repairs. She crumpled up a few sheets of the cream laid paper and made a trail to the big stack of yellowish wove paper she never used anyway. She took down the smoke alarm, removed the battery and pressed Emma's fingers against it; you never could tell what would survive a fire. Then she lit the match and carefully encouraged the flame to feed on the paper; she watched it grow bigger, almost getting lost in the pretty colours – she shook herself out of the flames' hypnotic trance, made sure it was strong enough not to go out again by itself and left the room, shutting the door behind her. Back in conservation she settled down on her chair, waiting for the smoke to reach a working fire alarm.

Marie was annoyed. First a dead body in her building, then Richard a thief, Olivia and Theresa dead and now she'd run out of dusters. How was she supposed to keep calm if she couldn't dust the books? Or the rest of the building for that matter – it was only too easy to imagine how quickly standards could slip. Then she had an idea – perhaps there was a pack in the basement store? Cleaning supplies were kept in her cubby hole, but there must be something in those disaster boxes she could use. She quickly went downstairs and opened the door to the store; the warmth of the handle took her completely by surprise and she stared in silent horror as smoke drifted out of the room and into the corridor. She could even see flames inside! She slammed the door back shut and hit the fire alarm seconds before the smoke alarm in the corridor went off. Then she burst into conservation, shouted at Jennifer that there was a real fire, waited till she ran past her, then followed her along the corridor and out through the fire exit.

Lucas was getting out of his car when he was startled by the sudden piercing noise of an alarm. He tried to work out where it was coming from when Nick shouted:
"It's the archive – they're all running out, it must be a fire!"
They both ran across the street.
"She must be trying to destroy evidence."
As they reached the group, they heard Frederick's frantic voice.
"Emma! Has anyone seen Emma? She's signed in, she must have been in the building."
Lucas felt as if the whole world turned into slow motion – it seemed to take him hours to turn his head towards Jennifer and the words he produced sounded as if they had travelled from a different planet.
"Where is she? What have you done?"
The small smile that very gradually formed on Jennifer's face was all the confirmation he needed.

Then suddenly the world snapped back into normal time and he heard Marie shouting "The storage room, the fire's in the storage room," and Lucas found himself running down the steps, through the fire escape and into a thick cloud of smoke.

This was stupid. He knew this was stupid. He could barely see anything in front of him, the smoke was already affecting his breathing, what the hell did he think he was doing? But he knew she was there, in that room and if there was any chance she was still alive he had to get her out. He should have seen it sooner, he hadn't been able to save Theresa, he wouldn't abandon Emma. He started crawling on his hands and knees now, vaguely remembering that smoke rises, desperately trying to slow down his breathing, anything to buy himself that little more time to reach her. He felt his way along the wall, then suddenly the texture changed and he knew he'd reached the door. He put his hand in the pocket of his jacket and managed to haul himself up on his feet; carefully he pushed down the handle and opened the door, making sure he moved out of the way as he did so. Still the smoke and heat knocked him off his feet and he collapsed against the wall. He tried to get back up, but could feel his legs give way and he fell back down again.

Strong hands pulled him up on his feet and started dragging him back towards the exit. 'No,' he wanted to scream, 'that's the wrong direction, she's in that room, save her' but all he managed were some strangled grunts. He was handed over to a shadowy figure as soon as he was outside and the fire fighter disappeared into the building again. The figure tried to take him further away from the building, but he found he couldn't move –his ears were still full of the roar of the smoke and fire, he felt totally disorientated and his surroundings were a jumbled mess of colours and shapes.
"Lucas!"
That word did somehow penetrate, a familiar sound. A second arm grabbed hold of him, pushed him on, helped him sit down on the pavement. The fog of shapes slowly started to come into focus and he recognised Nick, pale-faced and scared looking, kneeling beside him, talking to the paramedic. And then he saw the other paramedics, rushing around an ambulance trolley, frantically carrying out CPR. He tried to get up, desperate to see her, but his legs refused. The wailing of the siren signalled the departure of the ambulance and within seconds she was gone. Lucas took a deep breath and proceeded to throw up all over the paramedic's sturdy black shoes.

Twenty-eight

"Ok Nick, fill me in."

Lucas was still sitting on the pavement, a few metres away from where he'd sat before. His voice croaked, his eyes were stinging, his head felt like it was about to explode and his throat complained bitterly every time he swallowed. At least he was breathing a little easier, thanks to the oxygen the paramedic had thrust in his face. The poor man had eventually given up trying to persuade him to go to hospital, and had driven off fuming about pig-headed idiots who made his job impossible. The ambulances were gone now, as were all the archive staff and other police cars. One fire engine still blocked the street, but the fire fighters were walking around rather than running. Nick was sitting beside him, holding two cups of coffee – Lucas didn't trust his trembling hands not to spill his everywhere.

"After you ran off I arrested Jennifer Marr and handed her to the officers in the patrol car. The fire brigade arrived and seconds later they dragged you and Miss Baines out." He paused for a moment to compose himself. "Don't ever do that again, by the way."

"I think I can pretty much guarantee that. Any news about Miss Baines?"

"Nothing yet."

Lucas carefully grasped his cup with both hands and took a few sips.

"Go on."

"After I left you with the paramedic I talked to the other archive staff and told them to go home. Mr Samuels said he'd call Miss Baines' mother."

Lucas took a deep breath – he'd never take fresh air for granted again – and slowly rose, hoping his legs wouldn't crumble this time.

"Let's get back to the station."

Nick jumped up, ready to provide support if needed. Lucas tossed him the keys, steadied himself, and tentatively began to walk to the car.

He really ought to go and speak to Jennifer Marr. She was waiting for him in an interrogation room downstairs and had apparently waived her right to legal counsel. The constable on guard reported that she was talking enthusiastically to invisible people and seemed quite relaxed. Invisible people. Was that going to be her defence, diminished responsibility? Right now he couldn't bring himself to accept she was entitled to any kind of defence. He could still feel the heat crawling across his skin, the smoke searing his throat, the certainty that he was about to die...Still no word from the hospital.

"Shall I talk to her?"

"No thanks Nick."

"The loony squad are on their way, we may not get another chance."

Clever Nick. The one thing bound to get him into action – the fear of never knowing why.

"Hello Jennifer."

He forced his voice to sound pleasant, his hands to stay steady, his emotions hidden behind the calm façade.

"Are the manuscripts damaged, inspector?"

Lucas couldn't avoid the mask slipping and showing his surprise. Jennifer leaned further over the table.

"I really didn't want anything to happen to them – they were safe in the store, weren't they?"

Lucas still couldn't quite find the words.

"Inspector?"

"It's not something I've asked about, I'm afraid. I'll have to find out for you."

She seemed satisfied with that answer and sat back in her chair.

"Tell me about Hugo, Jennifer. Why did you kill him?"

She shifted on her seat.

"It was an accident. Sort of. He fell and hit his head."

"Why didn't you call for help?"

"There was no need; Simon helped me."

"Simon?"

"He used to talk to me a lot, but I hadn't heard him for more than a year. He was there when I needed him though."

"Simon talked to you after he died?"

She nodded.

"He told me it was all right. That I didn't have to feel bad."

"About his suicide?"

Jennifer's eyes lit up.

"About killing him."

"It's raining again, Jen, out there and in my head. Gloomy clouds, they just never go away. I can sense it all going dark again; maybe this time I'll just give in."

Jennifer was standing in the middle of the room, ready to go out to work.

"Have you taken your pills?"

"Yes, of course. I don't think they help any more. Nothing helps anymore.."

"I'll make you a cup of coffee before I go."

She took off her coat and went in to the kitchen. There she carefully ground up about half of the anti-depressants left in the bottle and watched the powder dissolve in the coffee.

"Drink up."
She watched as he drank the whole mug in several gulps, as he always did.
"You'll feel much better soon."
She put her coat back on and walked out of the house.

"Everyone just accepted it as suicide."
"Why did you do it?"
A cold stare met his eyes.
"Do you have any idea what it's like to live with someone who never, ever stops whining?"
She suddenly shook her head.
"Yes you did Simon, all the time."
"And the others?" Lucas raised his voice a little to be heard above whatever it was that was going on inside Jennifer's mind.

Another knock on the door. Olivia back again?
"Come in."
"Hello my sweet."
"Hugo! What on earth are you doing here?"
He quickly moved over to her and pulled her close for a kiss.
"Now answer my question."
"I sneaked in to see Richard and thought I'd say hello to you too."
"Why sneaked?"
"No need for you to worry about that my dear. I've made reservations at our favourite place for tonight."
"Don't be patronising, Hugo. Why are you holding that manuscript?"
Hugo hesitated for a moment, then smiled.
"I'll let you in to a little secret: whenever I need some extra cash, Richard finds something lovely for me to sell."
Jennifer couldn't believe what he was saying.
"You're stealing from the collection???"
"Don't look so shocked my dear, life's little luxuries do need to be paid for somehow. And no one will ever know – they're all manuscripts that couldn't be examined until you'd repaired them, so they're easy to remove from the catalogue."
Jennifer felt a cold rage descend on her.
"You bastard," she hissed, "how dare you sell my work."
She moved towards him with such menace in her eyes, Hugo was completely taken aback and slowly started moving away. His soothing words were meaningless against the fury that approached him; as she lashed out he swayed to miss the blow, stumbled, fell backwards and hit his head on the corner of the giant press. Jennifer stood frozen for what seemed like hours,

trying to apprehend what had just happened. Then she slowly picked up the manuscript from the floor; at least that was unharmed. Hugo had betrayed her, had used her – she hadn't meant to kill him, but who would believe that? Suddenly she heard Simon's laugh. Did you miss me, Jen? You didn't think I'd gone, did you? I'm sorry Simon, I didn't mean to stop listening. What do I do now? Don't worry – just do exactly as I say. With Simon's help Jennifer found a new resolve; no way was Hugo going to get the better of her. Of them. She went over to the disaster supply cardboard boxes, took out a large plastic sheet, lay it on the floor next to Hugo and rolled his body onto it. She moved some more boxes to clear a path and dragged the body beyond them; then she stacked the boxes up again and checked the view from the door – perfect, he was completely hidden. She cleaned up the blood stains on the press and the floor with some wet wipes. But of course the police had ways of still finding blood, didn't they? There was no bleach in conservation; try a solvent. Of course, solvents should do the trick; she took the large bottle of toluene out from the fire proof cabinet and poured a generous amount over the press and floor. She'd just finished when she heard a knock on the door – in a flash she ran to the other side of the central table, put the bottle in the fume cupboard, stood behind the table and picked up a document.

"Come in," she said and looked closely at the letter as Emma entered the room...

At a quarter to five Jennifer listened behind her door until she could hear Marie's footsteps going all the way to the fire exit – you had to admit, she was thorough – and then back again up the stairs. She dragged Hugo's body, still in the plastic sheeting, into the store and in between the mobile racking. Then she rolled him off the sheet and positioned him carefully so his skull would get crushed by the large rubber stoppers, hiding the sharp gash from the press. He was still surprisingly warm so maybe not actually dead, but it was too late to worry about that now. She walked about six rows down, then started heaving away at the big steering wheel, putting the racking into motion, feeling the great weight of all that history getting closer and closer to the body until she could feel some resistance; a final turn and she heard the crack of the skull. Quite poetic really, how the manuscripts were taking revenge on their thief. She couldn't resist rolling everything back and having a look – oh yes, it had definitely worked. Well done.

Jennifer washed the mugs as Olivia took hers, spooned in some instant coffee, switched on the kettle, sighed as she realised it was full to the brim and stormed out of the kitchen, back to her office. Dear, predictable, impatient Olivia. Jennifer hadn't thought about those leftover anti-depressants in her bathroom cabinet for ages, but Simon had reminded her. Egged on by Simon, who had now been joined by Hugo, she'd ground them into powder downstairs and now carefully added them to the coffee granules, stirring them in bit by bit making sure she didn't put more in than would be hidden. She'd topped up the kettle to make sure she'd have plenty of time; when Olivia finally returned, Jennifer was already making her way back down to the basement...

She signed herself out of the building at quarter to five, making sure Marie had seen her in the basement corridor and then quickly dashed upstairs and waited inside Olivia's office. She heard Richard's door close at ten past, waited another five minutes to be sure and then silently went to the first floor to get a kick stool from one of the libraries. There was no danger of Marie coming upstairs this late and risking a confrontation with Olivia, but she still had to be careful. Back on the second floor she took Olivia's mug from her desk and washed it up in the kitchen; then she roused Olivia from her deep sleep and while she was still in a very dazed state managed to persuade her to walk into the corridor and to the stairs. Hugo and Simon had been very clear, explaining exactly how it would all work. She helped Olivia get up on the kick stool, then leaned over the railing herself as if to point out something odd downstairs. Olivia began to lean over, then some kind of self-preservation instinct kicked in and she started to straighten up again. Too late though – Jennifer didn't even need to push with that much force to make her go over the edge. She stood still in the darkness as she heard Marie rush over below and then go back to her office to make the phone call; she was out of the door before she'd even been put through to the police.

"Jennifer? Jennifer! It's Theresa!"
Jennifer turned round, feigning surprise.
"Theresa, what on earth are you doing here?"
"The party, remember? The Black Circle's just down the road from here."
"Of course. Did you have fun?"
"It was fan-tas-tic! Tim came for a while but he left ages ago. I'm just heading for the bus now."
"I can give you a lift if you like; I'm parked round the corner."
"Wow, this evening is just getting better and better."
Theresa climbed in the car; Jennifer got in beside her, carefully placing her feet either side of the old iron that was waiting on the floor. Olivia was right – no matter what Simon and Hugo said, Theresa simply had to go.

"And they're still talking to you now?" Lucas wondered.
"Dear Simon and poor Hugo try, but Olivia is much louder than they are." Jennifer burst out laughing. "Oh Olivia, you shouldn't say such things." She looked apologetically at Lucas. "I'm afraid she made a rather rude remark about you; she doesn't like you much."
Lucas smiled back.
"The feeling's mutual." He glanced at the constable who was standing next to the door and then continued. "PC Flinders will stay with you until the doctor comes."
"Doctor? I'm not ill, inspector."
"Just routine, Mrs Marr. We like everyone to be checked by a doctor before they go to jail." He got up from his chair. "Goodbye Mrs Marr."

"Simon likes you. But then, he would."

Outside the interrogation room Lucas took a deep breath. Nick handed him a cup of coffee, but he didn't dare take it – his hands had started shaking again. He could see Jennifer through the one-way window, chuckling at something one of her voices had just said. He was glad it wasn't up to him to determine the state of her mental health - he wouldn't trust himself to be entirely objective. The ring of his phone brought him out of his reverie.

"Bohr."

"It's Elise, inspector."

Lucas stopped breathing as he listened to Elise's shaky voice.

"I thought you'd like to know – Emma's still unconscious, but they think she'll pull through."

He steadied himself against the wall and tried to sound calm.

"Thank you for telling me. I'll come to the hospital later."

As he held his phone in front of him to end the call, he realised he was squeezing it so tightly it was a wonder the screen hadn't cracked.

EPILOGUE

Emma began to open her eyes, but decided against it – even her eyelids hurt. The realisation that there was something covering her mouth and nose made her panic and she desperately tried to move her arms, trying to remove whatever was stuck on there.

"Easy sweetheart, it's all right, you're in hospital."

She wasn't entirely sure about the meaning of the words, but the sounds were soothing and the tone familiar. She relaxed her arms again and before she could think of anything more she drifted back to a deep sleep.

"How is she today?"

"They've reduced the dose of painkillers; she might become more responsive that way."

Painkillers? Why did she need painkillers? What had happened? She managed to open her eyes a tiny amount and saw a bright room – far too bright – with white walls, a woman sitting by the side of her bed – mum, she suddenly realised – and a man standing beside her. She was sure she knew him too, but his name wouldn't quite come. He was looking at her closely now.

"Emma? Elise, I think her eyes are open."

Elise rose up from her chair and leaned in closer.

"Emma? Sweetheart, if you can hear me squeeze my hand."

Mum's hand? She didn't even know where her own hand was. Think Emma, concentrate. Move your fingers.

"Oh sweetheart, I felt that."

Now Emma could feel a squeeze on her hand. Time to be even more daring.

"Mum." The sound that left her mouth didn't quite sound right, not at all as it had in her head. But it seemed to have had the desired effect, as the squeeze intensified. Time to find out what the hell was going on.

"What..." Damn, she couldn't get any more out.

"You were in a fire darling. This is a specialist burns unit." The squeeze again. "Don't worry, you're going to be fine."

Fire? She didn't remember a fire.

"Your feet caught the brunt of it. They're going to be sore for a while, but the doctor says you will make a full recovery."
What the hell was all this about a fire? She remembered... she remembered... Theresa was killed... something wrong in conservation...
"Jennifer."
Elise sat back and glanced at Lucas. He moved a little closer to the bed and bent forward.
"We've arrested Jennifer for all the murders." He paused for a moment. "You must have worked it out as well; she knocked you unconscious and lit a fire in the storage room. Fortunately Marie Thorpe discovered it and the fire fighters got you out in time." His voice broke slightly. "If you hadn't been unconscious the smoke would have killed you, but as you were barely breathing..."
Lucas. That was his name. And she drifted back off to sleep.

Emma was sitting up in bed propped up by several pillows, reading on her tablet; she looked up as she heard the door open, but she knew who it would be. He'd been there every day at the same time for the past two weeks.
"Hello Lucas."
"You're looking very chirpy today."
He sat down on the chair next to the bed.
"I'm being allowed out."
"That's great news."
"Tomorrow. I won't be able to walk yet, but at least I won't be in here anymore."
Lucas thought for a few minutes.
"I can give you a hand tomorrow...you know, bring the car, drive you to the flat..."
Emma smiled.
"Mum's picking me up. And I'm not going to the flat; I'm going to stay with her for a while, at least while I recover. I can have check-ups in the local hospital."
"In Derbyshire?"
Emma nodded.
"When will you be back?"
"I don't know. I'm not even sure I'll come back." She saw the shock on his face. "I certainly won't go back to the archive; I've no idea what I'm going to do instead."
They sat in silence for a while, each with their own thoughts.
"You know, Derbyshire is very beautiful. And mum lives near the Peak District. Cromford, Wirksworth, Matlock Bath - lots of people go there for a holiday."
She looked straight at Lucas.
"A wheelchair isn't exactly handy on those hills either... It would be nice to have someone to help."
Lucas gently placed his hand on hers.

"You do realise I've never driven on country roads. Or motorways."
Emma intertwined her fingers with his.
"Some risks are worth taking."
Lucas looked straight into her smiling eyes, leant in and finally kissed her.

The end

Read on to find out what happens next in

The Stencott Secrets

The second Baines and Bohr mystery

MONDAY 10 JULY

Fred positioned himself in between the five men who were studiously ignoring each other at the bus stop. He tried hard not to stand out, a skinny twenty-two year old college boy in amongst thick-set forty- and fifty-somethings with ill-fitting clothes and weathered faces. He almost audibly sighed with relief when a group of women joined the huddle – they must have been visitors, bringing a little sunshine into a dark place. His quarry boarded the first bus that arrived; Fred cautiously moved behind him, making sure he could see him at all times. They got off in a run-down area somewhere in east London, where Fred trailed him to a fish & chips shop. He watched as the burly crook sat down at a greasy plastic table, next to a suited, overweight, grey-haired, other kind of crook. Lawyer maybe? Fred entered the shop and cautiously kept an eye on them while waiting for his order; a small leather case passed between the two and was quickly stuffed in the black holdall his quarry had brought out of prison with him. Fred sat down with his back to the other men; he put earphones in so it wouldn't be obvious he was listening, and concentrated hard.

"You're supposed to stay in London, Martin. Don't do something stupid and break your parole."

"I'm not waiting any longer to collect. Did you book it?"

"Yes, they're expecting you. At least meet up with your parole officer tomorrow, so they don't start looking for you straight away."

"I'll leave in the afternoon. I need money for the train and food."

"Where is it you're going again?"

"Stencott. Derbyshire."

"Christ, you won't get there for less than a hundred quid. Come by the office before you leave, I'll get you some cash."

The scraping chairs indicated that the conversation was over; Fred didn't dare turn round and waited another ten minutes before leaving himself. Stencott. So that's where they were.

THURSDAY, 13 JULY

One

Detective Inspector Lucas Bohr crawled along the narrow road, holding his breath each time a car came flying past from the opposite direction. Country roads. Even worse than the motorway had been. At least on a motorway there was enough room in the lanes and everyone was going in the same direction, even if everything had to happen far too fast; these country roads were so ridiculously narrow and winding, he couldn't understand how anyone could drive along them feeling confident they weren't about to hit something. Or someone – ramblers actually used these roads to meander along on, simply assuming cars would get out of their way. At least there weren't as many cyclists as there were in London, although there were signs everywhere telling him to look out for motorbikes. Surely the bikers should be looking out for him as well? Damn. He slowed the car down even more and stared in disbelief as two riders on horseback came into view. The road had far too many bends to be able to overtake the horses safely, so he stayed behind them until they pulled in to a little lay-by to let him pass. Giving them as wide a berth as he felt he safely could, he swore never to complain about London traffic ever again.

Emma Baines opened her eyes in terror; gasping for breath she looked anxiously around her, trying to establish where she was and what was going on. A three-seater black leather sofa. White walls. A worn, dark, wooden floor. Red rug. Sunlight pouring in through a large bay window. Home. She forced herself to take slow deep breaths and the panic gradually ebbed away. Although she couldn't remember anything about the fire that had nearly killed her three months earlier, her body most certainly did. At least once a night she woke up feeling hot, gasping for air, confused and panicking. She'd been taught techniques to control the attacks and had been assured they would eventually go, but for now a good night's sleep was impossible to come by. Which is why she kept nodding off in the cosy armchair in the front room of the house she'd grown up in. She checked her watch – half past twelve. Lucas should have been here by now. She took hold of her crutch and savoured the cool sensation of the metal against the sweaty palm of her hand. She'd only been down to one crutch since yesterday – her left foot still needed a bit of support - but at least she was a lot more mobile now. She cautiously manoeuvred herself in front of the window – no, no sign of the dark green Golf anywhere. She resisted the temptation to send him a text he'd have to ignore anyway and hopped into the kitchen to make herself a cup of tea, pausing for a quick look in the hallway mirror. Her green eyes stared back at her, critically examining the black bob that framed her face. Maybe it was time to let her hair grow a little longer? She smiled as she saw that her mother had laid the table for lunch – a note explained that she'd gone shopping. Dear mum. Making room for the big reunion. Sipping her cup of green tea, Emma tried to work out how she felt at the prospect of seeing Lucas again. Excited, obviously. They hadn't seen each other since she'd left the hospital in London to convalesce up here in rural Derbyshire. But she had to admit she was nervous as well. What if that spark simply wasn't there anymore? What if part of the attraction had been the murders and the thrill of the adventure and she didn't feel the same way in the quiet of the countryside? Even worse, what if she still did and he realised he didn't? She put the cup down on the table and told herself sternly to snap out of it. Second-guessing what might happen was pointless. She looked at the clock again – nearly one. He should have been here by now.

Damn, damn, damn. Fred struggled through the trees, tripping over branches, slipping on the moist moss. He was tired, hungry, confused. And angry. Angry with himself for being such a failure, angry with the man who had disappeared, angry with the trees for being there. Why hadn't he returned? He stopped to catch his breath and looked down across the valley. No. He was not going to give up now. Not after all these years, not after all the planning, not after coming so close... He'd nearly touched him. He'd bloody well nearly touched him. But all these trees looked the same and he'd been so hopelessly lost. A small thought sneaked into his head: *what if he's gone back to London?* Fred shook his head vehemently. No. He had to still be here. He'd find him and...and... He unclasped the big grey rucksack, sat down in between the leaves and twigs and carefully removed a tightly rolled up plastic bag from in between his spare jeans and green fleece. Taking deep breaths he pressed the small automatic in his left hand, the feel of the metal calming him down. Yes. That's what he'd do.

Welcome to Stencott. Think bike. Every village he'd driven through had felt the need to mention bikers – just how many of those were there around here? Lucas pulled in to the car park of The Crowned Peacock and switched off the engine. Thanks to the calm, clear voice of the satnav he'd borrowed from his sergeant, he'd made it to Emma's village. *You'll see The Crowned Peacock first*, she'd said. *A large pub that prides itself on its food – lots of tourists go there.* And it has a useful car park to gather your thoughts after hours of driving, Lucas added to himself. In a few minutes he'd be at Elise's house and would see Emma again. He'd been looking forward to this moment for weeks, but now it was nearly there he was nervous as well. What if she didn't feel the same when she wasn't a damsel in distress? And what if she decided not to go back to London? He looked at his watch – ten past one. He'd optimistically promised to be there by twelve, so he'd better not waste any more time. He took a deep breath, started the car and drove back out onto the road.

Emma's grip on her crutch tightened as she watched the Golf pull up outside. He was here. She was partly annoyed that she couldn't run out of the cottage and greet him with the exuberance she felt and partly relieved she had a great excuse not to. She waited until he'd negotiated the garden gate, walked up the brief path and rung the bell, then she hobbled to the front door.
"Hello Lucas. Do come in."
"Hello Emma. Good to see you."

"That jacket looks great on you Elise."
It was said with only a tiny hint of jealousy: Lizzy had always been the bigger of the two and never had got the hang of sticking to a diet. Elise did another twirl in front

of the mirror – the large check pattern and autumn colours suited her and went will with her greying black hair. She yet again thanked whoever had come up with the idea for a petite range and strode to the till. Lizzy waited patiently till the purchase was completed and then suggested lunch. It only took the two friends five minutes to reach their favourite haunt: an old fashioned tea shop, *Olivia's cakes,* where they still hadn't heard of calories and gave you lashings of cream with your scones.

"So what's this Lucas like then?" Lizzy asked when the daintily cut sandwiches arrived. "He must be pretty special for your Emma to be all in a tizz – she was very choosy as a teenager, I remember."

Elise was glad she had her mouth full and therefore had an excuse to consider her reply carefully. What was Lucas like? She couldn't in all honesty call him handsome, but there was something charming about those short blond curls and startling grey eyes. He was the wrong side of forty, but that didn't seem to bother Emma; of course it wasn't that big a difference if she thought of Emma as an almost thirty year old woman, rather than her little girl.

"He's intelligent. Has a maths degree." She took another bite. "He's obviously good at his job."

"Funny way for them to have met."

Elise took another bite. *Funny* was one way to put it. Emma finding that dead body in the archive and then deciding to try and help find the killer. She had rather enjoyed going along with the adventure; well, not when they'd been held at gun point. And then Emma nearly getting killed in a fire.

"Elise! You still haven't answered my question – what's he like?"

"He seems quite nice."

Lizzy rolled her eyes.

"Talk about damning with praise!"

"Well, I don't know, I hardly know him. He's not my type, but then I'm not the one *all in a tizz.*"

Lizzy frowned. She'd known Elise for nearly sixty years, ever since primary school, and although their friendship had ebbed and waned over the years and they'd led very different lives, she felt they were close enough to broach a difficult subject.

"He doesn't have to be like Daniel, Elise."

Elise put down her scone, glared at Lizzy and marched off to the ladies' room.

Two

Lunch was proving to be as awkward as Emma had feared. They'd both attempted to get a conversation going in between mouthfuls of salad and pizza, but hadn't got much further than the weather and Emma's improving health.

"I hope I haven't chased your mother out of her home."

Emma laughed.

"I'd like to see anyone make my mother do something she doesn't want to. She's gone shopping with one of her best friends, Lizzy Shepley, who runs the village post office." After another mouthful of pizza she added: "She's being nice and giving us some space."

Lucas looked doubtful.

"I'm not sure she approves of me."

"She's never approved of any of my boyfriends..." Emma blushed "...eh, relationships. No one ever matches up to my dad, who was perfect of course."

Lucas put down his knife and fork.

"It can't have been easy for her after he died," he said gently.

Emma sighed.

"I can't really remember, I was only eight."

"Hasn't she had any other...relationships?"

Emma nearly choked on a cherry tomato.

"Mum? Other men?" She pushed her plate away. "Don't give me images like that!"

It was Lucas turn to laugh.

"She *is* a woman as well as being your mum, you know."

Emma got up.

"Let's change the subject, shall we? How about I show you where your cottage is?"

"Great idea. It looked very cosy on the website."

Emma just managed not to hit Lucas with her crutch as she wriggled into the car. He sat down beside her and looked across.

"Whereto?"

"Back to the main road and turn right."

It only took them a minute to drive to the little cottage Lucas had hired: the middle house of a row of three, all built in the local sandstone and all looking very old. He knew from the website that it was an 18th century lead miner's cottage; what he hadn't been prepared for was the view. The short garden ended abruptly at the edge of a cliff, from where he could see a lush green valley beneath and dark green tree-covered hills opposite. Emma hobbled beside him.

"Good view, isn't it?"

"Amazing."

The intensity of the reply surprised her and she felt a sudden surge of affection – he liked her home.

"Come on, I'll show you one of my favourite spots."

Lucas felt relieved as he followed her back out onto the street; he wasn't sure why, but the atmosphere had changed and Emma's eyes were smiling again.

"Hang on," he called after her, "Are you sure you're up to this?"

"It's only a short walk," Emma hobbled a bit further ahead. "Along the trees, gradually uphill, then down again in a loop and back to the village – it only takes half an hour."

Not with a crutch, Lucas thought, but he felt it best not to say anything. Emma was so happy, smiling so brightly, he didn't want to be the one to dampen her joy. Besides, there was no rush, it didn't matter how long it took them to get back.

Twenty minutes later, all the joy was gone. Emma had been determined not to give in, but she simply couldn't cope anymore.

"My hand's killing me," she confessed.

Lucas carefully took her right hand in his and saw just how red it was, blisters starting to appear on the palm.

"It might help if you wrap something soft round the handle."

"Really? And where do you suggest I find anything soft out here?"

Lucas counted silently to three to let the sarcasm wash over him.

"You're right of course, we'll need to get back first."

"I can't go on, the climbing is too painful." She hesitated for a moment, then admitted "Not just for my hand. I hadn't realised just how tiring this would be and how much my feet would ache."

"The we go back."

"Downhill won't be much easier."

"You can lean on me if it helps."

Emma took a deep breath – for heaven's sake, she told herself, don't turn into a pathetic wimp now. There must be some way out of here, just think. She turned round, scanning the area, when a blue and grey figure appeared as if out of nowhere on the path ahead. Of course – clever hiker!

"The bridle path."

Lucas looked confused.

"There's a bridle path along the stream – it's on even ground and goes all the way back to the village. It's slightly longer than the way we came, but should be a lot easier with the crutch. You can get down to it just behind those trees, but it's a bit steep to get to."

They walked over to where there was the gap in the trees the hiker had surfaced from; Lucas peered through and could see a bank of grass below.

"You'll never get down there."

"When we were kids we'd sit and slide down the hill."

"Seriously? You'd rather fall down a hill and risk breaking your legs than walk down the path?"

"Don't be melodramatic. Jess and I used to do this all the time. If you can bring my crutch, I can get myself down there." She saw he still wasn't sure. "In one piece."

"All right. But I'll go first."

Lucas took her crutch and carefully made his way down the steep hillside, gingerly placing his feet in between the bushes, each time checking the soil wouldn't slip away. As soon as he'd safely arrived Emma sat down on the edge of the path – it looked a lot steeper than she'd remembered, but not as far down. Ah well – no going back now. She put her hands on the soil and slowly slid down on her bottom, using her hands as breaks, trying no to put too much pressure on her feet. At least she was wearing trousers and not a dress! Lucas reached out his hand when she was nearly down and she gratefully took hold of him and pulled herself upright.

"There," she said, managing to sound a lot calmer than she felt, "easy-peasy."

Then she realised she was still holding Lucas' hand tightly and was standing very close to him; she turned her head slightly so she could see those beautiful grey eyes of his. He raised his other hand, stroked her short black hair, caressed her cheek, and gently pulled her even closer to him; they kissed each other slowly, fully embracing the closeness, their fingers entwined. They stood cheek to cheek for what seemed like an eternity, neither wanting to end the moment, until Emma finally felt the pain from her throbbing foot.

"Aw."

Lucas pulled away slightly.

"What's wrong?"

"I'm sorry, stupid way to spoil the mood, but I shouldn't be standing without..."

"...your crutch! Of course."

Lucas hastily bend down, picked up the crutch and handed it to Emma.

"Thanks. My right foot's not too bad, but the left one is throbbing manically."

"We'd better get you home."

They started to walk along the narrow path, Emma in front; she was beginning to feel very tired now and not fully concentrating on where she was going. Just in time she spotted she was about to put her crutch down in some freshly laid horse dung; she quickly moved it out further, but it slid away from under her and she found herself tumbling down the bank, towards the stream.

"Emma!"

Lucas ran down after her, half tripping over the crutch and just managing to stay upright enough not to actually fall. He crouched down beside her and felt a wave of relief wash over him as she sat up.

"Will you please stop doing this?"

"Doing what? Making you panic or finding dead bodies?"

With raised eyebrows Lucas followed her gaze down the stream, where a man's body was lying in the water.

"Both."

See how the story continues in **The Stencott Secrets**

26026323R00127

Printed in Poland
by Amazon Fulfillment
Poland Sp. z o.o., Wrocław